HERS TO PROTECT

by
Nicole Disney

2018

HERS TO PROTECT

ISBN 13: 978-1-63555-229-4

This Trade Paperback Original Is Published By
Bold Strokes Books, Inc.
P.O. Box 249
Valley Falls, NY 12185

First Edition: June 2018

CREDITS
EDITOR: CINDY CRESAP
PRODUCTION DESIGN: SUSAN RAMUNDO
COVER DESIGN BY JEANINE HENNING

HERS TO PROTECT

Visit us at www.boldstrokesbooks.com

Acknowledgments

Thank you to the entire Bold Strokes team for all the hard work that went into making this book a reality, from the beautiful cover art to the typesetting and everything in between. A special thank you to Cindy for helping to smooth the rough edges with her sharp eye for detail, mastery of grammar, and always kind guidance.

With all my heart, thank you to the extraordinary women in my life who have shaped me.

To my grandmother, for keeping my books on your shelf, my reviews printed, and my covers framed. You make my dreams feel real.

To my aunt, for spending a family gathering reading my entire first novel in one sitting. At an age when dreams are so easily crushed, you believed in mine.

To my mom, for screaming in the middle of a crowded restaurant when I won my first writing contest, for crying with me when I got my first contract, for making my dreams yours, and for your endless support and love. Your belief in me gave me everything I will ever need.

To my wife, for being by my side through the messy parts. For listening to me talk in circles about characters and plots and arcs, for reading and rereading every word, and for helping me find my way when my word tangles become jungles. This book would not be what it is without your patience, encouragement, and creative input. Thank you for always getting it.

Dedication

To Cassandra. You are my heart, my love, my forever.

CHAPTER ONE

Darkness tickled the edges of her vision. Hot fingers pressed into the sides of her throat and a sweaty palm squished the pliable elastic of her windpipe closed. Adrienne knew at some point it would snap, that it would happen in an instant, and that it would kill her.

"Gianna," she tried, but only spit and a squeak came out.

"Shut up!" Gianna screamed. "Don't lie to me! I saw the way he looked at you."

Adrienne usually tried to weather Gianna's episodes, but she was all out of courage. She couldn't believe Gianna was trying to kill her, yet she knew her life was in danger all the same. She couldn't die over a meaningless smile from the grocery store bag boy. That couldn't be the end of this ridiculous life.

Adrienne glanced around the room and quickly identified the lamp as the only remotely heavy object within reach. She swatted the air, desperately clawing for it. She felt her fingers brush the iron and grasped it. Gianna's eyes followed Adrienne's hand in time to see the shade swinging at her head. The bulb broke against the side of her face and sent the room into darkness.

Adrienne gasped for air when the vice of Gianna's grip released her. The frantic inhale ripped through her burning throat. She ran through the dark, eyes only able to distinguish vague outlines of the furniture. She toppled a chair and muscled through the obstacle and the pain with Gianna's string of curse words crashing after her. She slammed and locked the bathroom door just fast enough that Gianna's attempt at the knob amounted only to a violent, frustrated rattle.

She pulled her cell phone from her pocket and struggled with her trembling hand that didn't seem to be her own. She watched the foreign limb clumsily betray her, missing the buttons and nearly losing the phone completely. It seemed an irrational and panicked thing, incapable and helpless even as her brain felt hyper-focused.

"Open the door, Adrienne!" Gianna shook the doorknob. "What do you think you're going to do? I'm not going anywhere."

Adrienne heard a small voice from the phone she hadn't yet put to her ear. The screen showed a connection to 911. Her heart dropped. Had she really done that? She'd never called the cops before. It was a dangerous line to cross. Gi would be furious. You never snitch. If there was one rule not to break in this world, that was it.

"Adrienne!" Gianna was loud enough the phone picked it up. Adrienne heard the insistent operator still chiming from the other end of the line, reaching for someone, refusing to disconnect.

It went quiet. Gianna stopped yelling. Adrienne stood, paralyzed in the silence. It was almost worse. What was she doing? Adrienne's eyes rebounded around the drab bathroom, to the chipped paint, the floor laminate curling up at the corners. There was no way to barricade the door, no way to escape, and nothing to use to defend herself.

A massive thud shook the door. Adrienne jumped and backed into the corner by the sink. Another crash and the door shivered. She was breaking in.

"You don't want to make me do this, Adrienne."

"I'll open the door if you calm down." Adrienne tried to sound strong, but she knew she didn't.

"You're only making this worse for yourself."

"Please." Adrienne heard the fear in her own voice.

"Open the fucking door before I blow your head off!"

Adrienne put the phone to her cheek, surprised to find it slick with tears. "Four thirty-three West Sixty-Second Street. My girlfriend's going to kill me." She didn't wait for an answer or linger on the mangled sound that was her voice struggling through the tears in her damaged throat. She set the phone down behind the toilet where Gianna wouldn't notice it and left the line open.

Gianna slammed into the door again. The wood was cracking, surrendering to her weight.

"Adrienne!" Gianna screamed. "If you don't open this door right now I swear I'm going to beat your face in."

Adrienne heard herself crying, again feeling her body was someone else's. Her voice wasn't hers, her hands weren't hers, the aching in her chest wasn't hers. This life wasn't hers.

"Baby, please," she said, sliding down the wall, crumpling in terror. "Please, I swear I don't know who he is. I've never seen him before. Please."

"I don't believe you. I saw the way you looked at each other. You think I don't have eyes? You think I'm stupid?"

"No! I love you, please just stop. We'll talk about this, I promise."

"You're damn right, we will. Open the door!" Gianna slammed into it again without waiting for an answer. Adrienne knew it wouldn't hold much longer. Gianna was all muscle, built tall and thick.

"Hello? Ma'am?"

Adrienne heard the 911 operator still calling for her from the cell phone she'd left on the floor. Another crunch and splintering wood. They were going to be too late.

"All cars, be advised I'm holding a domestic violence in progress at Four thirty-three West Sixty-Second Street."

Carli sounded stressed out even though most people wouldn't notice. Her voice always came through the radio in the ice-cold, even tone that made for a good dispatcher, but ever since they started hooking up, Kaia couldn't help but pay closer attention to the subtle shifts in Carli's word choice and volume when she really needed officers to pick up a call.

"You want to grab that?" Kaia asked her partner, Reid. He glanced over from behind the steering wheel, a grin spanning his face.

"That your girlfriend dispatching?"

Kaia and Reid were part of a special street crime task force. They wouldn't be directly dispatched the way a patrol officer would, but they could volunteer if they were close or heard something of interest. Volunteering was an endangered practice, so much so Reid was able to assume Kaia's ulterior motives.

"She's not my girlfriend," Kaia said. "We're just…" She paused. "Yes?"

"I don't know. We're whatever. That doesn't mean I can't help her out, does it? It's right around the corner."

He smiled again and picked up the radio from the center console. "Seventy-seven sixty-two Baker, we'll grab your DV." He paused for Carli to give him the information and turned to Kaia. "It's not right around the corner, though." He winked.

Carli's voice scratched through the radio, moving through the details of the call at an all-business clip. At the pause, Kaia clicked the handheld radio hooked to her shoulder. "Copy."

"Thank you, ma'am." Carli's response to Kaia's voice was warm, the secret of their nights together playing in her tone, subtle but plain to Kaia nonetheless, and Reid for that matter.

"You're such a cliché, Sorano," he said. "Hooking up with a dispatcher."

"Shut up, Castillo. God forbid we take a call."

His smile was bright and sweet, standing out against his caramel skin. He'd been her partner and best friend for three years, and teasing each other was like breathing now.

"I hate domestics," he said. "What did you get us into, anyway?"

Kaia swiveled the screen of the MDT toward her and scanned the notes of the call. "Female gave the address, said her girlfriend was going to kill her, left the line open. Banging and yelling in the background, then lots of screaming and crying." The notes went on and on since the line stayed open, but that was the end of what she would describe as useful.

"Jesus, do you have a sixth sense for dyke drama?"

"I guess so."

Reid flipped on the lights and sirens and accelerated down the quiet street.

The house was dark when they pulled up. The red and blue of their lights painted the splintered wood and sliced through the night. The house's actual color was a creamy white, but the paint was peeling away and the structure looked warped. It wasn't a good part of town, well known for drugs, gangs, and shootings.

They glanced at one another and moved up slowly. There was a window without blinds, but Kaia couldn't discern anything inside from her distance. She listened for arguing, crashing, crying, but there was nothing. The lack of light or sound was eerie. It almost looked abandoned. Maybe the girlfriend really had killed her, then packed up and left. Then again, maybe it was just the wrong address. It certainly wouldn't be the first time.

Kaia knocked on the door. "Chicago PD, open up." She waited, on edge. She'd dealt with plenty of domestics, plenty of fights, weapons, the type that ended up bloody, endangered her life. She'd found bodies, seen people take their last breaths. The streets of South Chicago were as hard as they came, and she wasn't skittish by a long shot, yet every now and then something routine still made her hair stand on end. Sometimes she just knew something bad had happened, and that feeling was bothering her now. She knocked again, harder.

"We know you're in there. Don't make us break it down!" Silence stretched.

"Sorano." Reid was starting to move back down the driveway.

"There's something here," she said. She could tell he didn't agree, but he didn't say so. She loved that about him. He knew the value of instincts, respected them, even when they weren't his own.

Kaia got closer to the window, nearly touching the glass with her forehead, hand ready on her gun. She saw a dark smear on the wall and a lamp out of place on the floor.

"We have blood."

"Shit. I'll get—"

A loud rustle crashed through the bushes on the east side of the house.

"Runner!"

"Got it!" Kaia jumped off the porch and launched after the figure in black. She heard Reid yelling their direction of travel into the radio, falling behind while he tried to be understandable. She knew he wouldn't lose her.

The figure running appeared to be female, which matched the information from the call. She was tall and fast, black tank top, black pants, a blue bandana trailing in the wind from her pocket, denoting a gang affiliation Kaia didn't have time to guess at. The woman cut through the backyard and flung herself effortlessly over the fence. Kaia followed, pleased with herself for managing it smoothly.

"Freeze!"

The woman ducked into the alley and opened into an impressive sprint that had Kaia concerned she might not be able to keep up. She had to. She forced her legs to go faster, ignored the screaming burn in her thighs. She heard Reid's feet hammer the ground furiously, but he was still falling behind. Kaia heard a hint of fear in his voice as he yelled into the radio.

"Approaching Stewart, she's eastbound in the Sixty-first, Sixty-second alley."

Kaia's pulse thundered in her ear. This couldn't last much longer; one of them would be too tired. She just had to keep her eyes on this girl long enough for backup to box her in.

The suspect looked over her shoulder, checking her lead. She had big brown eyes, a cut on her cheek, darkish complexion, maybe Hispanic, shaggy brunette hair, muscular arms heavily tattooed. Kaia was trained to notice these things, break them down into pieces. The whole picture was that she was both beautiful and intimidating. Kaia had a height and strength advantage on most women she dealt with, but this one was going to be a struggle. She couldn't afford fear or doubt. She pushed it away.

The woman slid across the hood of a car that protruded into the alley. Kaia jumped it, using the wall to kick off. She heard Reid tumble over it five seconds behind her. Finally, she heard sirens. The woman slowed just slightly, discouraged. Her head swiveled in search of a better escape route as the alley split at someone's backyard. She veered north and sprinted on.

"Freeze!" Kaia tried again and forced herself to find yet another reserve of energy. The woman ignored her, but Kaia could taste the catch. She was on her heels. She lunged. Her palms hit square in the woman's back and sent her tumbling to the asphalt. The momentum sent the woman sprawling and she scraped several feet across the ground and groaned.

"Bitch!"

"I said freeze!" Kaia rushed to pin her before she could compose herself. She put her knee on the woman's back and yanked one hand behind her before the woman processed it enough to resist. Despite Kaia's lead, the woman pulled her arm back toward herself as hard as she could and yanked Kaia off balance. Kaia's shoulder hit the ground hard, but she wrestled back on top even as the woman managed to prop herself up with her free hand. Kaia was determined not to lose control and more than a little nervous about that possibility. Kaia grabbed the woman's arm with both hands and drove her weight down. Reid caught up and grabbed the other arm. Without its support, the woman's face hit the pavement chin first and she grunted in pain. Even then, getting the cuffs on was a struggle. Finally, Kaia heard the satisfying clicks. She backed away a few paces and tried to catch her breath. Reid sat the woman up, then stood for a breather himself.

Kaia reached for her radio. "Sixty-two Baker, we have one in custody. Next units into the house." Carli echoed her and stated the time to document it; again their nights together seeped out in the sound of relief.

"Hey, assholes, these are too tight."

Kaia spun to the woman on the ground. Part of her always wanted to tell criminals to shove it, what nerve they had to run, resist, and then complain. But she had vowed when she started in law enforcement not to get too cold, not to lose sight of compassion. She leaned over and checked the cuffs.

"No, they're not," she said. "What's your name?"

"Fuck you."

Reid searched her pockets, hoping for an ID.

"Don't have one, home boy."

"I guess we'll start with Hernandez," he said, pointing to a tattoo of the surname across the woman's chest, arching like a necklace.

"Yeah, 'cause there aren't many of those," Hernandez scoffed.

"Yeah, you got me there," he said, his good nature remaining intact. "Why'd you run?"

She stopped answering.

"You got warrants?" he tried. Nothing. Kaia's eyes wandered to Hernandez's most prominent tattoo, "WAK" in bold letters on her neck next to an assault rifle. She didn't know what it stood for, but she knew it was a gang.

"Hey, Blondie, you're bleeding."

Kaia's hair was dirty blond, almost brunette, but this wasn't the first time a suspect used it to try to make her feel like a Barbie. Her arms did burn, though. She didn't have to look to know she'd rubbed them raw on the ground during the scuffle.

"So are you," she said. The concrete had done its work on Hernandez's palms and under her chin, and her cheek was still freshly ripped from whomever she'd been fighting.

Kaia keyed up her radio. "Do we have anyone with the victim yet?"

"I've got her." Kaia recognized Murray's voice scratching through the radio. "Adrienne Contreras. She'll need to be looked at, but she's fine."

Kaia's breath caught in her chest and she felt herself go pale. It couldn't be *her* Adrienne, could it? She hadn't seen her in almost ten years, not since they were teenagers. Since they were lovers. Since the night that changed everything.

Kaia looked back at the cuffed Hernandez. This was Adrienne's lover now? Beautiful, she had to admit, but coarse, rough and tumble, a gang member and brash enough to put her hands on sweet Adrienne? What could she be thinking? It was so insane Kaia couldn't even buy it.

"Reid," she said. "I'm going to check our victim."

"Right," Hernandez said. "Victim."

Kaia's cheeks flushed for reasons she couldn't even pinpoint. She ignored the comment. It was probably just a coincidence of name anyway.

"You okay?" Reid asked. Kaia realized she was still standing in a lifeless stupor.

"Yeah," she said. "I'll meet you at the house."

"Will do."

As Kaia walked back, she realized how far she'd actually chased Hernandez. There had been a moment she wasn't sure she'd catch her. Another where she wasn't sure she could overpower her. What if Hernandez had gotten away? What if she'd let Adrienne's attacker escape? The thought enraged her. But what was she thinking? Adrienne wasn't hers to protect, hadn't been in years. Memories of those times rarely even surfaced anymore. Why did she feel so possessive? Then again, your first love would always be yours in a way.

Kaia used the gate to the backyard this time and found the back door to the house open with patrol officers gathered in what seemed to be a kitchen. She knew they must be questioning the victim, but Kaia couldn't see her. She took a deep breath, suddenly extremely self-conscious as she stepped inside.

"Hey, there she is!" Murray greeted her. He was an old friend from before she moved to the street crime task force. They used to patrol on the same shift, had taken plenty of calls together.

"Murray." She accepted the slap on her back she knew was his way of approving her willingness to go hands-on.

Kaia couldn't focus. She passed him, eager to see the victim, still hoping to see a stranger. Kaia heard her voice before she could get around Murray, and her heart dropped into her stomach.

"I don't want to press charges."

Adrienne saw Kaia right away and their eyes locked. There was a thickness in Kaia's throat she recognized as tears trying to sneak up. Adrienne's eyes were darkened with bruising that still had a ways to go before they would be done. Her lip was split; a smear of blood was wiped along her jaw. Kaia pushed away the emotion. She couldn't cry. For so many reasons, she couldn't do that.

"Why is she in cuffs?"

"She was pretty rowdy when we got here," Murray said. Kaia would doubt anyone else, but she knew Murray, knew how he worked. He was a good guy, exceedingly patient for someone with ten years on the force. Kaia raised an eyebrow at Adrienne, but she looked away.

"Give me a minute with her, guys."

"Sure, sure." They were more than willing to disperse. It wasn't uncommon for them to ask her to talk to women for them. There was a presumption women responded better to other women, which was sometimes true and other times completely wrong. She told herself that was the only reason they scurried away so quickly, that no one was picking up on her recognition of Adrienne. Kaia waited until they were out of earshot, well into the backyard. She wanted to close the door, but that would look odd.

Kaia met Adrienne's eyes again, searching for the girl she'd known and loved, would have done anything for. There was no trace of her, only defiance and a surprising hardness.

Kaia walked to Adrienne's back and fit her key into the cuffs, releasing them. She shivered as her fingers brushed Adrienne's wrist.

She walked around again and pulled up a chair, facing her. She rested her forearms on her knees, reminding herself of the tender scrapes.

"What if I attack you?" Adrienne asked.

Kaia felt disarmed by the question. Adrienne, attack her? "You won't."

"You don't know that. You don't know me anymore."

"No, I guess I don't. You're..." she paused, "rowdy now, huh?"

"That's what they say."

"Is it true?"

Kaia saw a glimpse of vulnerability. Adrienne's eyes were almond shaped, brown, infinitely warm, and in no way predisposed to this coldness she was trying to wear.

"I had to be," she said. "She can't think I'm cooperating with you."

"You know you have to press charges, right?"

"Why? So she can get out tonight and beat me for that too?" Adrienne seemed to pull away from her own words, like she just realized who she was talking to all over again, embarrassed. Kaia dragged her hand down her own face in anxiety. This couldn't be real.

"We can help you." Kaia reached and grabbed Adrienne's hand before she could think better of it. Her heart stopped, but she left it there. "Let me help you."

Adrienne pulled away. "You can't. She'll get out and she'll find me. Don't get involved in this, and for the love of God, do *not* let her find out who you are to me."

Kaia couldn't fight the warm buzz up her spine at being someone to Adrienne, yet she couldn't believe she was hearing the same old argument from Adrienne she'd heard from so many others. Cops hated domestic violence calls because the victim was almost never cooperative and often forced officers to leave them in the same dangerous situation they'd called about. Kaia had always understood why, the fear, the love that endured even when they were treated terribly, but hearing it from Adrienne brought back soul-crushing sadness and empathy she hadn't felt in a long time.

"I'm taking her to jail with or without your cooperation. She ran and resisted."

"Good. Take her. Why put myself at risk?"

Kaia didn't bother pressing anymore. She knew a hard no when she heard one. "Okay, but you need to be gone when she gets out. Pack and go the second we leave."

Adrienne shook her head but didn't say anything.

"What, Adrienne? What is it? Why would you stay?"

She didn't answer.

"You still love her?"

Adrienne looked up. "Gianna?" She laughed. "Wow, I haven't really thought about it that way in a while. Love. Yeah, I guess I do."

Kaia pretended it didn't sting and just mentally noted the first name Hernandez had denied them. Gianna.

"She'll kill you someday, Adrienne. It doesn't get better."

"I know that," Adrienne snapped. "God, don't cop talk me."

Kaia heard the distaste for police in the word "cop." She'd masked it a little, but not well. Adrienne saw Kaia register it. She expected an apology, but Adrienne surprised her again.

"I can't believe you're a fucking cop." The animosity was plain. Kaia felt anger fighting shame in her chest. She was hated for her uniform on a daily basis, but it rarely hurt anymore. From Adrienne, it did. She grit her teeth. Kaia had immediately assumed a familiarity and warmth, but all Adrienne saw was a uniform.

"Fine." Kaia slapped her card down on the kitchen table without explanation. "You can give your statement to Officer Murray."

Kaia saw the surprise pass through Adrienne's delicate features, but Adrienne made no move to stop her.

CHAPTER TWO

Adrienne locked the door behind Murray. The statement she'd given him was useless, deliberately riddled with excessively vague information and inconsistencies. She knew Kaia would read it and that she'd be furious. She hoped Kaia would know it was intentional, at least. Adrienne could live with Kaia disagreeing with her decision, but she didn't want to come off as dumb or as a liar. She observed the fact that she cared what Kaia thought of her without emotion, refusing to linger on why. She had more important things to worry about than running into an ex from another life, even if Kaia *was* still tomboy gorgeous with her dirty blond hair, blue eyes, and a body Adrienne suspected was even more toned than before, if hidden under that obnoxious, boxy vest. It didn't matter. If Kaia hadn't already forgotten her, she would certainly write her off now. The urge to redeem herself was pure ego and not in her best interest.

Adrienne went into the living room and picked up the lamp from the floor. She gathered the pieces of the light bulb gingerly, remembering the cut one of these shards had inflicted on Gianna's face. Gianna was probably poking at it right now while she ruminated in rage.

A knock at the door made Adrienne jump. She tightened her fingers around the shards of glass before they could slip apart and felt the edge grip her flesh.

"Pigs are gone. Open up," a voice called from outside.

Adrienne recognized it as Celeste's voice and turned the deadbolt. Celeste paused when she saw Adrienne's face, then came in and shut the door.

"You okay?"

Adrienne nodded. She firmly resisted the urge to get emotional, but Celeste must have seen through her.

"Come here." She raised her arms for a hug as if she didn't really want to. Adrienne quickly hugged and released her.

Anna and Christina came in without knocking. They were both in wifebeaters; boxers showed from the tops of low-slung jeans. They wore their tattoos like armor. They lived by intimidation and toughness above all else. They had to if they wanted to maintain control of the fifteen square blocks they'd claimed as their turf, despite being a small and young gang.

"Heard your address on the scanner," Anna said. "What happened?"

Adrienne gestured at her beaten face.

"Okay," Anna sneered. Anna was Gianna's best friend, every bit as deep with the Wild AKs and fiercely loyal.

"They came for that, arrested her for running."

"That's your fault," Anna said. "You dimed her out."

"I did not."

"I just told you I heard the scanner, didn't I? Woman said her girl was going to kill her. That's you. You did this."

"I didn't file charges. I didn't give them anything they could use."

"And I'm supposed to believe that? Like it even matters? You brought the cops here, what did you think would happen?"

"I had to," Adrienne said. "She *was* going to kill me."

"Please."

"She was."

"I hope she does, snitch."

"Gianna can deal with that when she's out," Celeste interrupted. "That's her business."

Adrienne knew the sentiment was to her benefit, but she still didn't like feeling like property, like she was Gianna's belonging to deal with. Celeste had tried to convince Adrienne to join up a dozen times. She'd be a person if she became a Wild AK. The gang would care about her and how she was treated. Gianna wouldn't be able to beat her with impunity anymore because she too would be family to Anna, Christina, Marco, and all the others. She couldn't pretend it wasn't tempting. She missed being an equal.

"They find anything?" Anna asked.

"No."

"Good. Let's get on with it then."

It was a pickup day and Gianna's arrest wasn't any reason to slow down. When Adrienne first started dealing weed and coke to the WAKs they'd respected her. They'd shared their connections with each other as they made them. They'd grown together, moved into harder drugs and bigger quantities together, out of poverty into comfort and even occasional extravagance.

Adrienne stopped having to deal at the street level and started only dealing with bigger quantities for the WAKs and others like them. It was simpler when she was just their drug dealer. Things got complicated when she started dating Gianna. It had been a status jump, and maybe it still was to outsiders, but she'd felt like less and less of a human ever since, and Gianna's treatment was contagious. Anna stopped respecting her when Gianna did.

"I'll take Gi's too," Anna said. "I'll move it for her."

Move meant sell. Adrienne wasn't sure how Gianna would react to her giving Anna her extensive stash of drugs. There was a time Adrienne would have gone on the corners and done it herself in Gianna's absence, but Anna and the crew had the reputation and firepower to survive the streets. Even so, she didn't relish the idea of letting Anna walk away with thousands of dollars worth of Gianna's drugs. Anna saw the hesitation.

"People don't stop buying just because one of us spends a weekend in the pen. I'll run dry without Gi selling her share, and we can't be dry. Ever."

"She'll still get her cut of the cash," Christina said. "She'd want this. And anyway, you don't want that much product here if your friends in blue come back to check on you."

"What, you think I'm stealing from one of our own?" Anna stepped closer. "Get the drugs, bitch!"

"Okay, fine." Adrienne accepted the cash from each of them and went to the bedroom to retrieve their drugs. She closed the door. She knew it would make Anna even angrier that she felt the need to conceal the safe's location and code, but no matter how much Gianna trusted Anna, Adrienne never would. She put in the combination, a series of dates that meant something to her and Gianna back when their relationship was intensely romantic, back when being part of the Wild AKs was more about protection and having friends in a neighborhood that could chew you up and spit you out. The gang had since swallowed Gianna, and Adrienne knew she had to either follow or get stamped out.

The safe held a scattering of drugs, marijuana, methamphetamine, cocaine, bags of pills, of both the prescription and party drug variety. Adrienne had already divided them into the portions each of her buyers wanted, including Gianna's share. She noted the stacks of cash, knowing that although a large portion of it was hers, Gianna thought of all of it as her own. A pistol sat on top of the cash as if it were guarding the entire contents. Adrienne grabbed the bags for Celeste, Christina, Anna, and Gianna, ignoring the lurch in her stomach as she grabbed the last.

Anna snatched the bags from her hands when Adrienne returned. "You call me when they're letting her out."

Adrienne nodded and locked the door behind them even though she knew they had keys. The Wild AKs were free to come and go from her life whether she liked it or not.

Adrienne went to the bedroom and stripped, examining her scrapes and bruises as she went. Most of them were turning purple. Officer Murray had photographed the obvious ones but missed many more, including the light blue ones across her throat, the ones that had made the fight life threatening and could have made Gianna's charges more serious. Incompetent. Cops couldn't see past their noses, so sure they had seen it all before and already knew the story that they scarcely bothered listening or truly looking.

Every time she'd had to deal with cops they'd been arrogant, rude, and eager to escalate the situation they claimed to be there to remedy. She'd seen them abuse their power, seen them pocket drug money rather than arrest the dealer, knowing there was nothing a criminal could do to report them. She'd grown to believe only a certain type of person wanted that job, and that they were usually overbearing, power-hungry animals who didn't think for themselves or know how to listen. She couldn't reconcile that image with the one she had of the patient, kind, and understanding Kaia, yet she still couldn't help but think of Kaia as lost to the badge. Whoever she was before, it wouldn't survive the job. Maybe that Kaia was gone before the uniform, buried ten years ago when she'd put a baseball bat to Adrienne's father's head.

Chapter Three

"Y ou sure you don't want those arms looked at?" Reid obviously knew something was wrong, but he also had to know it wasn't a little road rash. Kaia wished he'd stop bringing up her injuries with Gianna in the backseat. They had to transport her to the station and Kaia hated giving her the satisfaction.

On cue, Gianna leaned up to the partition separating the backseat. "You going to cry, Blondie?"

Kaia elbowed the cage at Gianna's face level. Gianna jumped but quickly recovered with a smirk.

"What's wrong, boo? I was just checking on you. You look like you need someone to take care of you."

"That's enough," Reid said.

"Are you two together? Is that what it is?"

"No."

"Yeah, I didn't think so." She turned back to Kaia, getting as close as the partition allowed. "You like pussy, don't you?"

"Shut the fuck up, Hernandez," Kaia snapped.

"Enjoyed our little tangle, did you? If you wanted a feel all you had to do was ask."

Kaia forced herself to stop responding. Prisoners loved razzing her, always had, but she didn't usually fall into it so easily.

"You're not still in the closet, are you?" Gianna persisted. "I mean, come on, everyone knows girl cops are gay anyway."

They finally pulled into the lot. Kaia opened the back door. "Out."

"Goodness, you're an angry one."

"Get out."

"You just need to get laid, sweetie. It'll help you with that urge to be a bitch."

Kaia grabbed Gianna's upper arm and yanked. Gianna stiffened and pulled back. She rolled onto her back and kicked in Kaia's direction. Her foot mostly missed, brushing her thigh, but it still hurt. Kaia grabbed the foot and yanked, dragging Gianna out and letting her slam to the ground. With her hands still cuffed, Gianna was unable to control her fall and landed hard, headfirst.

"Fuck!"

Kaia hoped it hurt. It was an unusual sensation for her, but she couldn't stop seeing Adrienne's swollen, purple eyes. Kaia knew the force this monster could generate and she had no problem smashing Adrienne's face, but a little tumble to the ground and suddenly she was a victim.

Reid pulled Gianna to her feet. "You done?"

"Not even close. I'm going to get you crooked cocksuckers for that. You think excessive force is a toy you can play with anytime you want."

"You can't assault an officer and not expect to be stopped," he said.

"Shut up, pretty boy. You should be able to arrest someone without bringing them in bloody."

"You can talk to the serge—" Kaia started.

"Please, I'm not going to talk to your stupid boss who's probably just as crooked as you. You'll get street justice, Blondie."

"You don't want to make threats, Hernandez," Kaia said. "Just shut up and stop resisting."

"That's fine. You'll get yours though, I promise you that."

Kaia was relieved to hand Gianna over in the station. The desk officer was eager to get away from the phone and took over without being asked. Kaia went to a free desk to start the report, but as she sank into the chair, the deep ache in her overworked muscles sprang to the surface and all she wanted was a drink and a nap. Reid leaned into the room.

"Hey, let's get out of here. I'll buy you a drink," he said.

"I have to—"

"They're doing the paper. You can add your info tomorrow. Come on, screw this night."

Kaia smiled. "I can agree with that."

"Good, let's go."

Kaia changed clothes and met Reid at their favorite after work spot. Some bars were somehow destined to become cop bars though no one could explain how it happened. Reid didn't say a word until they each had a beer.

"So." He took a swig.

"They're just road burns, Reid. You're going to start offending me if you ask if I'm okay again."

"Fair enough. Something did shake you up though."

Kaia wasn't sure she wanted anyone to know, but she did trust Reid.

"The victim on that domestic is my ex."

Understanding settled on his face. "Were you serious?"

"We were kids, but yeah, we were serious," she said. "We were sixteen when we met, seventeen when—" She stopped. She couldn't bring herself to tell him. Not even Reid. "When she moved."

"And you didn't keep in touch?"

"No. Her mom had a problem with us, wouldn't let us talk. I was in Evanston; she moved to South Side. It might as well have been across the country at the time. It's been ten years, though. She could have contacted me along the way. I figured her mom must have brainwashed her so deep into the closet that she didn't want to. I half expected her to be married to a dude living in the suburbs by now."

"And now you find her here. With a woman." He nodded again, putting it all together. "An asshole at that."

"Exactly."

"You can't take it personally, Sorano. No one means to end up in those relationships. I'm sure that brute started out lovely. Maybe she met Hernandez when she moved, and by the time she thought she could contact you things had gotten ugly. Afraid to set Hernandez off."

"Yeah," Kaia said. "Maybe. But what am I supposed to do now? Hernandez will probably be out Monday. Am I supposed to just let her drown in this?"

"Nothing you can do if she won't let you. She knows you're there if she needs it."

Kaia frowned. "Kind of."

"What do you mean?"

"I offered to help, gave her my card, but I didn't exactly leave off warm and fuzzy. She was anti-cop and I took it like a child."

"Oh, fuck her."

"Reid."

"These people want to call for help when they're in trouble, but the second we're there it's 'fuck the police.'"

"I know, Reid."

"All right, sorry."

"I should probably just leave her alone. Hernandez is out of control, though. You see that neck tat? WAK? You know anything about that?"

"Not really. I've seen their tags, but that's about it. Seem small time."

"Didn't act like it."

"I'll ask my buddy in the Gang Enforcement Unit about them, see what I can find out."

"Thanks." Kaia glanced at her phone for the first time in hours. She had five messages, all from Carli. The first was plain on the screen without her opening it. "Are you okay?" She was sure the rest were similar in nature. She still wasn't used to how much Carli worried. From dispatch, she knew when Kaia got into drama and when it ended, but usually not the specifics. Kaia texted back quickly, but it was already too late to save her much anxiety. Kaia didn't want to stress her out. She didn't particularly want to see her either, though.

Chapter Four

Adrienne sat in the jail parking lot. She'd stared at the bundles of cash in the safe for hours, calculating how far it would take her, how long it would last. She wondered if it even crossed Gianna's mind that she might take it and run. She doubted it. Gianna knew the hold she had on Adrienne. She knew how to alternate between love and terror as needed, always knew what to say to keep her there. As much as she hated it, as awkward as it had been to admit to Kaia, she did still love Gianna, even if it had warped into a different and ugly kind of love.

Gianna was crossing the lot. She had spotted Adrienne and looked happy. That was a good start. She opened the car door and slid in. She kissed Adrienne, a casual, familiar kiss on the lips that somehow communicated the five years they'd been together.

"You okay?" Adrienne asked.

"Of course."

Adrienne reached for the shifter, but Gianna covered her hand with her own before Adrienne could shift into gear. She looked into Adrienne's eyes.

"Are *you* okay?"

She looked so sincere, so warm. She cupped Adrienne's face with her palm, eyes exploring the bruises. Gianna's eyes shimmered, the closest thing to crying they ever did.

"I'm so sorry, baby." She kissed Adrienne's face gently. "I've been trying so hard to do better."

Gianna's cool touch was soothing to her sensitive skin. She wanted to ask how hard it could possibly be not to beat her senseless, but digging for more wasn't worth it. If Gianna felt her apology wasn't believed and accepted, she'd snap back into being the same person she claimed she wasn't. Three years ago, Adrienne had fallen for the apologies wholeheartedly. Two years ago, she'd been skeptical, but still foolishly hopeful. Now she knew it wasn't true, but couldn't truthfully say she didn't still love hearing it. She let Gianna pull her closer, wondering how it felt so safe being with Gianna even though she'd hurt her far more than she'd ever protected her.

"I'm nothing without you baby," Gianna said. "I've been getting better. You make me better."

Adrienne let go of the part of her that wanted to stay mad. To deny her would be a waste of Gianna's rare affection and would plunge them directly back into misery, and then she'd wish she had just enjoyed this moment instead of ruining it.

Adrienne drove home. When they pulled up to the house, Gianna saw the reunion of the Wild AKs waiting for her on the lawn, behaving as if she'd been gone for months rather than the three days she actually was. Anna jumped on the hood of the car, bottle of tequila in hand.

"Get out of the car, motherfucker, let's party!"

Gianna smiled as she got out and hugged all fifteen or so of them. They piled inside and tequila shots started flowing. Adrienne watched Gianna talk to everyone, the way they all wanted to please her. She was at once intimidating and warm, charismatic but ruthless. Adrienne knew she would be the leader of the Wild AKs one day, and that all the associated dangers of that would follow Adrienne too. She knew it was juvenile to be so fascinated with the money, drugs, power, guns, the fearlessness, the rebellion, but she couldn't help it. It was a life that felt different. It felt real. Not a life commanded by needs, clocking in and out of some worthless job, being crushed by constant struggle. She knew the dark side of this life well, but most of the time when she looked around she saw smiles, friends, money, and family who would die for one another. A huge part of her wanted to jump in and wear that WAK ink, and she was finding it harder to remember any benefits of not doing so.

Anna bounded up and handed Gianna a roll of cash. "I sold your share for you."

"All of it?"

"Yeah. Count it if you want. Your girl thought I was trying to rob you or something." Anna glared at Adrienne.

"She's just looking out." Gianna beamed at Adrienne and pulled her close. Adrienne wrapped her arm around Gianna's waist and squeezed, absorbing Anna's glare like a smug sponge. Gianna raised her shot glass toward Anna. "You *do* look sketchy as hell," she teased her.

"All right, that's cool," Anna said. "She called the cops on you, though, bud. You know that, right?"

"Yeah, I know. She didn't give them anything to work with, though. No harm done."

Adrienne was shocked. Gianna was obviously still trying to get back in her good graces, but she never expected that transgression to go unpunished. Anna looked like she was going to explode. Adrienne squeezed Gianna's ass and lightly bit her neck before Anna could press it again. Gianna's eyes flashed with lust, and Adrienne knew she'd won. Gianna could be hotheaded and selfish, but she was crazy about Adrienne. Even though the cost was too high, Adrienne loved the way Gianna looked at her like she was the sexiest, most desirable thing on the planet.

"That's weak, man," Anna said, pulling them both back.

"Nah, it's okay."

"It's not okay, man. She got you arrested. I don't want a snitch around us."

"She didn't give them anything."

"Snitching is snitching."

"It's not snitching if she didn't give them anything." Gianna leaned forward, mildly posturing on Anna and signaling she was out of patience. "She's ride or die, Anna. Give her a break."

Anna laughed and directed her piercing gaze at Adrienne. "You ride or die?"

"Of course."

"Prove it. We got some business to do. Need a driver. Think you can get some dirt on your church dress?"

"What does that even mean?"

"You coming or what?"

"Now?"

"Hell yeah, now. The night is young."

Adrienne glanced at Gianna, who shrugged casually. There was no pressure, but Adrienne had an opportunity to truly shut Anna up, to be something other than Gianna's girlfriend and punching bag.

"Let's do it."

Twenty minutes later, they pulled onto a street lined with what were obviously multimillion-dollar homes.

"Kill the lights," Gianna said.

Adrienne did as she was asked, heart thudding heavily in her chest.

"This guy has been buying from us for months," Gianna said. "Suddenly thought he didn't have to pay anymore. He obviously has the money, as you can see."

"So now he's going to pay plus interest and a beat down," Anna said.

"Stop here."

Adrienne stopped. She could barely breathe. This had transformed from words to reality in minutes, and now she was one twist of chance away from jail, maybe worse. She didn't have the personality for this. She'd always felt like the good kid trying to fit in with the bad ones, the one terrified person in the group of delinquents, except she was twenty-seven now. She suddenly felt so stupid and out of place, like she'd risked her whole life for the satisfaction of talking tough. She shook it away. She wasn't going to be scared and weak. She'd been trying to overcome that version of herself her whole life. Gianna looked at her, scanning her for a reaction.

"Be safe," Adrienne said. "I'll be here."

Gianna smiled and kissed her. She and Anna got out and moved quickly in a crouch toward the back of the house. Adrienne saw the subtle bulge of a gun in each of their waistbands. Adrienne strained to hear, but there wasn't a sound. She got paranoid some nosy neighbor was calling the cops, or worse yet that someone had cameras.

Gianna and Anna finally came creeping back out, apparently not in any hurry. They got in with sly smiles.

"Got it, let's go."

"Hold on," Anna said. "Someone just turned on behind us."

"Cop?" Gianna asked.

"I don't know. Duck, let him pass. He's probably just driving through. He's alone."

Adrienne lowered herself in the seat, trying to disappear. Her pulse thundered in her ears. They waited in silence for the car to pass, but it didn't. Gianna lifted just enough to look in the side mirror.

"Shit, he's behind us. It's a cop." She slowly took her gun from her waistband. "He doesn't know if we're in here yet. Go."

"What?" Adrienne hissed.

"Go. He won't chase for this."

"He's got our plates by now."

"They're not ours. I stole them. He's walking up, Adrienne. Go!"

"Shit." Adrienne straightened up and hit the gas hard. The tires squealed, then finally got traction and the car jumped forward. Anna sat up and watched out the back window.

"He's running back to his car. Damn, he's going to try it. You have to hit it, girl."

"You said he wouldn't chase!"

"Yeah, well, we got a cowboy." Gianna pulled the slide of her pistol.

Adrienne saw a flash of Kaia in that car, being shot at. She knew it was unlikely, the odds were absurd, but it was all she could think about. She tried to shake it away and hit the gas harder. The speedometer climbed through the 60s, 70s, up into the 80s, which felt like light speed in the quiet neighborhood. The red and blue lights were pulsing furiously, the sirens screaming. She turned, slowing a quarter of what she knew she ought to. They screeched around the corner and nearly lost control.

"You got it," Gianna said, cool as could be. Adrienne was shocked to find it actually helped. The street was narrow and curved constantly, impossible to speed through the way she wanted. She turned again. More of the same stretched in front of her.

"How the fuck do you get out of here?"

"Straight, left at the school," Gianna said. "We're okay."

"I still hear him," Anna said.

"He's going to have backup soon," Adrienne said, panic creeping up again. The lights flashed around the corner again and sped toward them.

"God, fuck off!" Adrienne yelled.

Anna laughed. "I got it." She rolled down the window, leaned out from the waist up, and fired three shots. His brakes locked and Adrienne flew ahead. She spotted the school and turned onto a wider suburban road. She accelerated into the 90s. Before she knew it they broke 100. She approached 110.

"Yeehaw," Anna said.

"All right." Gianna touched her leg. "Slow down up here and go right. He's not following anymore."

"Did you hit him?" She glanced in her rearview at Anna.

She shrugged. "Doubt it."

They pulled over and Gianna got rid of the stolen plates, putting their own back on before they went home.

Back inside the house, Anna and Gianna each emptied their pockets, producing thousands of dollars. Anna counted out a thousand and handed it to Adrienne. "You did good."

Gianna did the same and kissed her. "Get something you've been wanting."

What she wanted was out of this relationship and away from this gang, wasn't it? Gianna leaned over and kissed her again, wrapping her arms around Adrienne's waist and pulling her close. Gianna's tongue teased at her lips, parting them slowly. Adrienne accepted the advance. There was something about belonging to Gianna that still made her lose her mind. She was gorgeous, strong, devoted. Despite everything, Adrienne loved being hers. Being accepted by her and Anna felt exactly as good as she'd predicted. But why was the touch of Kaia's hand on hers still tingling days later?

CHAPTER FIVE

Kaia woke to her phone humming across Carli's wood nightstand. She glanced at Carli, still in a sound sleep. She'd tossed the comforter aside during the night and her bare back was exposed. Kaia hadn't particularly wanted to come over, but she'd always had a hard time turning down sex, even when she didn't much want or need it. She finally processed Reid's name on her phone and picked up.

"Hey." Kaia slipped out of bed and tiptoed to the living room.

"Got a minute? I asked about that WAK tat for you."

"Shoot."

"Gang Unit just recently started watching them. Wild AKs. They're up-and-coming. Started small, now they're dealing drugs and guns with the big boys, expanding in a hurry and getting ugly about it."

"How ugly?"

"Whole deal. They came out shooting. Caught a couple homicides. The founder was suspected in two, but they didn't have enough on him and he walked."

"Who is he?"

"Marco Woods. Started the group up as a neighborhood loyalty thing. They have guys, girls, kids, you name it. All you need to get in is the right zip code and a bad attitude."

"So they could be anyone."

"Exactly."

"What else?"

"Not much. They were flying under the radar, but they're getting a lot of attention now. Pretty sure a group of them fired at an officer last night fleeing a B and E."

"What?"

"Yeah, they didn't hit anyone, but they got away. The Gang Unit is taking a hard look at them now. My buddy was curious what brought me in. I think he'd really like to talk to you."

"I don't know if that's a good idea."

"It's a fantastic idea, Sorano. I thought you wanted to be in the Gang Unit."

"I did." She sighed. "I do. But, I don't know, this isn't an opportunity to me. It's personal."

"Can't it be both?"

Kaia paused. She wasn't sure if it could be. "Isn't it a conflict of interest?"

"They're shooting at cops, Kaia. What if you can help? And if it gets you your promotion and gets your ex's crazy girlfriend put in jail isn't that a win, win, and more win?"

"Well, when you put it like that."

"I'll tell him you'll come by. Ask for Davis."

"Okay, Reid. Thanks."

"Everything okay?" Carli padded in, barefoot and still groggy. Her wavy brunette hair was tousled. She'd thrown on a T-shirt that swallowed her small frame.

"Yeah, sorry. I was trying not to wake you."

Carli threaded her arms through Kaia's and kissed her collarbone. "Breakfast?" she asked.

"No, I have to go to work. Someone shot at an officer last night."

"Everyone okay?"

"They missed. He's fine. I just have to go. Might be related to that domestic from the other night."

"Your foot chase?" Carli was plainly distressed. "That means they could have shot you."

Kaia hadn't thought of it that way. "I guess so, but I could always be shot."

"Comforting."

"I didn't know you needed comforting."

"I don't," she said. "I'm sorry. It's not like I don't know what your job is like. You just scared me. Reid sounded panicked when he called it out, and he kept saying 'she's in the alley, she's going eastbound,' and I knew he meant you, not the suspect. Like he was losing you. I know it's not fair, but I was mad at him he wasn't doing more."

"Reid is top-notch. I wouldn't take the same risks I do if he wasn't."

"I know Reid is great. It was just in the moment. And then you weren't texting me back."

"If I was hurt, you'd know." Kaia had only been in the dispatch center a few times, which was more than a lot of officers could say but not enough in her opinion. She did know enough about the way it worked to know an officer injury was a big deal and sent the place into chaos.

"I know. I just…" she paused. "Never mind. It's stupid, you're right."

"Hey, I didn't mean it like that," Kaia said. "What's wrong?"

"You're just acting different."

"Different?"

"Yeah, but you don't have to explain. I just wanted to make sure you're really okay."

"I'm okay."

She thought about just telling the truth, filling her in on Adrienne. They weren't committed enough for Carli to get jealous. They'd always been more friends than anything else, and the sex was casual, though she sensed now that somewhere along the way that line had become blurry for Carli.

"I have to get going," Kaia said.

"Okay."

She knew she left Carli feeling empty, falling far short of the reassurances she'd wanted. All she could think as she took the stairs down was that it was about time to break things off with her, at least take a breather from the sex long enough for things to fall solidly in the friend category again. She didn't even know why. Would it be the end of the world to have a proper relationship? Carli was beautiful, smart, certainly not anti-cop, and as a dispatcher she knew enough about the job to understand, while not really being a coworker. There was a reason dispatchers and cops always dated. It worked. She'd just never been able to stomach the idea of a girlfriend after Adrienne. She'd bounced from flirtations to flings to one-night stands without ever questioning why she liked it that way. Why not try real dating? Adrienne had figured it out, and she'd had to battle a much more homophobic upbringing, had a harder road. But even as she tried to entertain it, Kaia knew she didn't want to be with Carli beyond their wild nights together.

When Kaia got to the gang unit building, she asked for Davis. They sent her back to a man with a military buzz cut, sunglasses, and a hard, round, beer gut.

"You must be Kaia Sorano," he said.

"I am. And you're Davis?"

"Jackson Davis. Parents forgot to give me a first name, gave me two last ones." He chuckled at his own joke and opened a door to a conference room. The walls presented pictures of felons and known gang affiliations.

"So, Sorano. I hear you ran into a friend of ours last week?"

"Yes." Kaia spotted Gianna's mug shot and pointed to it. "This charmer."

"Gianna Hernandez. She's your ex girlfriend?"

"Oh, no, I arrested her. She's dating my ex."

"Right, sorry. I'm sure Castillo said that. I'm swamped right now. Everything is getting a little fuzzy. So that would make Adrienne Contreras your ex?"

Kaia nodded and spotted her picture, not a mug shot but a snap obviously taken during a surveillance outing. Kaia stopped in front of it, fighting her eyes as they tried to wander to Adrienne's long, slender legs. Then the picture next to it grabbed her eye, a snap of Adrienne from when they responded a few nights ago. Murray must have taken the pictures for the report. She hadn't even registered it was Adrienne until she looked directly at it. The bumps and discoloration hid her features. A lump formed in Kaia's throat, and a stone of anger fell into her gut as she absorbed the image.

"Okay, I'm with you." Davis picked up a stack of papers and started flipping through them. "Adrienne Contreras." He settled on a page and scanned it. "Don't have much. Dating Gianna Hernandez, who is on her way to quite a reputation. We can't even tell if Adrienne is a member or just a lover. She's been spotted at some shady events, but seems mostly social, and no identifying tats."

"Adrienne isn't a member," Kaia said.

"You sure?"

"She talked about not being able to leave because of Gianna, but she never said anything about being tied to the gang."

"Would she tell you that?"

"They usually kind of advertise it, right? No big secret. They tattoo this shit on their necks."

"True enough, but not always. Not the ones with brains."

Kaia almost blurted out that she was sure, that there was no way, but she knew she couldn't promise that. Adrienne had directly warned Kaia that she didn't know Adrienne anymore. Could it really be that Gianna was the least of her worries? That it was the gang she was committed to?

"It's been a long time since I was close to Adrienne," she admitted. "I don't think she's a member, I highly doubt it, but I guess I don't know for sure."

"Can you find out?"

This was exactly what she'd been afraid of when Reid suggested she come in. She did want to reach out to Adrienne again, find these things out, but she didn't want to spy, or trick her, or stumble into an obligation to send her to prison if that's what it came to.

"I don't know," she said. "Probably not. I don't matter to her anymore like I did, and she knows I'm a cop."

"But she trusts you?"

"I don't know." She doubted it. Adrienne could hate her for all she knew. Between the way they'd ended, Adrienne's distaste for police, and the fact that she hadn't shown any interest in finding Kaia for the last ten years, she doubted she meant much to her. She didn't want to say that, though. It hurt to think about it too much, and she wanted on this case. She wanted to help.

"I know you've been looking at promoting over here," Davis said. "When Reid brought you up I looked through your application. It's been on ice for months, but it looks good."

"Thank you."

"I won't make you do anything you don't want to, but if you want on this, I do need the help. I think you can help. We can treat it like a trial run, a working interview. A really intense one." He chuckled and sat in a heavily reclined office chair, interlacing his fingers. "Let me know."

Kaia glanced back at the faces spread across the wall, back at Adrienne. It felt like a betrayal. It felt two-faced. But Reid was right, putting Gianna away helped Adrienne, not hurt her. Adrienne seemed fine with Gianna being arrested; she was just afraid to be the one responsible for it. What if Kaia could take it out of her hands?

"I'm in."

"Excellent. I'll let your sergeant know I'm stealing you. Have a look at these. They seem to be the players closest to Contreras. These will be the ones you can get the most intel on. He slid the papers across the table. When he left the room, Kaia sat and picked them up. It was strange hearing Adrienne referred to as "Contreras." It brought the reality that Adrienne was a suspect crashing down. She didn't want to investigate Adrienne; she wanted to investigate Gianna and put her away.

Kaia studied the first picture. Celeste Romero. Light skin, dark curly hair, sweet smile. Like Adrienne, she didn't quite seem to belong, but her criminal history included drug charges and an assault.

Marco Woods. Spiky black hair, deep set eyes, an assault rifle tattooed on the side of his face. Recognizable enough. He looked like a baby but was really thirty-five, an age most in his line of work didn't see. His history was surprisingly light. Still, usually people had to kill their way to power in the gang world. She hoped his cleanish record was more luck than intelligence.

Anna Fields. White girl, very thin, almost gaunt. She was pictured both in a mug shot and a surveillance snap holding an assault rifle in one hand, pointed to the sky. The other hand was flashing what had to be a WAK sign. There were notes describing a very close relationship with Gianna. Kaia hated her on sight. Her rap sheet went on and on, assaults, drugs, weapons, eluding, resisting arrest, breaking and entering. It was unbelievable to Kaia that these people could build such a résumé so young. It should be a physical impossibility, as any one of these crimes should have put them away past their current age. How did they keep getting out of jail so fast?

Christina Vickers was next. There were notes that she was ambitious and actively looking to climb the ladder. She was one to be aware of as she was liable to do anything to gain the street cred she needed. Like the others, she had dark hair and numerous identifying tattoos.

The last page was Gianna. Strong features but still feminine, wide jaw, broad shoulders, six feet tall according to her description. Good, she hadn't imagined it. Dark hair, large wide set eyes, tattoos just about everywhere, the very bold, legible "WAK" stamped on her neck the most prominent. Her history looked like a duplicate of Anna's. They'd probably done most of it together. Kaia spotted a scar from a bullet just center body of her right shoulder. *Jesus, Adrienne, what'd you get into?*

Davis walked back in. "All right, we're squared away. See any friendly faces?"

"Are they in the gun world?"

"Oh, yeah. They've got big guns and lots of them. Modified, fully auto, you name it. Weird part is we have an undercover with Los Hijos de la Santa Muerte. They're the big players in that game, and they aren't dealing to these guys. They're friendly, but not in business. We don't know where they're getting the ghost guns, but they're selling them all over town. My undercovers think they might have something worked out with someone over the border. That seems a bit over their heads to me, but whatever it is it isn't local and we haven't been able to figure it out yet."

"I'll work on that," Kaia said.

"All I need you focusing on right now is figuring Contreras out. Don't ask her the big stuff too fast or it'll just end up in Hernandez's ear. We need to know if Contreras is a member, where her loyalty lies, does she want out, and can she be flipped? Gianna's a big player; if we have someone cooperative in her house we could do a lot of damage."

Kaia's stomach hurt, but she nodded. "Got it."

"Whenever you're ready there's a soft car in the lot for you. I'll let you do this whatever way you want to do it. Just let me know what you need."

"I guess I'll touch base with Adrienne for starts."

"Good. But don't forget, Sorano, these are some real bastards. They know they're going away for a long time if they get caught so they're running and they're fighting, and if all else fails they'll just try to do as much damage as possible before they go down. They're not afraid to shoot. Feel Contreras out, but do not trust her and do not forget who she has chosen to be close to."

Kaia nodded, but she still couldn't bring herself to be remotely afraid of Adrienne. Gianna, on the other hand, she knew would absolutely kill her given the chance.

"Reid said you think they were involved in the shots fired at an officer last night," Kaia said. "Do we know that for sure?"

"Can't prove it. Carl started the unauthorized chase. Didn't call it out so he didn't have backup. He let them go when they fired. Came back and had to explain the shot up cruiser with his tail between his legs. So, no IDs and nothing solid enough to make an arrest. It wasn't their turf either, but I just have that feeling. They fled in a gold Corolla. Wrong plates, but guess who has a gold Corolla."

"Gianna."

CHAPTER SIX

Adrienne's stomach turned when a car she didn't recognize lurched up beside her. She didn't know who she was afraid of, but she'd never known a slow rolling car to be friendly. The window rolled down and the car stopped.

"Kaia?"

"Got a minute?"

Adrienne looked over each shoulder. She'd come out alone, but the prospect of being seen chatting with a cop was horrifying.

"I scoped it out," Kaia said. "No one to worry about."

Adrienne looked back. Kaia's face was half covered with dark sunglasses. She wasn't in uniform. The car was a beater. If this wasn't work, what did she want?

"I don't know." Adrienne stepped back. Uniform or not, if a wayward glance from the bag boy could set Gianna off, this would make her insane.

Kaia pushed her sunglasses to the top of her head. "Please?"

Damn it. Kaia had always known how to work her with those brilliant blue eyes.

"Five minutes." She practically jumped into the car, paranoia raging.

Kaia seemed to realize she wasn't going to be able to focus until they left the area and pulled away, leaving WAK territory in a hurry. Adrienne's eyes wandered to Kaia's toned tan arm as it rested on the steering wheel. She looked like herself again without the uniform, and Adrienne couldn't stop her eyes from soaking the familiar Kaia in.

"Going to church?" Kaia teased her.

"Shopping. What are you doing here?"

"I wanted to make sure you're okay, for starters."

"Of course I am. They're just bruises."

"I know, but Gianna's out."

"She's been fine. Great, actually."

Something flashed across Kaia's face that Adrienne couldn't read. It felt so foreign not to know her. She became self-conscious, remembering how her swollen face looked and wondering if that's what Kaia was thinking about.

"You do want out, don't you?" Kaia asked.

Adrienne couldn't look at her. She shifted. "I don't know."

"You don't know?"

"I never promised you I was leaving."

"Are you serious right now? You're smarter than this."

"This isn't even your business."

"So you're just going to let her smack you around whenever she has a bad day? I don't get it, Adrienne. Talk to me."

"I don't know how to talk to you right now, Kaia. Who are you? Are you a cop? Are you my friend? My ex?"

"You know I can't stop being any of those." Kaia seemed to surprise herself and her cheeks flushed. Just witnessing the warmth in her face felt intimate. A flash of herself kissing Kaia's neck intruded into her mind with unsettling force and clarity. She knew if she entertained it, memories would overwhelm her.

"Are you investigating me?" she asked.

"I'm looking into the gang."

"So, yes?"

"Are you a member?"

"No." Adrienne found herself eager to convince Kaia of that much even though she'd felt ready to commit to the gang just last night. Something about being with Kaia made her want to be the version of herself she'd spent so much time trying to bury. Kaia made the gang feel risky, violent, and stupid. Gianna made it feel like family, like unconditional love.

"I'm looking at the gang," Kaia said. "If that's not you, then I'm not investigating you."

Adrienne's heart fluttered. Why was Kaia being so direct? Why was she assuming Adrienne's friendship, even loyalty?

"I'm not going to help you, if that's why you're here."

Kaia nodded, seeming to be in deep thought. Her hair was pulled back, a few blond strands escaping.

"Kaia, if you're doing this for me, don't. I'm okay. I'm not going to be a mole for you, and Gianna will…" she couldn't finish.

"What? Hurt you if you help?"

"I don't want to help. I don't want them in trouble, okay? I know you think that's stupid, but I don't."

Yes, Gianna would hurt her if she helped, but what she'd really stopped short from saying was that Gianna would hurt Kaia, kill her if she had a chance. Adrienne thought of Anna shooting at the cop car last night. No hesitation. It wasn't Kaia, she'd known the odds of that were astronomical, but if Kaia started snooping, following them, next time it could be.

"Just leave it alone. Get back to your life." Adrienne tried her best to sound cold. The less she seemed to care the better. If Kaia really knew who she'd become she wouldn't care what happened to her. If she knew Adrienne had driven the getaway car while Anna shot at one of Kaia's cop buddies, she'd throw her in jail and forget about her.

Never mind that Kaia's smell still made her head swim or that showing up here in street clothes was exactly the way to make Adrienne remember how much she'd loved Kaia. They weren't sixteen anymore, and all they had in common now was a possibility Gianna would kill them. Her life with Kaia ended ten years ago.

"Let me out."

Kaia pulled over. "Do you still have my card?" Adrienne could feel the resentment.

"No. I can't keep that shit around, Kaia. Don't you get it? You're a cop. That's all Gianna knows about you and it needs to stay that way. Why would I keep a cop's card unless I was going to snitch?"

"Put my number in your phone then."

"Why?" Adrienne snapped. She couldn't keep this up. Why was Kaia making it so hard?

Kaia winced. "In case you need help. In case…" Kaia slowly raised her hand. Adrienne had time to move away, but she couldn't.

Kaia's fingers brushed the deep blue bruises around Adrienne's eyes. Adrienne turned her face into Kaia's warm palm and closed her eyes. *Just for a second.* When she opened her eyes, Kaia's were waiting.

"I have to go." Adrienne moved Kaia's hand and got out of the car before either of them could say another word. She went against traffic so Kaia wouldn't be able to follow.

"Shit." If she knew anything about Kaia, she wouldn't drop this. And if she knew Gianna, she wouldn't forget the cop who outran her and yanked her out of a police car by her foot. Gianna had told her everything in a rage, and though a piece deep inside her was smiling, it wasn't worth the danger it put Kaia in.

Adrienne took Kaia's card from her wallet. She had kept it, but what she'd said was true, it wasn't safe to do so. She didn't want Kaia's number, but she couldn't make herself throw it away.

CHAPTER SEVEN

The knock on Kaia's door came well after eleven. Kaia answered in her sweatpants and tank top. Carli stood in the doorway with a bottle of wine in one hand and a bottle of whiskey in the other.

"I admit I'm starting to really like you." She held the wine bottle up. "And I would love to romance you."

Kaia opened her mouth, but Carli cut her off.

"*But* if you're not ready for that, I can do crazy whiskey night too. Just let me do one of them. I'm your friend and I know you're going through something. You don't have to be afraid to tell me what."

Kaia opened the door wider and smiled. "Come on in." She led Carli into the kitchen and found a bottle opener. "Can we do something somewhere in the middle?"

Carli smiled and hugged her. "Of course." She sat on a barstool while Kaia opened the wine.

"Do you want to talk about it?" Carli was in a T-shirt and jeans. Kaia suspected that was her way of saying she wasn't here for sex, but she still looked sexy. Kaia poured each of them a glass of wine and rested her elbows on the counter.

Kaia knew she had to tell her something. "That domestic we went on that keeps coming up. My ex was the victim."

Carli took the information with a straight face, revealing nothing of how she felt. "Is she okay?"

"Seems to be. But she's mixed in with gangsters, and Gang Enforcement thinks she might be involved too."

"Jesus," Carli muttered. "Did you ask her?"

"Yeah, but I don't know if she's telling the truth. Why would she? I'm a cop."

"But you have history."

Kaia shook her head. "I don't know that it matters much. It's been so long. And, I don't know, maybe I overestimated how much she cared in the first place. I mean I haven't talked to her in almost ten years. It's not like she wanted to keep in touch, obviously."

Carli seemed to think for a long time before she answered. "Do you still love her?"

Kaia laughed. "Did you not just hear me say it's been ten years?"

"Why'd you break up?"

Kaia looked down at her marble counter, tracing the swirls with her fingers. "Her mom didn't approve and moved her away." That was the standard answer she'd been giving for years. It was true, but it wasn't the whole story by a long shot.

"So you never got closure. Do you think it's kept you from moving on?"

"No," Kaia said. "I moved on. Life doesn't give you a choice. You move on or you get left behind. I have a life and it's had nothing to do with Adrienne for a long time."

Carli squeezed her hand. "It's okay to care what happens to her."

"Yeah, but she doesn't want me to. She's moved on and she doesn't want me in her life. I'm just someone getting in her way. I think she kind of hates me, honestly."

"That's ridiculous."

Kaia wanted to take comfort in that, but Carli didn't know everything. She felt her eyes watering as her mind tried to jump to the past, to everything that had really torn them apart. The move may have set their demise in stone, but it didn't fall out of the sky. They grew up a couple of blocks from each other, and as kids they practically lived in one another's homes.

As they got older, Adrienne's parents became less welcoming, especially her father. He was a sensitive looking guy, mild mannered, but sometimes Adrienne would hint at his dark side. Kaia never knew what it meant, and even when they started dating, Adrienne wouldn't share anything but the vaguest allusions. The night she did finally find everything out shattered their world.

Adrienne had snuck her in to spend the night. They heard him coming up the stairs, so Adrienne hissed at her to hide in the closet. She did. She expected him to say good night, maybe ask if she'd done her homework, but instead he started taking off her clothes, and she was saying the weirdest stuff. That she didn't feel well, that she had a test tomorrow, like what he was doing was normal and she just wasn't in the mood. He pulled down his pants and got on top of Adrienne. She was crying.

Kaia didn't even think about what she was doing, she just grabbed the baseball bat that was in the closet, came out, and swung it at his head. She hadn't meant to hurt him so bad, didn't think she had until the blood started to pool.

When Adrienne's mom found out she couldn't get Adrienne far enough away. She was a strict Catholic, and her daughter's lesbian lover had just rendered her sexually abusive husband brain dead. The incident had to have shaken her to her foundation, though Kaia never saw her again to know. She thought about Adrienne's dad frequently. She felt like she had killed him. He was a vegetable, so she ended his real life. And she never knew what Adrienne thought about it. She was gone in a flash and never came back.

Carli wiped a tear from Kaia's face. She hadn't realized she started crying. Damn it.

"Maybe this is a whiskey kind of night after all," Carli said.

They both laughed and Kaia broke into the bottle. They moved into the living room.

"You still have a thing for Adrienne, though," she said.

Kaia couldn't help but laugh. "What?"

"Uh-huh, and you need to work that shit out."

"You're crazy."

"Don't tell me that if it's not true." She became serious. "I'll be your friend if that's what you need, but don't string me along while you test the Adrienne waters."

Kaia loved how direct Carli was. It had attracted her, but she didn't want to admit she was even thinking about Adrienne like that. If she let that idea in she might not be able to get rid of it.

"I don't know what to say. Adrienne and I are ancient history," Kaia said. "She's in love with a gangster. I really don't think there's anything there."

"Forget how you think she feels. You don't know how *you* feel about *her*."

Kaia hated that idea. She didn't want to be some weirdo who couldn't get over an ex from a decade ago while Adrienne had been in love with someone else for years and never even thought of Kaia. But Carli was right, just because she didn't want to have feelings for Adrienne didn't mean she didn't.

"I guess you're right. I don't know. But God, that's not fair. She's dating some lunatic and hates cops. We would never work." Kaia took a shot of whiskey. "You and I are such a better match."

Carli smiled shyly. "I agree. But you can't fight what you feel, and if we try to force this, you'll just hurt me."

Kaia was baffled by Carli's composure, her kindness. She'd never seen someone take what was basically rejection with such grace. "I do care about you," Kaia said. "I'm going to miss you."

"Miss me? Girl you still have to deal with me. I'm going to give you every shit call in the queue until I'm over you."

Kaia laughed. "Fair enough."

Kaia woke with an empty bed and a pounding headache. Wine and whiskey, what was she thinking? The clock showed 10:00 a.m. already. She pulled on a sweatshirt and stumbled out to the Lincoln that Davis had checked out to her. She could get used to this kind of work. No uniform, no start time, all about the long game. Her phone rang as she turned the key. It was Davis.

"Sorano," she answered.

"Get anything from your girl?"

"She says she's not a member, but I'm going to push it a bit. I need more time with her. I'm going to do some surveillance on the house today."

"Good enough. Need a surveillance buddy?"

"No, I'm okay."

"Gets boring."

"I know, but I'm okay."

"All right, don't forget to be careful. Even if Contreras is your buddy, these other cats aren't."

"Don't worry, I know."

Careful was not what she had in mind today. She wanted to be seen. She wanted the pressure on Gianna, who obviously couldn't control her emotions. She wanted her to know she was being watched and she wanted to see what Adrienne would do.

Chapter Eight

"Marco says the pigs keep watching his place," Gianna said. She was pacing, thinking.

"What's he want us to do?" Anna asked.

"Just be careful, especially when you're carrying. Don't do anything stupid."

Anna went to the only window that had blinds and peered through them.

"They'll realize they have nothing to go on and move on to bigger fish," Gianna said, mostly to herself.

"We have plenty of money." Adrienne looked up from portioning out the last of the cocaine on the coffee table.

"Yeah." Gianna spun. "So?"

Adrienne shrugged and added some more of the white powder to the scale until she was satisfied with the weight. "We could lay low for a while."

Gianna shook her head. "No. If people can't buy from us they'll go somewhere else, and I'm not having that. We can't go backwards."

"Yo, Gi, we got a problem out here."

"What?" Gianna powered to the window. Adrienne closed her eyes. She'd seen Kaia parked across the street in the same Lincoln she'd been in the other day. That was hours ago, and Adrienne had hoped Kaia had had the good sense to move by now.

"Looks like an undercover car to me," Anna said. "Some cat just sitting inside. What do you think? They on us too now?"

"Hold on." Gianna motioned for Anna to be quiet and squinted. "That looks like the same blond bitch who locked me up last week."

"The one that threw you on the ground?"

Gianna squinted again. "I don't know what she's doing here in that thing, she was a uniform, but I'm pretty sure that's her."

"If it's the same chick she's probably just following up on that," Adrienne said. "Checking up on me."

Gianna looked over her shoulder at Adrienne. "Maybe," she said. "But why the undercover car? She's up to something. Doesn't want people to know she's a cop. Bet she's here to take another cheap shot 'cause I threatened her."

"Alone?" Anna asked.

"These Blues think they're gods just because they have a badge and a gun."

"She got one of these?" Anna picked up the AK-47 from the coffee table.

"She's about to get the wrong end of one," Gianna said. "I warned her."

"Hold on," Adrienne said, forcing herself not to give away her panic by standing up. She mechanically dumped the portion of coke from the scale into a small plastic bag. "I can get rid of her. I'll just go show her I'm fine and healing and she'll go away."

"She's got justice coming her way still," Gianna said.

"Not like this, not in front of our house. You'll go to prison. Just let me try." Adrienne's heart felt like it was going to explode. She couldn't tell if she was believable. Gianna's eyes were narrowed.

"I don't like it," Gianna finally said. "No telling what she'll do. She's crooked."

"Kaia's not crooked."

"What did you say?" Gianna and Anna both advanced.

Adrienne sat up straighter and met their eyes, furious with herself. She'd been so terrified Kaia would give away their past, but she'd been the one to get sloppy. She tried to blow by it.

"I didn't mean it like that. She shouldn't have—"

Gianna charged over and slapped her with a loud clap that made her teeth clack together and left her dizzy. "What did you call her?" Gianna yelled.

"Kaia. Her name is Kaia."

"How do you know that?"

"She told me when she interviewed me."

"Bullshit! They use last names."

"She did! And she left me her card. She wanted me to call if—"

Gianna slapped her again. "If I hit you? You going to turn me in?"

"No! I didn't. I wouldn't."

"You're such a fucking liar! Everything out of your mouth is bullshit. What makes you so sure she's not crooked? You know this broad, don't you? You been talking to the police behind my back?" Gianna was screaming at the top of her lungs and getting closer with every word until Adrienne was plastered to the back of the couch with Gianna towering over her, leaning close to her face.

"No, of course not," Adrienne said. "She's going to hear you, baby."

"Good. Let her ass come in here. I dare her."

"Yo," Anna interrupted. "If you do know this chick that could come in handy."

Gianna stopped and looked at Anna, processing it. She turned back to Adrienne.

"All right," she said. "I'm going to ask you again and I want the truth. I will find out if you lie, believe that. I'm going to find out where this bitch lives, where she's from, where she went to school, where all her family and friends live, what she fucking eats on Tuesday nights, you get it? And if anything or anyone links you to her, even if you just crossed paths in the fucking street and you lied to me, I swear I will kill you. If you tell me right now, maybe Anna is right and we can find a use for that. Now what's it going to be? Do you know her?"

Adrienne's tears were falling from her chin. Over Gianna's shoulder she thought she saw a glimmer of sympathy on Anna's face as she nodded at Adrienne to speak up. Adrienne didn't doubt Gianna's ability to find Kaia's family and friends, and they could all link the two of them. Looking up Adrienne's high school would reveal Kaia went there too. A lie would never pass scrutiny.

"She's my ex."

"Jesus." Gianna backed away from her face. "You dated a cop and you never thought you should tell me that?"

Adrienne shook her head. "She wasn't a cop. We were only seventeen. I haven't seen her since then. I had no idea until she showed up here last week. I swear."

Gianna stared at her. It felt like hours. "That's it? That's everything?"

She nodded.

"Get rid of her."

Adrienne started toward the door. Gianna grabbed her and pulled her back. She wiped her sleeve roughly down Adrienne's face, pressing the sensitive bruises carelessly as she brushed away tears.

"She's not going to leave if you're crying."

When Adrienne got close to the car, she heard the locks pop. She ignored them and went to Kaia's window. It rolled down. Kaia had had a rough night. Adrienne recognized her favorite hangover attire, sweats, a ridiculously old T-shirt, sunglasses, her hair in a messy bun, and coffee in the cup holder.

"Good morning," Kaia said.

"Are you out of your fucking mind?"

"I told you I was looking into this."

"Ever heard of discretion?"

"Never been for me."

"You're supposed to be undercover. They're not going to do anything when they know you're out here, genius."

Kaia smiled. "See, I knew you wanted to help me. Got any other pointers?"

Adrienne scowled at her.

"I'm just making them uncomfortable," Kaia said. "I know I'm obvious, that's the point. Just ruining a few days."

"The only day you're ruining is mine. Now will you please leave before I lose my face?"

Concern mixed with anger flashed across Kaia's features and she pulled her sunglasses down and let them hang around her neck. "Did she hit you? I'll go take her back to jail right now and we can be done with this."

Adrienne shook her head and rested her forearms on the window, making sure to make eye contact. "You have no idea what you've gotten into, do you? They're at the window right now with an AK-47. You try to arrest Gianna they will literally kill you."

"I doubt that. They know that's game over for them. It's just tough talk."

"No, it's not, Kaia. They'll kill you. Please just leave. You are such a shit cop. You have no idea what you're doing."

Kaia laughed.

"Seriously. It's not funny."

"I am not a bad cop. I arrest people who do illegal shit, hitting someone qualifies. I have every right to go arrest her. I don't care how much backup I have to call in to do it."

"I never said she hit me, I said she's going to if you don't leave."

"And you think I believe that? You think I don't see the mark on your face? Or smell the weed on you? Or know that white dust on your shirt is coke? I mean, Jesus, Adrienne."

"Oh, is there coke on my shirt?" Adrienne snapped.

"Yeah, there is."

"You going to arrest me?"

"Of course not. Would you just—"

"Go on, Kaia, arrest me. Serve justice." Adrienne held her wrists forward for cuffs.

"You know that's not what I want. I told you I'm investigating the gang."

"You can't arrest Gianna because *I* smell like weed."

"We both know what I'll find if I go in there."

"Please, like you've never smoked a joint before."

"So far from the point, Adrienne."

"And what is the point? That you're going to just barge in there because you want to and find the evidence later? Use a little cocaine you found on me to arrest Gianna? That the kind of cop you are?"

"Of course not. We both know Gianna's the dealer. I know she's making you—"

"No, Kaia. You can't be that naïve."

Kaia's eyebrows raised. "What is that supposed to mean?"

"I'm not a member, but I *am* a dealer. It's how I met Gianna. The coke is mine."

Kaia rubbed her temples, and Adrienne felt herself hanging on to the silence when she should be walking away. Finally, Kaia looked up.

"I'm not going to mark up your record and give you an excuse to say this life is your only option. I can help you, Adrienne."

Adrienne wanted to believe that, to trust Kaia, to let her be some knight in shining armor who was going to just whisk her away from all of this and into the sunset, but she couldn't. She thought of how incredible it would be to just get in this shitty car and leave, never return. But that wasn't real. All she was going to do was get Kaia hurt if she leaned on her.

"Please go, Kaia. Please."

"We'll get you to a safe house." Kaia wouldn't let up. "Change your identity if you want. We can get you out of town. Gianna will go away for a long time with even a little of what you know."

"Why can't you understand I don't want that? I don't want to put her in prison. I just want you to leave me alone," Adrienne said. "I have to go. I've already been out here too long."

"Look, I'll leave now, but I want you to call me. This isn't you, Adrienne. Whether you go down with her or she kills you, this doesn't end well. It's just a matter of time. Let me help you."

Adrienne walked away without responding. It was the second time Kaia asked Adrienne to let her help, and it had melted her both times. She couldn't let herself believe in a way out, though. It would crush her.

Anna and Gianna were waiting at the door.

"Well?" Anna asked.

"She's leaving." Kaia had already started rolling down the street.

"No shit," Anna said. "What did she say?"

"She was worried about me."

"She's not looking into the drugs?" Gianna asked.

"She didn't say anything about drugs, or the Wild AKs. I think she's just trying to see if we're still fighting."

"Why the car?"

"She's on her own time. She's my ex, I'm not sure it was exactly supervisor approved to come by."

Gianna nodded. "So this is all about you? That's it?"

"Seems to be." If Gianna thought Kaia was a threat to the Wild AKs the whole gang would get involved. That was the last thing she needed.

Gianna walked over and lightly grabbed Adrienne's face. "You did good," she said. "I'm sorry I hit you. I thought you were double-crossing me."

"I'm not. I just didn't know what to say."

"You love me?"

"Of course."

"Good. We can flip this on her then."

"What do you mean?"

"You can get information from her," Gianna said. "She's a cop, right? She has to know or be able to find out what they know about us. And then you can nudge them another direction. She'll ask you about us. You can make them think there's nothing to find. Get these assholes off our case."

Adrienne's heart dropped. All this effort to get Kaia to leave and now Gianna wanted them in contact.

"You want me to meet up with her again?"

"She seems willing enough."

"Yeah, but she doesn't know anything. Why get her interested by bringing it up? Then she really won't drop it."

"If you feed her bad information you can get this whole case thrown out. Convince her we're not in the game. Then she'll go tell all her little cop friends and we're in the clear again."

"I don't know. I don't think I have that much power over her."

"I think you do," Gianna said. "And anyway, she's still snooping around looking for another domestic violence charge. She has to go. Either you convince her to leave it alone the nice way or I can do it the bloody way."

"Fine, I'll try." She turned.

"And, Adrienne." Gianna pulled her chin back. "Betray me, you're done."

CHAPTER NINE

The novelty of detective work was already wearing off. Kaia hadn't uncovered anything useful the last two days. She'd spent it researching the gang members but didn't find anything she hadn't already assumed. She knew it would piss Adrienne off, but she had to get back out there, and to do that she needed to ditch the Lincoln. She pulled up in the gang unit lot and went to Davis's office. She set down her keys. "I'm going to need a different car."

Davis didn't look up until he finished typing. "Are there bullet holes in it?"

"No."

"Whew. They're getting real testy about that at the garage. What's wrong with it?"

"They know it now."

"Okay, you got it. Update?"

"Adrienne isn't a member. I'm sure. She had hours to tip them off and didn't when I was doing surveillance, and when they finally spotted me she came out herself to get rid of me safely."

"That doesn't mean anything other than she likes you."

"Doesn't a gang trump that if she's really in it?"

"Supposed to, but it's not really like these are the rule abiding sort of people."

"We talked about it. She said she's not a member and I believed her."

His face wasn't exactly one of doubt, but Davis was clearly mulling it over.

"Sometimes you just know when you're hearing the truth," Kaia said.

Davis nodded. "I can understand that. We should look at flipping her, then. You think you can?"

"I think so. With more time."

"All right, keep working it."

"Anything new I should know?" Kaia asked. She felt guilty she hadn't provided more herself yet, but Davis had made her mission clear. Turn Adrienne. She preferred to look at it as rescue Adrienne, but she understood. Adrienne must have more than enough information to put Gianna in checkmate if only she'd provide it.

"Davey is set up at Marco's most days now," Davis said. "Heavy traffic in and out of the home. We've been working on finding out who they all are. So far they're small-timers. Corner dealers. I'm not even that interested in their drug game, to tell you the truth. I've seen it before. I just want to know where they're getting these guns and shut it down. We don't need our streets that heavily armed. They have way more firepower than our guys in uniform. It's a matter of time before someone gets hurt."

"Got it."

Kaia's phone rang. She ignored it while she made her way out of Davis's office, but it went off again. She silenced it again. On the third call, she gave in and pickup up, even though she didn't recognize the number.

"Sorano."

"Kaia, Reid is hurt." She couldn't process who was even talking to her. "We're on our way to the hospital, meet you there."

"Wait, what happened?" Her heart slammed into overdrive while she ran to her car.

"We don't know exactly. We found him badly beaten." Kaia finally placed the voice as her sergeant's. "He didn't even get a call for help out. The guys went to his GPS location to check on him when we couldn't get him to answer the radio, but we don't even know how long he was there before we got him."

"Suspects?"

"Long gone."

"I'm on my way."

Kaia knew his room by the horde of officers around it. Some were praying, others huddled in small groups, more still simply stood quietly on their own. They moved out of the way when they saw her. Her sergeant from the street crime task force found her and grabbed her arm.

"It's bad. Brace yourself."

When she walked into the room, she realized she had not braced herself. She should have. Reid had a tube down his throat and his face was mangled. It was bright red and lumpy to the point his adorable features weren't even recognizable.

"Oh, Reid."

"He's going into surgery soon. They say they'll know more after, but he's critical right now."

Kaia put her hand gently on his forehead. "I'm here, Reid. I'm so sorry." She looked to Sergeant Cruz. "I should have been with him. This shouldn't have happened."

"You didn't do anything wrong. You know that. You can't always predict this stuff."

"Is he going to be okay?"

"They don't know."

"Oh God." Kaia's throat swelled and tears ran hot.

"Hey, they're not writing him off. He's got a hard road, but he'll make it. He's young and strong."

Kaia nodded. "What happened, Sarge? How could he not have even been able to hit his emergency button?"

"We have the scene secure still. They're talking to witnesses, checking cameras. We'll figure this out and we'll get the sons of bitches."

"He got jumped?" It was the only conclusion she could draw from his scattering of bumps and injuries.

"Or hit by a car. But my money's on jumped too." He paused. "I haven't let many people see this yet, but there's more." He waved Kaia to the corner where he handed her Reid's shirt. "WAK" was spray-painted across the chest.

"Motherfuckers!" Kaia spun for the door, but Cruz grabbed her.

"That's why I haven't told people. Don't make me regret telling you. Don't get crazy. I don't want you trying to handle this yourself and getting hurt too."

"Why are we acting like we don't know what happened? Why aren't we doing something? They claimed him. Like a fucking achievement."

"We'll get them, but we don't need to be idiots about it."

"Where is the scene?"

"What?"

"You said the scene is secure. What scene? Where?"

"Garfield and Wentworth."

"I'm going."

"They have it. You should stay with Reid."

"Reid is going into surgery. The only useful thing I can do right now is make sure no one misses anything or fucks up the scene. That is right in WAK land. The more of us out there the better. They're going to be threatening witnesses and trying to mess with evidence."

She knew he didn't want her to go, but he nodded. She brushed Reid's hair with her fingers one more time. "Be strong, Reid. You're going to be okay."

Kaia screeched into the square at Garfield and Wentworth fast enough to alarm the officers until they recognized her. She received a dozen hugs before she could get them to focus. Finally, a rookie named Jason took her to the corner where they'd left Reid. There was more blood than she expected, and she had to gather herself.

"They left him to die," she said.

"Oh, yeah. My guess is they were pretty sure he was done for or they'd have kept going. It was no quick beat down. They wanted to kill him."

"Get anything from the witnesses yet?" Kaia spotted seven stores within sight.

"No, they're not talking. Scared shitless."

"See any Wild AKs trying to sneak a look?"

"Wild AKs? Don't know 'em. Wouldn't know how to spot them."

"They fly blue and most have it stamped right on them. W-A-K or rifle tattoos. Could be any race, male or female."

"Got it. I'll keep an—"

"They're right there. Come on," she said. "You too." She pointed at two more officers. "They're nasty and probably armed." Kaia powered over to the group without a second thought to her safety. Gianna, Anna, and Celeste were sitting at a restaurant's outdoor patio watching them like it was a show.

"You're going to need a really good explanation for why you're here," Kaia said.

Gianna sipped her drink, then held it up. "They have good margaritas." The group chuckled.

"You need to leave." Kaia hated that she couldn't just arrest them on the spot. A WAK tag on Reid's shirt didn't mean it was them; there were a lot of members. It wouldn't hold up in court, anyway, but she knew it was. Hate filled her body.

"Leave? We just got here. Loosen up. Let me buy you a drink," Gianna said.

"I think you've been here for hours, on the other side of the square. This is a secured area, you need to leave or I will escort you out."

"Escort me, is that what you're calling it now? You know, you should really ease up with the inappropriate use of your power, the excessive force. People can really get hurt." Gianna winked.

"I'll give you excessive force." Kaia felt herself raise her fist. Jason's arm wrapped around her upper body and pulled her back. Gianna laughed.

"Damn, I think I underestimated you, Blondie. Now I kind of like you a little." Gianna turned to Jason. "Don't worry, rookie, I won't make a fuss about you harassing us or your buddy's temper. We'll even leave nice and orderly for you. Bye, Blondie."

Kaia headed across the street, back to the scene. Jason was in her ear.

"What the hell was that?"

"They're the ones who attacked Reid. I can't prove it yet, but it was her. She is not to be in the area. She's the one scaring our witnesses quiet."

"What if someone calls internal affairs?"

"Did you not just hear me say they beat down our boy?"

Jason flushed. "I know, I didn't mean—"

"We have legitimate cause to remove them from the area. If you're referring to the disagreement back there, you heard her, this is a quiet zone. They do not report. The only one who would tattle on me is a no good rat of a cop."

"Shit, I didn't see a thing."
"All right then."

Kaia felt frozen inside when she woke up. Reid's beaten face was her first thought, and it came the moment she was conscious. It was like she went from a nightmare to the reality that it was all true seamlessly. She sat up and looked at her phone for updates on Reid. She had a message from Cruz that simply said, "All same." When she'd last checked on him he was out of surgery but still critical, so the same wasn't great. She also had a voice mail. It was from a number she didn't know, but since Reid got hurt she was getting calls from all sorts of law enforcement she didn't have numbers for. Adrienne's voice surprised her.

"I heard about your friend. I'm so sorry. I don't know if you can, but I want to meet you. I'll be at the coffee shop at Racine and Taylor at ten."

Kaia looked at the time. She needed to leave soon to make it. She didn't really want to see Adrienne right now. It was her psychotic girlfriend that did this. Adrienne could have pressed charges that would have put Gianna safely behind bars and Kaia could have been with Reid to watch his back. She knew it wasn't fair to hold Adrienne responsible for everything, but her heart hurt too much to stop feeling it.

Still, Adrienne knew about Reid, which probably meant Gianna told her. And now she wanted to meet. Adrienne might finally be ready to give her a lead, and she couldn't ignore that.

Chapter Ten

Kaia showed up in sunglasses again. Another rough night. Adrienne knew this one was probably from crying. She got up and walked toward her. It was a compulsion she couldn't stop. She wrapped her arms around Kaia and held her tight.

Kaia felt stiff. It took her a long time to return the embrace, but she finally did. Adrienne released her and sat.

"How is he?"

"Not good, but fighting. He's alive. You can tell Gianna that."

Adrienne heard venom in Kaia she wasn't used to. "I will if that's what you want."

"Please tell me you're here to give me a statement that Gianna did this."

Adrienne pulled back. She should've seen it coming, but she hadn't. "No."

"What the fuck are we doing here, then?"

Adrienne winced. Kaia had never talked to her that way. Had she lost her? Pushed her away too well? Did she not see all this coldness was just to protect her? Adrienne had assumed she was transparent and that Kaia would always be hers in their own way. Maybe that had been arrogant. She wanted to explain herself, to go back to when Kaia first walked into her kitchen after tackling Gianna in the alley and give her the gratitude she'd deserved.

"Kaia, I'm so sorry about your partner. I really am. He didn't deserve that."

Kaia wiped away a tear. "No, he didn't."

"I can't give you a statement because I don't have any proof. Gianna went out with the gang like always, but I don't know where she went or what she did. She didn't tell me she did it."

"How did you know it happened then?"

"She told me it happened, just not who was responsible. She told me she ran into you, that you were accusing her of it and that you tried to hit her. Kaia, are you out of your mind?"

"Give me a break. I'm not afraid of your stupid thug girlfriend. I walk around with a gun too. I wish she would."

"Kaia."

"Fine." Kaia raked her fingers through her hair. "So she didn't tell you she did it, how do you know she did?"

Adrienne cocked her head in surprise. "The same way you do."

"Well, shit." Kaia ran her hands through her hair again. It was down today, the first time Adrienne had seen it that way since Kaia came back into her life. The unruly dirty blond tresses fell into her face. She probably hadn't bothered even touching it today. Adrienne smiled, remembering how Kaia would scold Adrienne for calling her hair blond, insisting it was brunette even though it wasn't. If only she knew she was gorgeous just as she was.

"So what did you want to talk about then?" Kaia asked.

"Gianna found out you're my ex."

Kaia finally took off her sunglasses and leaned forward. "What? How? What did she do?"

"It was my fault. It was stupid. I accidentally said your name."

Kaia raised a suggestive eyebrow to tease her and caught her completely off guard. Adrienne felt her cheeks flush. "Shut up, not like that. In conversation."

"Did she freak?"

"Yeah, but not as bad as I thought she would. She wants me to pump you for information."

"What kind?"

"I convinced her you're just following up on me, but she wants me to get you to find out how much the detectives know about the Wild AKs."

"Really?"

"Yeah, then she wants me to convince you they have it all wrong and that the Wild really just deal a little weed and that Gianna hitting me was a crazy fluke so you'll all leave us alone. She thinks all you're doing is making sure I'm okay."

"That is what I'm doing."

Adrienne felt a warmth travel down her spine. "I'm taking a leap of faith here, Kai, telling you this instead of trying to actually do it. What do I tell her? What am I supposed to take back to her?"

"I don't know. I'll have to ask Davis what he wants to reveal."

"What? No. I'm not a mole. I'm telling *you* this, not the department. And I'm only telling you because she wants me to play you and I'm not going to do that."

Kaia smiled. "Thanks for that. I was afraid you were."

"I'm not playing you. I'm trying to keep your stupid ass out of danger."

"Not going to happen."

"Yeah, I'm getting that. So what do I tell Gianna?"

"Tell her her plan might've worked, but now I know she hurt Reid and no amount of you lying or saying you're okay is going to stop me."

"I don't want you in a war with her, Kaia. I know you're pissed and want to fight right now, but she's not going to fight fair. The Wild are everywhere now. There are dozens of them."

"Dozens? Really? How many dozens?"

"Several." This felt too much like snitching, but she had to make Kaia understand the danger. "And they are all armed. Heavily."

"Yeah, what's up with that? Why so many guns?"

"To scare people, obviously. They're taking over everyone's territory by sheer force. You can join or get gunned down."

"Where are they getting them?"

Adrienne pushed back in her chair. "Come on, Kaia."

"You come on. I know you know this stuff. You say you can't leave and you keep telling me how scary they are, help me disarm them. Let me fix it. You don't have to be trapped. You're doing this to yourself."

"If they find out—"

"I know. They won't."

"You don't know that. You want to find my body in a ditch with no fucking skin? Because that's where this goes."

"Okay, okay."

"Thank you."

Adrienne watched Kaia try to hold back. She could barely control herself. "Oh, for Christ's sake, what?" Adrienne asked.

"Don't go back," Kaia said. "If you'd let me get you out of there this wouldn't be a problem."

"You really think it's going to be that easy? She *will* find me."

"She'll be in jail once you give us what we need."

"I'm not going to send her to prison."

Kaia shook her head. "So you're just here because she sent you? That's all there is to it?"

"No. I came for you too, but I'm not going to do what either of you want. You could have arrested me the other day. I told you to, but you didn't."

"Of course not."

"Well, I feel the same about her. We might not be flowers and chocolates anymore, but I still can't ruin her life."

"It's a bit more serious than lackluster romance."

"You know what I mean."

"The middle is dangerous, Adrienne. You're going to have to make a decision."

Adrienne smiled weakly. "I know. But not right now."

Gianna was waiting in the dark when Adrienne got home.

"Well?"

"She's not going to stop," Adrienne said.

Gianna shot to her feet and crossed the space to the door. "Why not? What did you say?"

"I told her I love you and I'm fine. She doesn't care."

"She have a death wish?"

"She said it started about me, but now it's about her partner, Reid. She knows it was you."

Gianna reached out, grabbed her neck, and squeezed. Adrienne forced herself not to move. It only got worse when she fought back.

"Did you tell her it was me?"

"No. I wasn't even sure it was, but she is."

Gianna studied her, then released her. "Yeah, it was me. What's she going to do about it?"

"She wants you to know he's okay."

"She said that?"

"Yes."

"This bitch. Oh, I'm going to kill her."

"Gianna, just let it go."

"Excuse me?"

"Baby, if you kill a cop you're going to prison. I love you. I want you here. Let's just stop." Adrienne looked into Gianna's eyes, trying to communicate her love, searching for the tender soul she knew was buried under all the pain.

"She got to you, didn't she?" Gianna said.

"No. I didn't give her anything. I just want you safe."

"I'm not going to prison." She shocked Adrienne by reaching out and hugging her. "If I let her get away with talking trash I'll lose everything. I won't be safe here anymore. You know my respect is everything."

"They do respect you."

"It's not a one-time earn, babe. You have to live it every day. She should have never chased me. It's been shit ever since then and we can't go back now. She has to defend her partner. I get it. Cops ain't nothing but a rival gang, and we're at war."

"I miss you," Adrienne said. "I miss what we were before the Wild AKs."

Gianna backed up, all business again. "The gang comes before anything. You know that."

Adrienne dropped it before she made Gianna mad. "I know. I just care about you."

"Yeah, well, you sound like your cop friend. Don't let her mess with your mind."

"I'm not."

Chapter Eleven

Sometimes Kaia couldn't stand the gray of Chicago. It felt like the city was composed almost entirely of concrete and the criminals were just as cold and hard. She liked being able to say she was an officer in one of the roughest cities in the nation, but on those days she needed a little help, the old-fashioned neighborhoods where everyone grew up being told to never tell cops anything were suffocating and lonely. Nevertheless, she went into the salon that had a direct view of Reid's assault and hit the bell at the counter. A bite-sized over-tanned teenager came to the front.

"Can I help you?"

"Chicago PD, I need to talk to you about an event from last night."

"We already talked to someone. We didn't see anything and our cameras only monitor; they don't record."

"I find that hard to believe."

"Don't know what to tell you. That's the way it is."

"Uh-huh, were you working last night?"

"Yeah, but I didn't see anything."

"You said that. I was going to ask if anyone came in here, maybe stole your equipment? Maybe threatened you? You can be anonymous."

"Lady, what are you talking about? This is a salon. Only time I get threatened is when I'm doing a bikini wax."

"All right, if you remember anything give me a call." Kaia slid her card across the counter.

"There are three employees here," she said. "How anonymous do you really think I can be?" She slid the card back to Kaia. Kaia nodded and turned to leave. She understood, and as much as she wanted to catch Gianna, she didn't want to get this kid killed.

She exited the salon while trying to return her card to her wallet and almost bumped into someone. When she looked up, it was Gianna. It took her a second to process Gianna's face, then take in Anna, Celeste, Christina, and Adrienne beside her.

Gianna beamed at her. "You want me to go in with you? You can ask her if she recognizes me."

"That'd be great, thanks."

"You don't get it, do you?"

"Oh no, I get it. I know you terrorized these people with your fake macho shit. We know, you have a huge dick, Gianna."

She caught a glimmer of a smile on Celeste's face, but Adrienne was a pro actress.

Gianna stepped closer. "You keep poking around where you don't belong you'll get my huge dick right up your ass."

"They're not going to be afraid of you forever."

"Oh yes, they will," Gianna said. "You will be too one way or another."

"You messed with a cop," Kaia said. "You fucked up. They know you fucked up, but they won't tell you." Kaia pointed to Christina, Celeste, and Anna. "And you're all going down for it. Someone always does the right thing eventually."

"Fuck you, pig," Anna jumped in. "We didn't do shit."

Gianna held up her hand. "It's okay. She's trying to make this a legit investigation, but we all know it's personal. You're just mad I'm fuckin' your ex. I know it hurts, but you have to pull yourself together. Let it go."

Gianna grabbed Adrienne's chin and kissed her. Adrienne seemed to expect a peck but Gianna licked her lips and coaxed her into a french kiss.

Kaia's hands felt numb, but she knew the others were diligently studying her for a reaction to report. She gave away nothing, even hoped Adrienne would pull it off seamlessly, well aware of the beating she'd probably get if she didn't. But if Adrienne was uncomfortable with the display, Kaia couldn't tell. Adrienne laced her fingers into Gianna's hair and met her lips passionately. When they finally parted, Kaia felt drained and tingly, a rock heavy in her chest.

"Very nice," she said. "I'm sure you'll write every day from prison."

She passed them, not trusting herself to look at Adrienne.

"Give my best to the cripple," Gianna called after her.

Kaia flipped her off over her shoulder and got in the marked unit she'd decided to drive today.

Kaia waited outside Reid's room, hoping that obstructing the hallway would force someone to update her. A nurse finally stopped.

"He's doing really well," she said. She looked like Dorothy from *The Wizard of Oz*, in personality more than literally. She wasn't sure this woman was capable of bearing bad news and doubted her information.

"Does he have more surgeries?"

"Yes, two more. But he's already through the worst of it. Keep your head up."

"When will he wake up?"

"It'll be a while. He's got some brain swelling right now, so we don't want him to wake up yet. Don't let that stop you from talking to him, though." She moved on to the next room unceremoniously.

Kaia went into Reid's room and pulled a chair next to the bed. She interlaced her fingers and rested them on the side of the mattress.

"You're going to be okay, Reid. I know it. And I'm going to catch these bastards. I'll catch them if it kills me. I know you're going to wake up and tell us it was them. They're saying you might not remember, but I know you will."

She watched the monitors. She didn't know what it all meant, but it seemed steady, peaceful. She sat with him for hours, happy to have some time alone with him. Reid's warm and silly personality won him lots of friends. Everyone wanted to be there for him, and there had been a steady stream in and out since he was hurt.

Kaia knew her people would show up for her too, but not the kind of turnout Reid had. She had family, supportive parents. They hadn't loved it when she came out, but they took it on the chin, hugged her, loved her. She had a brother in Australia who was a sweetheart, but she only saw him around Christmas, and some years he missed that too. Her dating habits were shallow and erratic. Reid was her family. The longer he was gone the more she realized how alone she'd been walking through the world.

Kaia walked out of the hospital late, after midnight. The cold air ripped through her, humidity from the lakes giving the temperature a sharp edge that cut through her layers. She was heading for her car when she heard pops. She couldn't process what it was for an instant. It sounded like fake gunfire, like a toy. Two massive impacts hit her chest like a baseball bat and sent her to the ground. She hit pavement flat on her back and lost her breath but didn't let the pain slow her down. She scrambled behind her police car, opened the passenger door, and hit the emergency button to call for help. She glanced at her chest and confirmed there were two rips in her shirt where bullets had found her vest. She didn't think either had made it through, but she didn't have time to check.

A black Escalade she'd never seen rolled by with the windows down. A handgun was leveled at her from the driver's window, the back windows revealed assault rifles pointed her way too. The gunmen's faces were covered with blue bandanas. She gave up the limited cover her car provided and ran in a crouch, hearing bullets thumping after her, stirring up dirt and bits of concrete. She cut behind a thick brick wall that surrounded the hospital dumpsters. She waited for the inevitable pause and returned fire.

She hoped they would speed off, but they actually hit the brakes and another barrage from the rifles whizzed mercilessly at her. They weren't making it through the wall. She heard a car door open and her heart leapt. She couldn't let them close the distance between them. It would be over. She risked the exposure and peered around the wall. She fired at the Wild AK on foot. A fountain of blood erupted from the Wild's chest and they went down. Three others jumped out. Kaia fired at them too, emptying the rest of her magazine and hitting another, who dropped to a knee. She scrambled to reload while they screamed at each other and tried to gather their wounded friend.

She knew she could outshoot them, but she only had one magazine left. She had to be careful with it. She let them drag the down member back to the Escalade while the other limped back. Kaia chanced another look around the wall and fired at the side panel. She'd considered the driver, but if she killed him they'd be stuck here and they'd be forced to shoot it out. She didn't have the ammo for that. She fired one more round and the driver finally sped away.

Kaia checked herself for wounds. She knew adrenaline could be strong enough even to mask a gunshot wound, but all she found were the two initial shots to her vest. She was okay.

Cop cars showed up fast enough she pointed after the Escalade in hopes they were dumb enough to be close by still. The third car ignored her gestures and pulled up. Sergeant Cruz leapt out and ran over to her.

"Are you hit?"

"Just the vest."

He keyed up his radio. "Sixty, I'm on scene, shots were fired at an officer. We're code four, but we need more cars checking the area on this." He turned to Kaia. "You catch a plate?"

She shook her head and gave him all she had. He relayed the description into the radio and helped her up.

"You recognize them?"

"WAKs for sure, but I don't know who. Their faces were covered with blue bandanas."

"Got it."

"Sarge," she said. "I got two of them."

"Attagirl. Dead?"

"One in the leg, one in the chest."

"You're a fucking boss, Sorano."

Kaia nodded, feeling a million miles away from Cruz.

He walked over and rested his hand on her shoulder. "Look around, Sorano. You see all this?"

Kaia surveyed the damage, the casings, the bits of concrete chipped from the ground and walls.

"Most would be dead," he said.

She nodded. "I'm going to go inside. I need a minute."

"Of course."

Kaia went to the bathroom and threw up. She looked under her vest. Purple bruises marked where the bullets had hit. They were vital areas. If she'd ignored her instincts to wear the vest all the time these days, she'd be a goner. If she'd been hit by the rifles instead of the handgun she'd be dead. With bullets flying the way they had been she could easily have taken one to the head. Gianna definitely meant business. First Reid, now this?

She couldn't get her hands to stop shaking. She wondered if either of the people she'd shot would die, and if either had been Gianna. She knew it was a long shot. Gianna's build was pretty unmistakable. She waited for some kind of crisis of conscience over shooting two people, but it didn't come.

CHAPTER TWELVE

The front door slammed open and blasted into the wall. Five people rushed inside, two carried a pale young woman, and Gianna carried a teenage boy.

"Clear a space!" Gianna screamed. Adrienne jumped up and shoved everything off the kitchen table.

"What happened?"

A trail of blood followed them in. She cleared a second place on the floor. Gianna was shimmering in sweat from the effort of carrying the boy. Adrienne had seen him before but never met him. Gianna laid him down on the table. Anna and the uninjured recruit carried the young woman in and lowered her to the floor. Adrienne went to the guy on the table first and pulled his blood-soaked pants down. He had a gunshot to his thigh. It made Adrienne's chest seize looking at it. It was smaller than she'd imagined it would be, a perfect black circle.

"Gianna, what the fuck?" she yelled.

"She's dying over here, man," Anna yelled from over the girl on the floor. Adrienne and Gianna both switched their attention to her. Gianna pulled down the girl's shirt from the neck and revealed two wounds a few inches below her collarbone, just right of center, centimeters from one another.

"Fuck," Anna said. "That's not good."

Gianna grabbed the girl's hand. She was choking on her own blood, panic in her eyes.

"You went out shooting," Gianna said to her and stood again.

"Gianna, you have to take them to a hospital," Adrienne yelled.

"They won't make it there."

"He will." Anna nodded at the guy. Gianna looked at him and he nodded, quiet desperation in his pale face.

"If we drop them off they'll know it was us," Gianna said.

"Gianna!" Adrienne yelled.

"She's not going to make it." Gianna pointed at the girl on the ground.

"Gianna, stop it!" Adrienne knelt by the girl on the floor, who was trying to turn on her side to stop choking on the blood. Adrienne helped turn her and put pressure on the wounds. The girl rested her head in Adrienne's lap. Adrienne rubbed her back, trying to soothe her.

"And we can take care of him ourselves." Gianna gestured at the teenager on the table. "There's no reason to put the whole gang on the chopping block. If we go out in that Escalade right now they'll be all over us before we get anywhere near the hospital."

"We could steal a different car," the uninjured recruit said.

"There's no time to steal a car," Adrienne said. "Gianna, you have to go now."

"I'm serious, Adrienne, we'll never make it to the hospital in that thing. We'll get arrested, probably shot, and those two will die in the backseat while the cops scratch their dicks."

"Well, we have to do something with it 'cause it's in your driveway right now," Anna said.

"Fuck." Gianna looked around the room. "Fuck!"

"There's a used car lot down the street," Adrienne said. "Dump the Escalade there and get something else."

"Cameras?" the recruit asked, halfway to the door already.

"No cameras," Anna said. "But wear the bandana anyway." The new guy nodded and ran out the door.

"Gianna, what happened?" Adrienne asked again.

She didn't answer. Adrienne looked back to the girl in her arms. Her eyes were glassy. She was dead.

"Oh God." Adrienne set her down and stood up, revolted she'd been holding a corpse without knowing it.

Gianna's eyes were cold and hard. "See, she's gone. We should bury her and patch him up ourselves or this is all going to blow back on every single one of us."

"We can just dump them in the ambulance bay," Anna said. "They won't see us."

"It won't matter, the second we drop off a Wild at the hospital they're going to be so far up our asses—"

"They're recruits," Adrienne said. "They're not even inked."

"Adrienne—"

"I'll drop them."

Gianna and Anna exchanged quiet looks. The newbie pulled up in a Suburban.

"I said I'll drop them," Adrienne yelled. "You going to help me get them in the car or what?"

"All right, fine. You." Gianna pointed at the terrified recruit on the table. "She's going to drop you off. You'll be in the backseat. You push the body out and then get your ass out of the car and I mean fast. And if any of our names come out of your mouth I'll give you a bullet somewhere worse than your leg." Gianna turned to Adrienne. "The moment they're out of the car you tear out of there. You find a busy square and ditch the car. You walk away and then you call me and I'll pick you up."

Adrienne nodded and accepted a pair of gloves from Anna. Gianna reached for her cheek, but Adrienne swatted it away and powered for the Suburban.

They loaded the body into the back so the recruit could push it straight out the rear. The moment they closed the hatch, Adrienne zipped away. The quiet roads were at odds with her raging thoughts. She tried not to drown in them. She had to accomplish this first.

"Hey, thanks for this," the recruit said from the back.

Adrienne nodded. "What's your name, anyway?"

"Jeremiah," his voice was a whisper. She wanted to ask if he was okay, but she knew he wasn't. There were a million things she wanted to ask, actually, but it didn't seem right in his condition.

"Any hospital but Christ Advocate," Jeremiah said.

"What? Why?"

"Cops," Jeremiah huffed out the word like breathing was a struggle.

"Cops?"

He didn't answer.

"Jeremiah, you with me? Hang in there." She took his small groan as enough and sped for the next hospital. The building crept into sight and her heart raced as she choreographed the drop in her head.

"We're pulling up," she said. "You ready?" He didn't answer. She looked over her shoulder and saw he was unconscious. "Shit." She stopped the car a block away and climbed into the back. She shook him, but he didn't wake up. She searched the car for an idea but came up short. She could go back home, but she knew Jeremiah would die if she did. She could call Gianna for help, but the idea disgusted her.

She lowered the backseats so they were flat, removing the barrier between herself and Jeremiah. She removed her jacket and shirt, tied the shirt around her face, and put the jacket back on. She climbed back to the driver's seat and took a deep breath.

She hit the gas and pulled into the ambulance bay. She pulled past the door, as far away from the staff as she could to allow herself time, then threw the car in park. She climbed over the front seat, crawled to the back hatch, and opened it. She pushed the dead girl as hard as she could. It was harder to move her than Adrienne expected, but the panic helped her muscle through, rolling the body until it thumped to the ground outside. People saw her now; they were jogging over. She put her feet on Jeremiah, one on his shoulder, the other by his hip, and pushed as hard as she could. He thudded to the ground.

She slammed the hatch shut and dove for the front seat. People were screaming at her to stop, but she threw the car in drive and hit the gas. A man in a security uniform slammed on her window, but she was already rolling away. She hit the gas harder and tore into traffic. A symphony of horns and screams berated her, but she powered on. Her face was covered and the car wasn't hers. She could be a maniac if that's what it took.

She screamed through traffic and weaved her way out of the area. She waited for sirens behind her. Nothing yet, but she knew she couldn't be in the car long. Gianna wanted her to leave the car in a busy shopping center. It would take longer for anyone to notice it was out of place that way, but Adrienne was afraid of cameras. She didn't want to walk down the streets of Chicago with her shirt tied around her face, so she pulled into a quiet neighborhood instead.

She jumped out and put several blocks between herself and the car before she took the shirt off her face. She found a dark corner to put it back on, then cut for a main road where she could disappear into the crowd. She glanced at her phone, but she couldn't make herself call Gianna.

A pink neon sign caught her eye. The flickering words read "Irish Pub." Yeah, she could use a drink.

❖

It was four in the morning when Adrienne fumbled with the lock to the front door. When she got inside the lights were dim. Her eyes adjusted slowly, and finally she could make out the graffiti WAK letters sprayed on her walls. She'd stopped noticing them a while ago, but they leapt at her now. Music came from the kitchen, but all she could make out was the bass.

When Adrienne made her way to the kitchen, Gianna was lounging in a dining room chair with a woman on her lap and a joint hanging from her mouth. One arm was tightly wound around the woman, the other held a bottle of tequila. Gianna's eyes met hers and she let out a cloud of smoke.

"Come on in," Gianna said.

Adrienne thought the hours away might help, that by the time she saw Gianna again she might not hate her anymore, but she still did. She still found this person who was willing to let her friends die a stranger, and even though she knew she should be afraid of what might happen next, she couldn't muster fear of this person. She saw a coward.

Adrienne pulled up a chair and sat. "Who's this?" She nodded at the girl on Gianna's lap.

"This is Amber," Gianna said. She wrapped her hand around the back of Amber's neck and pulled her into a kiss. Adrienne knew Gianna cheated from time to time, but she'd never had it rubbed in her face. She knew Gianna wanted a fight, wanted Adrienne to scream, to cry. She stood and started for the bedroom instead.

"Where do you think you're going?"

Adrienne glanced back. "To bed."

"Are you drunk?"

"Yes."

"Come back here."

"Why? You're busy."

Surprise filled Gianna's face, but it quickly turned to a smile. "Join us."

"It's been a long night, Gi."

"Sure has. Where the fuck have you been? Getting some of your own? That why you don't want to join us?"

"No, I actually have no idea how you can think about sex right now."

"Oh, please, don't give me that. Don't act like this happened to *you*. You weren't there. You didn't lose a member."

"Excuse me?" Adrienne whipped around and went back into the kitchen. "This didn't happen to me? I didn't just have a girl die in my arms? I didn't just shove two bodies out of a car while you sat here getting shitfaced and fucking some bitch?"

Gianna was speechless for a moment. She patted Amber's hip. "Scram."

Amber seemed more than happy to scurry away. Gianna didn't move a muscle until the front door closed behind her.

"The fuck do you mean you shoved two bodies out of the car? What happened?"

"No, you tell me what happened."

"What happened to Jeremiah? Did he die?"

"I don't fucking know, Gianna. Maybe."

"Why didn't you call me? I've been calling you for hours."

"I turned off my phone."

Gianna stood and slammed the bottle on the table. "Why? We had a plan. You call me, I pick you up. And if you had complications you should have called me."

"Yeah, well, I didn't want to."

"This isn't all about you and what you want. This is serious!"

"You think I don't know that?" Adrienne yelled. "That girl died in my arms. Now tell me why."

"Because of your fucking blond friend, that's why. She did this."

Cold tickled up Adrienne's spine. "Kaia shot them?"

Gianna took a swig of tequila. "Yep. She did. There were five of us. She was alone and off duty checking on her boyfriend partner. It should have been a no-brainer. None of us should have died."

"You did a drive-by on Kaia at the hospital?" Jeremiah telling her not to go to Christ Advocate Medical Center rang back through her brain.

Gianna leaned close to her face. "You're Goddamn right I did. I took every big gun in the closet and every recruit with something to prove and I lit that fucking lot up."

Adrienne felt a tingling sting, the impact of her hand on Gianna's face as a loud clap sounded with it. She and Gianna were equally stunned by it. She couldn't breathe. She didn't care if she breathed. Paralysis melted off and something inside snapped. She swung at Gianna again with everything she had this time.

"What is wrong with you?" Adrienne screamed.

Gianna's booze-lazy face finally registered what was happening and caught Adrienne's wrist in the air.

"I lost a member today!" Gianna yelled. "I don't need your shit!"

"Yeah, *you* lost a member. This is your fault. I told you to drop it. I told you to lay low, but you're too fucking selfish, and now people are dead!"

"Your stupid cop isn't dead, Adrienne. She's fine." Gianna slung Adrienne's hand away. Adrienne realized she was crying, near hysteria, figuring it out only as she came down from it. Kaia was alive.

"That's all you care about, isn't it?" Gianna said. "You don't care about the recruit. You don't care about me."

"I—"

Gianna spit in her face. Adrienne tried to wipe the spit from her eyes, but she felt hands around her neck and they were toppling to the floor.

"You've just been playing me," Gianna screamed. "Using me." Adrienne's head was shoved into the corner. Gianna was on top of her, a knee on each shoulder as her hands drove down on her throat. She couldn't move. She was losing consciousness.

Gianna was dragging her. Had she passed out? She didn't resist. Better Gianna not know she was awake until she could see straight. She was being dragged across the kitchen. Adrienne wondered if Gianna was taking her to the backyard to bury her. Did she think she'd killed her? But Gianna dropped her feet. Adrienne heard the faucet turn on and water sprinkled on her face from the sprayer. She didn't move.

"Damn it, Adrienne."

Gianna's footsteps left the room. It was now or never. Adrienne jumped up and went for the sliding door that let into the backyard.

"You fake bitch." Gianna ran after her. She grabbed Adrienne's hair and pulled her back. Gianna slipped on the water on the floor and they both crashed to the tile.

Gianna tried to wrap her arm around Adrienne's neck from behind. Adrienne bit her forearm and clenched her jaw as hard as she could. She felt skin rip and tasted metallic blood. Gianna screamed and let go. Adrienne scrambled up and grabbed a knife. Gianna looked at her own arm, then at the knife.

"What're you going to do with that? You going to stab me?"

"Don't make me."

Gianna rushed her and Adrienne slashed, connecting with Gianna's shoulder, biting into it enough Gianna jumped back.

"Yeah, you don't care about me. Never did. You want to stab me? Stab me!"

"Just let me go!"

"Where? To your cop?"

"Away from you before you kill me."

"Please, I'm not going to kill you."

"Yes, you will. You don't know what you're doing when you're doing it."

"Don't be such a baby. I didn't almost kill you. But I will if you don't put down that fucking knife."

She moved toward Adrienne again. Adrienne swiped. Gianna caught it, but by the blade. Adrienne ripped it away and sliced her hand open.

"Fuck!"

Loud knocking sounded at the door, and Adrienne could just barely hear someone calling Gianna's name, someone looking for drugs. Gianna glanced away just long enough for Adrienne to bail out the back. She heard Gianna hot on her heels and ran with everything she had. She made it out the back gate and ran down the alley. Gianna sounded close. Adrienne couldn't breathe, but she couldn't stop.

"Help!" she screamed.

"Shut up!" Gianna hissed.

"Help!"

House lights started turning on and Gianna fell back.

"This isn't over, Adrienne."

She knew it wasn't, but she didn't care right now. She ran until she found a heavily populated street. She slowed, gasping, and fished for Kaia's card from her wallet and dialed. She held her breath, praying for Kaia's voice.

She answered. "Adrienne?"

"Kaia!" She knew Kaia probably couldn't understand a word she was saying she was crying so hard, but she couldn't calm down. "Pick me up. Please, Kaia, I'm sorry. Please come get me."

She was vaguely aware Kaia had said okay, but she couldn't stop crying. She stayed on the phone the whole time she waited. Finally, Kaia pulled up. She started to open the driver's door, but Adrienne frantically climbed into the passenger seat.

"Let's go. Please, go. Hurry. Get me away from here and I'll tell you everything."

Chapter Thirteen

K aia had been a little afraid the cop car she was in would spook Adrienne, but she barely seemed to notice. She wanted to hug Adrienne, calm her down, but she followed instructions and sped off, eagerly counting the blocks out of WAK territory. Once they were well outside the area, Adrienne reached across the seat and wrapped her arms around Kaia's neck. Surprise and warmth traveled down her spine, and Kaia squeezed her arm in return. Kaia could only guess what happened. Adrienne was still flushed, but she looked basically uninjured. She released Kaia's neck.

"I thought you were dead," Adrienne said. "They said…" She didn't finish.

"I was wearing a vest."

Out of the corner of her eye, Kaia saw Adrienne continuing to look at her and reached for her hand. She squeezed it and they both fell quiet while Kaia drove home. She didn't know if that was what Adrienne had in mind, but she didn't know where else to go and Adrienne didn't comment when they pulled up to Kaia's apartment. Kaia could always breathe easier once she made it back to the north side of town, away from the criminals she angered on a daily basis. Adrienne followed Kaia inside, watching as Kaia dead-bolted the door.

Adrienne looked around the clean but understated apartment. Kaia marveled at the simple wonder of Adrienne in her living room.

"Beer?" she offered.

"God yes," Adrienne said. Kaia smiled and grabbed two from the refrigerator, then handed one to Adrienne. She led Adrienne to the balcony and sat. She was on the tenth floor and had a great view of the twinkling city and the lake stretching as far as the eye could see. It looked nice at night but seemed to be crumbling by day, a sad and abandoned quality to everything despite the dense population.

"You want to talk about it?" Kaia asked.

Adrienne looked over, long dark hair framing her face. Her lip was almost completely healed, the bruises light. Kaia was relieved and confused not to see fresh wounds. What had terrorized her into calling? What had made her hysterical on the phone?

"They brought in two recruits that were shot. Gianna said it was you."

"It was."

"Are you okay?"

"It hasn't sunk in. I wasn't sure how bad I got them until they turned up at the ambulance bay. I knew it probably wasn't good for the one I got in the chest, but you never know."

"She died in my arms."

Kaia felt a shot of adrenaline fly through her veins. "You weren't…"

"In the Escalade? God no, Kaia, I would never shoot at you. Are you kidding?"

"I didn't think so. I just…" she paused. "What happened, then?"

"She died on my kitchen floor while Gianna was trying to figure out how to dump the fucking Escalade."

"I'm so sorry."

"All that talk about family. Wild for life, ride or die, loyalty, and she couldn't be bothered to take them to the hospital. Said she was a goner and we should just bury her so they wouldn't get caught." Adrienne shook her head, eyes lost in space.

"How did you convince her?"

"I didn't. I took them myself."

"That was you?"

Adrienne nodded, tears filling her eyes. "I didn't want to dump them like that, Kaia. I didn't mean to treat them like trash, shoving them onto the ground and running. I just didn't know what else to do. Jeremiah was supposed to help, but then he died in the back on the way."

Kaia reached out and grabbed Adrienne's hand. "Jeremiah didn't die."

"He didn't?"

"No, he's stable. You probably saved his life, Adrienne."

Tears spilled down her cheeks. "Thank God. I was so angry with Gianna. I'm sure you're not surprised, but I was. I really was. I know she's street tough, but she loves her members like family. Or I thought she did."

Kaia nodded. Gang loyalty was a well-known phenomenon, but she'd seen those bonds break over less. "Getting caught shooting at an officer would ruin her life. She should have just left them. We were already at a hospital."

"She probably thought you'd kill them."

"Jesus," Kaia said. "They really think we do that kind of thing?"

"Yeah."

"I would never. That's insane. I mean, I guess I *did* kill her, but not because I wanted to. Not maliciously. Not if she was down." Emotion finally bubbled up that she had ended a life. Adrienne made it real. "Not—"

"You did what you had to," Adrienne said. "I wouldn't trade you for any of them, Kaia." Adrienne's eyes filled to the brim again too. "I thought I could control her. I thought I could keep this from getting so bloody."

Kaia nodded, finally understanding.

"Are we safe here?" Adrienne asked. "She'll look for me. She'll look for me with you. Will she find us?"

"Probably, but not tonight. Even if she does, there are undercovers watching the doors for her."

"There are?"

"Yeah. In case they try to finish what they started. We'll have to figure something else out eventually, but we're very safe right now."

"Oh, Kaia." Adrienne shook her head. "God, I'm so sorry. I'm so sorry I got you into this."

"It's not your fault."

"The hell it's not."

"We'll stay somewhere else after this until they arrest her."

"You need me to go on record for that to happen, don't you?"

Kaia shook her head. "No, actually. The manpower they have on this is unbelievable. They pulled every camera around for miles. She slipped up. Put gas in the Escalade without the bandana. Got her on camera. They know she was one of the shooters. They'll move heaven and earth to get her now."

"When are they trying to pick her up?"

Kaia frowned. "They already did."

"She got away?"

"Yes."

"She escapes all the time," Adrienne said. "I can't even count the times. It's unbelievable. I can't believe you caught her on your own."

Kaia smirked. "Yeah, she did not appreciate that."

Kaia saw Adrienne's eyes wander over her body. Her skin tingled under the gaze.

"So you're in really good shape," she said.

"Have to be." Kaia laughed. "The guys can get fat and lazy, but I'm already at a disadvantage as a woman. It's dangerous for me to get weak."

She could see Adrienne searching carefully for words, but she landed simply on, "Why are you a cop?"

"You can't still think we're all bad, can you?"

"Of course not, but you have to admit a lot are."

"A lot aren't as nice as they could be, I grant you. Too many years on the job being hated, too judgmental, impatient, some too jumpy. But corrupt? You hear those stories sometimes, but it's mostly bull. Gangs like saying they own corrupt cops because it keeps everyone afraid to talk to us, but it's rarely true. Every cop I know wants to protect people from bad guys, to be strong for the weak. That's what I wanted."

Adrienne nodded. "When I saw you in your uniform I was afraid you'd turned into an asshole. It's not even that anymore. Now I'm just afraid you're going to get hurt. Even most straight-laced people don't like cops. You risk your life, people hate you, I hear the pay is just okay. And in Chicago? Are you crazy? Why would you choose that? You could do anything."

"You don't expect the hate when you sign up, not at that level anyway, and you accept the risk going in. I didn't have anyone to worry about when I got the job." Kaia felt her cheeks flush. She didn't have anyone to worry now, either. Adrienne wasn't hers. "Adrienne, why didn't you ever contact me?" The question forced itself out. She couldn't fight it anymore. Adrienne looked like she'd been waiting for it and nervously ran her fingers through her hair.

"I was going to," she said.

"What happened?"

"I ran into you at a bar. You didn't see me. I even bought you a drink, thought I'd come over and surprise you."

Kaia smiled. "But?"

"But when I turned around you were with someone. She was gorgeous. Really gorgeous, Kaia. And you were both smiling so much, touching. You were obviously together and you looked so happy, and she looked so perfect. I just couldn't imagine what you'd want with me when you had that. It had already been four years. I just doubted everything. I knew all I could do was fuck up whatever you had going on, so I left."

Kaia grabbed her hand. "I would have dropped her in a heartbeat. I can't even tell you who she was. No one has meant what you do to me. Not ever."

Adrienne smiled sadly. "I guess I missed out, then. I met Gianna not long after and of course she'd never let me reach out to an ex, so I never got to try again."

"And all that time I thought I wasn't hearing from you because you switched to guys."

Adrienne laughed. "Seriously? Come on, you knew that would never work."

"I knew you were gay." Kaia laughed. "Doesn't stop some people."

Adrienne shivered. The night was cooling fast. They moved inside, exhausted but stranded awkwardly by the bedroom threshold. They looked at each other, paralyzed. Adrienne looked like herself again, small, feminine features unmarred by the bumps Gianna had given her. Her tender brown eyes pulled Kaia in.

"I can sleep on the couch," Adrienne said.

"That's silly."

"Is it?"

Kaia's mouth went dry. "Yes."

Adrienne nodded. "Okay." She was wearing a cotton button-down. Kaia wanted to help her out of it, wanted to pull the buttons apart, but she couldn't move.

"We can handle the same bed without anything happening," Adrienne said.

Kaia raised an eyebrow. "Of course we can." Shit, what was she thinking? Adrienne had escaped her abusive ex hours ago; she didn't want to have sex. Kaia tried to blink her beer buzz away. *Pull it together.*

In the bedroom, she undressed discreetly, her back turned. She reached for the T-shirt she had ready on the dresser, but Adrienne's hand stopped her.

"Can I see?"

Kaia's heart pounded. She knew Adrienne meant the bullet marks, but Adrienne hadn't seen her in just a bra since they were teens. She relented and turned. Again Adrienne made no secret of her wandering eyes. Finally, she reached out and touched the two purple bruises where the bullets had hit. Her fingertips barely brushed her at first, then her palms were flat on Kaia's stomach, moving to her sides, then up her back, pulling her closer. The intensity in Adrienne's eyes sent a tingle of arousal shooting through her. Their lips met hard. Adrienne pressed herself against Kaia and parted her lips. Kaia deepened the kiss, the air in her lungs escaping in a soft moan. She pulled Adrienne toward her, hands moving from her hips, up her sides, she laced her fingers through her hair. She kissed Adrienne's neck, felt her shudder and pull back. Kaia stopped.

"I'm sorry," she said.

Adrienne was breathless. "You're sorry? That was me."

"Did I do something wrong?"

"God no. I just—" She stopped.

"I understand, Adrienne, it's okay if—"

"No, no. Kaia, shush. It's not Gianna." She met her eyes. "It just hurts." She pulled the collar of her button-down apart, revealing dark bruises around her neck.

"Oh my God." Kaia wanted to kill Gianna. "What did she do?"

"She choked me. I passed out."

Kaia felt her pulse in her temple. She couldn't explode; that wouldn't help anything. "We should take you to a doctor."

"I'm okay," she said. "Really. Just tender."

"What do you need?"

Adrienne glanced at the bed. "Sleep?"

"We can do that."

Adrienne reached across the bed, feeling for Gianna but finding it empty.

Kaia's voice from the other room slowly registered. She opened her eyes. She was in Kaia's bed. She had thought that would never happen again. Kaia's walls were pale blue, the furniture sharp and modern, her comforter was a rich crimson color. Adrienne let yesterday's events wash over her, trying to recover from the disorientation. The shooting, the fight, Kaia. They'd kissed. They'd nearly slept together.

Her pulse quickened just thinking about it, but she was glad it hadn't happened. Just because she'd been terrified Kaia had died didn't mean it was right to jump directly into bed with her. She was still tumbling through the dark matter, clawing for a vision of what her life was going to be now.

Adrienne heard another voice and realized Kaia was talking to someone at the door. She strained to make it out. She caught Gianna's name, but nothing useful. She heard the door shut and ventured into the living room.

"Morning," she said.

Kaia looked like she'd been up for hours. She was dressed and looked fresh and bright.

"Hey." Kaia smiled and Adrienne lost track of what she'd been doing. Kaia patted the kitchen barstool and she complied.

"News?"

"They haven't found her," Kaia said. "Your house was empty. She got out somehow and she knows she can't go back. No sign of her here either. They rounded up some WAKs, but the interviews haven't turned anything up."

"Of course not."

"My Gang Enforcement superior wants to talk to you."

Adrienne took a deep breath. "Of course he does."

"I'll be right there with you. It'll be okay."

❖

A man named Davis met them at the door. "Welcome." He waved Adrienne in and hugged Kaia. Adrienne couldn't help but soak up the sight of Kaia in her element, in a world that clearly adored her. Davis led them into a conference room and slid a bottle of water across the table to Adrienne.

"So, I'm sure you understand we need to ask you some questions."

"I do."

"Let's jump right out of the gate with the most important one," Davis said. "Do you know where Gianna Hernandez is?"

"No. The last time I saw her was at our house."

"And do you have any guess where she might go?"

"Nowhere you don't already know about. Members' houses. Anna Fields most likely or Marco Woods."

"Checking clear."

"I don't know then."

"She doesn't have family?"

"Not really. Foster parents, but she hated them."

"You'll get me that address?"

"Don't know their address. I'll get you their names if you want, but she won't go there."

"Sorano explained to me you called her for help last night. Can you tell me why? What made you leave the house?"

Kaia was watching, concern written plainly on her face, but Adrienne recounted everything in detail from the moment Gianna came inside with the bodies, hiding nothing. Davis took notes while she talked.

"And you're ready to go on record on all this?"

"She's going to need protection to do that," Kaia said.

"Of course," Davis said. "You'll have it."

"And immunity," Kaia interjected again.

Davis chuckled and Adrienne forced herself not to smile at Kaia's protection.

"I'm not interested in getting you in trouble," Davis said to Adrienne. "I'm interested in catching someone who tried to kill two of my officers."

"I'll give you what you need," Adrienne said.

"You're sure? You're not going to recant on us?"

"I can't go back even if I wanted to. I'm not safe until she's in jail."

Davis nodded solemnly. "None of us are. All right, so where do they get the guns?"

Adrienne was taken off guard. "Their guns? From Los Hijos de la Santa Muerte."

Davis let several seconds pass, then folded his fingers in front of him. "Look, Contreras, I hesitate to bring this up because I do believe you got stuck in a shit sandwich and Sorano here has your back, but the truth still remains that you've been around some serious illegal activity. You've witnessed some very serious crimes. I'm going to need your full cooperation to let you off the hook for all this."

"Davis," Kaia said. "Sir," she bashfully corrected herself. "She's cooperating."

"I want to believe that, but you can't give me bad intel. You tell the truth or you tell me you can't tell me. No lies."

"It's not a lie," Adrienne said. "They get them from the Hijos de la Santa Muerte. They usually meet once a month. On the docks at four a.m."

"Then why does my undercover know nothing about the Wild AKs?"

"Who, Kitchen? Because he's Gianna's, not yours."

Davis's face went pale. "Excuse me? Detective Benson does not belong to Gianna."

"Yes, Detective Whatever. His street name is Kitchen because he cooks the best meth on this side of town. You guys teach that in the academy? Gianna bought him years ago. He's dirty. She gives him a cut, he forgets to bring up the Wild AKs and tips them off if the heat is getting too hot."

Davis looked nauseous. When Adrienne looked to Kaia she was equally stunned and confused. Did they really not know crooked cops existed? In Chicago? It was so naïve.

"I'm sorry," Adrienne muttered. "I didn't mean to be insensitive about it."

Davis cleared his throat and continued, subdued. "We know Gianna was part of the attempt on Sorano's life, but we don't know who else. Can you put Anna Fields in that car?"

"Yes."

"And the others?"

"The two at the hospital, obviously, and there was only one more. He was just a recruit. I don't know his name, but I could point him out."

Davis reached for a stack of papers, straightened them on the desk, and handed them to her.

"I'll need you to write down as much as possible. When you're done, assuming it's all true, you can consider yourself immune. We'll claim you as a cooperative asset."

Davis stood and motioned for Kaia to follow him out. Adrienne nodded at them as Davis pulled the door closed. She stared at the lined sheets. There was a list of questions for her to answer paper-clipped to the front.

Adrienne picked up a pen. Her hand shook as she placed it to paper. She might as well be signing a war declaration. She closed her eyes and let go of Gianna forever.

CHAPTER FOURTEEN

Gianna sank low in the Honda Accord she'd stolen until Blondie and Adrienne passed. A thrill shot through her that they'd been feet away without knowing it. She could have shot them both before either knew what happened. But she didn't want it like that. She wanted the cop to feel it. She wanted to see fear in her eyes as she realized her life was ending. As far as Adrienne, she had to admit, what she really wanted was to have her back, but she knew that was a dying fantasy.

Adrienne and the cop walked through the apartment complex parking lot to a car Gianna had never seen. It had to be the cop's personal vehicle, a blue Ford Taurus. Gianna waited until they were already turning out of the lot to start the engine. She felt like she was going to lose them, but a cop would have a sharp eye for tails and she couldn't be caught.

She followed them to a restaurant in an uppity part of town well north of anywhere Gianna spent time. She knew Adrienne lived even farther north before they'd met, just outside Chicago in Evanston. Even knowing that, it was strange seeing Adrienne in this setting. She preferred to think of Adrienne as the poor, tough girl she'd met in South Side, not some upper middle class kid from the suburbs. She parked a couple of rows away from the Taurus, confident her dark windows hid her.

Adrienne looped her arm through Blondie's. They were smiling, relaxed. They went into the brunch restaurant like they didn't have a fear in the world, like they were on a Goddamn date and like Adrienne hadn't just abandoned her, like the cop hadn't just killed someone.

Gianna gripped the steering wheel in anger. The cut on her hand split and blood rolled down her arm. They thought they won, that they could get away with this. How could Adrienne not know better? After five years together, could Adrienne really think she was going to just drop it?

The anger built, threatening to explode. She wanted them to know she was here, that she could take them whenever she wanted. She wanted Adrienne to know she was betting on the wrong horse. She wanted to put a bloody end to this hearts and rainbows fantasy they thought they could live.

But watching them from the safety of anonymity was also thrilling in its own way. She could torture them. She found a scrap of paper and scribbled down a message. She pulled up to the car and stuck the paper in the window, then sped off.

Kaia saw a scrap of paper propped on her window as they approached the car. She smoothed it out.

I see you.

She refused to look over her shoulder. Gianna wouldn't be visible, and seeing panic would give her exactly what she wanted. If she was here to hurt them, she'd have done it.

She met Adrienne's worried eyes but simply crumpled the paper and got in the car. Once they'd left, she handed her the paper.

"Shit," Adrienne said. "I told you."

"I know."

"I told you, I fucking told you. She is going to find me and kill me. God, and now I'm a rat on top of it. Why did I do that to myself? Shit!"

Kaia calmly put her hand on Adrienne's knee. "She assumed you were a rat the second you called me. The only difference it made is you gave us a real chance to put her away for a long time. It's going to be fine. This is good."

"Good?"

"Yes. She's shown herself. I'll give the info to Davis and he'll be all over it."

"I'm going to die," Adrienne said. "You too, probably."

"No, we're not. We'll stop by my place, get some stuff, and move to a safe house."

"What if she follows us there?"

"She won't be able to. There are safety measures to prevent it."

"You're sure?"

Kaia spared a glance from the road to look Adrienne in the eye.

"I'm sure. This is exactly what they're for. And now we know she's still in town. We'll lay low and they'll find her. Every cop in the city is looking for her."

Kaia pulled into the apartment parking lot. She knew Adrienne's stomach couldn't handle being here long. It didn't feel safe anymore. As she swung into her space she noticed Carli's car pulling in behind her.

Carli hopped out of her car and jogged to Kaia's door. Kaia got out, and Carli plowed into her, pulling her into a tight hug.

"I came as soon as I could, but your security wouldn't let me up last night. Are you okay?" She let go and backed up.

"I'm okay," Kaia said. "Still on high alert around here, but they should have let you up. You could have called me."

Carli waved it away. "I figured you needed rest. They told me your vest saved you."

Adrienne's car door opened and she walked over, eyes combing Carli head to foot. Carli glanced from Kaia to Adrienne and back.

She finally extended her hand to Adrienne and introduced herself. Adrienne tentatively shook her hand. Kaia shifted uncomfortably. Their tension was contagious.

"I'm so glad you came," Kaia said. "We're going to have to move to a safe house. It would have been a shame to miss you before that. Who knows how long it will be."

Carli's eyes went wide. "A safe house? That's necessary?"

Kaia explained everything, feeling self-conscious as she caught Carli unable to hide a few glares Adrienne's way.

"Well, you take care of her," she finally said to Adrienne.

"I will."

❖

Adrienne and Kaia slowly unpacked the one bag they'd shoved both of their things into. Adrienne had chosen several of Kaia's clothes to hold her over and bought new toiletries. She was too scared to go back to her house for belongings, even, or maybe especially, with Kaia and other officers with her.

The safe house was pristine, on a large plot of land, wood floors, pale walls, and stone counters. Everything felt hard and sterile.

"Have you ever had to do this before?" she asked.

"No," Kaia said. "Doesn't happen often." Kaia's hair was pulled up in a messy bun, strands falling free over her bare tan shoulders. Adrienne wanted to kiss their warmth, breathe in her smell. She studied Kaia as she casually went about finding places for her things.

"So," Adrienne said. "You didn't tell me you have a girlfriend."

Kaia wandered to the refrigerator and studied the contents. "Hey, they gave us beer. Guess they knew we'd be stressed out."

Adrienne's cheeks flushed. God. Kaia had a girlfriend all this time. It was just like the time she'd seen her in the bar. Her stomach turned with jealousy and her chest deflated. What did Kaia need with her? She was a common criminal, and Kaia obviously had high caliber suitors. Why lead her on?

Kaia walked over and handed her a beer. Adrienne accepted it with numb fingers.

"She's not my girlfriend," Kaia said.

Adrienne tried to hide the relief. She didn't even know why she was. Had she not just this morning decided she wasn't going to jump into anything with Kaia?

"That's good," Adrienne said. "Thought I was messing up your relationship for a second."

Kaia shook her head. "Nope. I don't really do relationships."

Adrienne's heart sank again. Damn it, what was wrong with her? She sat on the bed, ignoring the clothes she'd yet to put away. Kaia did the same, leaning against the headboard.

"So what was she then? You seemed…familiar."

Kaia nervously rubbed her own neck. "She's a dispatcher. We're friends."

"With benefits?" Why was she putting them both in this awkward position? It wasn't her business and she didn't even really want to know. "For a while."

"When did it stop?"

"Uh." Kaia took a drink. "A few days ago."

"I see."

She'd been with Gianna until yesterday, what could she really say? "She seems nice. Pretty."

Kaia looked over at her. "She is. But it wasn't right. It wasn't there."

"And you never date? Never been in love?" Adrienne knew Kaia had loved her, but were there others?

"I like to keep it simple." Kaia shrugged. "Love is messy."

Adrienne nodded. Love *was* messy. Loving Kaia had ended in terror and chaos. Loving Gianna had ended like this. Maybe Kaia had the right idea.

Kaia abruptly switched subjects. "Do you ever go see your dad?"

"Ted?" She hadn't thought Kaia would mention him. "I did a few times. Been a long time now." Adrienne saw pain she didn't understand on Kaia's face.

"Is he…"

"The same."

"And your mom?"

"We don't talk. We stopped when I came out. Or when I told her the conversion therapy wasn't working, rather."

"Conversion therapy?"

"Yeah, the whole teach you how to be straight thing."

"No, I know," Kaia said. "I just didn't know she made you do that. I'm sorry."

Adrienne shrugged. "I lived."

"That was all my fault. I got us caught when I…" she trailed off again.

Adrienne wanted to comfort her, tell her it wasn't her fault, but she'd never completely believed that. She knew Kaia had acted out of love, but it had still taken her father's life, destroyed her mother, gotten her moved into a poverty-stricken neighborhood and enrolled in one sadistic Catholic program after another. She'd be lying if she said she didn't wish Kaia had handled it differently. She could have handled it differently herself, too, though. She could have told Ted Kaia was in the closet before things got out of hand. He would have been mad, but Kaia wouldn't have had to see what she did and she wouldn't have grabbed that baseball bat.

"Everything happened so fast I never even knew how you felt about it," Kaia said. "Everyone told me I did the right thing, but it never felt so clear-cut to me. I never stopped feeling guilty about it."

"Everyone told me you did the right thing too. Except my mom, of course."

"Did I?"

"I don't know, Kaia. I understood you, but it wasn't what I wanted. He was a sick fuck, but he was my dad. I was so afraid of what would happen to your life after that, but then I realized mine was the only one changing."

"Mine did too."

"Not like mine. You still had your home, your family, and everyone thought you were a hero. For me it was therapy and church and my family hated me. We moved to the ghetto because my mom couldn't afford anything else and Ted's hospital bills were crazy. That's how I first started hanging out with gangs and dealing drugs. Out there, everyone was in one, it was normal. If I needed two things they were money and to feel like I had a family. That might as well be the brochure for gangs. It barely fazed me when Gianna jumped into the Wild AKs. I figured I'd follow soon enough."

Kaia slammed her beer. She didn't say a word. Adrienne looked down at the bed, guilty. She'd said too much. It wasn't Kaia's fault her life turned out the way it did, that her mom was homophobic or that her dad had raped her. She didn't mean to blame Kaia for everything, and yet she couldn't deny there was some anger, anger she couldn't name or rationalize. She grabbed Kaia's hand.

"The results sucked, but I never blamed you."

"I never meant to hurt him that bad," Kaia said. "I just wanted him to stop."

"I understand." She'd never known that. She'd assumed Kaia felt no remorse, then or now, that she hadn't cared what the results were. No one else did. A child rapist doesn't receive much sympathy.

She turned to Kaia, but she was already turning away. Kaia pulled the blanket over herself. It was still early, but Adrienne didn't know how to help. She was too mixed up about it herself. She stared at Kaia's back until she faded off to sleep.

CHAPTER FIFTEEN

Gianna rolled up Marco's alley at his second, secret home. She knocked on the back door, using the pattern he'd told her to. The door opened slowly. The person opening it was hidden behind the door in the dark until he shut it again behind her. He was an athletic looking black man with a scruffy beard. He pointed at the stairs.

"He's waiting."

Gianna climbed the stairs two at a time. Marco was sitting with his arms spread along the back of a leather couch. A stripper pole was fixed in the middle of the room. One girl danced while another lay faceup across his lap while he ran his hands over her. An AK-12 was propped against the armrest, much like the one tattooed on the side of his face.

"Come on in," he said. His thinness and crazy eyes suggested heavy drug use. Gianna sat as close as the woman's legs allowed. It was bizarre watching her lie there while he felt her breasts and caressed her legs as he pleased, sometimes wandering between them. The woman provided understated reactions to him that made sitting next to them extraordinarily awkward.

"You want one?" he asked.

Gianna was too nervous to think about girls. "Nah."

"Suit yourself." He reached into his pocket and produced a piece of paper for her. "That is a list of all the times and places we've had cops up our asses. Notice anything?"

She searched for a pattern but couldn't find one. "No."

"No? I'll tell you. It's fucking constant! Every member. We can't do shit. I'm sitting on fifty kilos I can't sell. That's a lot of fucking cocaine, Gi."

She looked away. She hadn't known Adrienne was able to hook him up with that much, but she wasn't going to question him. Adrienne's connections had surprised her from the start; it was possible.

"You know why they're all over us?" he asked. It seemed he was cutting into his giant supply himself. "Do you?"

She didn't answer. He fished in his pocket, sprinkled a line on the girl's chest, and snorted it. "I'll tell you why. Because they're looking for you."

"I'm sorry."

"You're sorry. I don't need I'm sorry. I need my money. We have a gun run coming up, and if we don't sell this shit we're not going to be able to pay for them. Guess what they'll do with the guns if we can't pay for them. Go on, guess."

"Find another buyer?"

"They'll fucking shoot us with them is what they'll do. *Then* they'll find another buyer."

"Can we sell it in—"

"Shut up. I didn't bring you here for ideas. Your ideas are obviously shit."

Gianna looked at the ground and waited. Marco slapped the thigh of the girl on his lap, signaling her to get up. Free of her, he crossed the room and opened a cabinet. Gianna couldn't see what was inside, but her pulse quickened. She checked the accessibility of the pistol in her waistband.

"You know, Gi. I always thought you were dumb, letting that little girl have such a hold on you. You let a little pussy get you into a real mess. Look at you, making a fool of yourself, going to jail for slapping her around. It was dumb, but it wasn't my business." Marco crossed the room, fitting brass knuckles to his hand. "But now you're making it my business. You're messing with my money, my respect."

"It wasn't even like that, Marco. It was the cop that fucked everything up. She was coming at us, I had to—"

"No, it's about your girlfriend, and I'll tell you why. She is the reason that cop got involved, and instead of just cutting her loose the second that happened, you let your emotions make you make stupid choices. You got my people shooting at a cop, dying in the street over your personal shit, and you couldn't even be bothered to do it well? You didn't even get her, and you showed your face on a camera."

"Marco—"

"You're on the Goddamn news! Weather, Gianna Hernandez's stupid face, sports, Gianna's fucking dumb face again!" he screamed. "One of my people died in the street and the cop doesn't have a scratch!" The punch came so fast Gianna couldn't defend herself. The brass knuckles split her face, a dull, solid thud marked the impact and made her ears ring.

"You got too big for your britches, and you need to fall in line." He punched again, this one sent her to the floor.

"I'm sorry, Marco."

"This is not your gang. They are not your minions. They are my members. They make me money and they protect the WAKs, not run fucking errands for you when you get pissy. And you, what good are you now? The second you show your face you're going to prison. What good are you to me?"

"I'll be your security. I'll do the pickups on the docks. I'll do anything, Marco, please."

He removed the knuckles. Gianna had seen him beat people much worse. She was shocked by the pain of just two punches.

"All right, get up," he said. "Sit down, have a girl." He snapped at the dancer. "Sweetheart!" She came over and danced in front of Gianna enticingly, touching her legs. Gianna could barely see, her eyes were still watering from the blows to her head.

"Here's what we're going to do," he said. "I have a case out there right now and it's leaning the wrong way. You're going to take care of the judge for me."

"Take care of him?"

"You said anything, didn't you?"

"Yeah."

"All right, well, that's what I need. You want to survive around me, be needed."

Gianna nodded. "And my warrant?"

"Don't get caught."

"Can you hook me up with a new identity?"

"Sure, but it's not going to help you if you can't stay your happy ass away from the girl. Can you?"

Gianna paused. "I want her to pay."

"Christ, you're being such a pansy. She's just a girl. Let it go."

"She lived with me for five years; she knows things. And now she's with a cop."

"How much does she know?"

"Nothing she shouldn't," Gianna said. "But—"

"How much?" Marco leaned forward, danger flashing in his eyes.

"Nothing she shouldn't," Gianna repeated. "But she knows who was in the car when we shot at the cop and knows who the members are and where most of them live. Could have something to do with that list you showed me."

"So you're saying she's a rat?"

"I think so."

"Fine," he said. "Get the judge, get the girl. Then we'll get you a new name and setup."

Kaia woke to the softest of morning light seeping through a small part in the drapes. She'd gone to bed too early and now woken at sunrise. She turned carefully toward Adrienne, trying not to wake her, but her eyes were already open. She smiled.

"Good morning."

"I thought you were sleeping."

"Not for hours."

Kaia got up and made coffee. She heard Adrienne riffling through clutter behind her. "So, we're not allowed to leave, are we?"

"That's the idea," Kaia answered. "Don't want to be seen."

"Makes sense, but would it have killed them to give us some entertainment?"

Kaia laughed as she poured her coffee. "What do we have?"

"An encyclopedia, really bad movies, and Monopoly."

"TV?"

Adrienne turned it on. A hiss of static answered her.

"Well, shit."

"You want to play Monopoly?" Adrienne asked.

"God, no. I'd rather read the encyclopedia. Hate that game."

Adrienne laughed. "I guess it's just you, me, and our brilliant minds then."

Kaia laughed, squinting into the open closet. "Are those fishing poles?"

"Yeah, but what can we do with them?"

"I saw a pond not far when we drove up."

"Does it have fish? Are we allowed?"

Kaia shrugged. "Don't know why else they'd be here."

"What about bait?"

"Guess we'll have to find it."

"Find it?"

"Yeah, girl. It's early. Let's go get some worms while they're out."

The lake was about a mile away, farther than she'd remembered but still easy to find. A small gravel path led the way. Trees came in patches and gatherings, a quiet hiss of wind whipped through the delicate buckthorns. It felt secluded and safe, like they were surrounded by miles of private land no one could touch.

Adrienne was in Kaia's clothes, an old T-shirt with paint stains and well worn jeans.

"Hey!" Adrienne said. "Found one!" She crouched next to a worm on the path. Kaia smiled and held out the cup for collection. Adrienne looked at the worm, then back at Kaia with disgust.

"Really?" Kaia laughed in surprise.

"He looks really slimy. And fat. And why is his ass half black?"

Kaia couldn't control the smile burning her cheeks. "You better get him."

"You do it."

"What kind of lesbian are you?" she teased her.

"Oh my God, fine, but I am *not* putting him on the hook."

"Deal." Kaia extended the cup toward Adrienne. She pulled away the first time she touched it, then actually picked him up, tossing him frantically into the cup, feet dancing in place.

"Yuck, yuck, yuck. I hate bugs."

Kaia collected the rest along the way. At the water's edge, they found a large, flat boulder that was perfect to sit on. Their legs dangled off the edge and Kaia made good on her promise to hook the worms.

They cast their lines into the water, laughing at their first pathetic attempts and trying again until they had the feel for it. Leaves were just starting to fall from their branches and were landing in the water, stirring gentle ripples.

"Is it bad for me to love this?" Kaia asked. "I know everything is messed up and we're in hiding, but I can't help feeling like I'm on vacation."

Adrienne looked over, warm brown eyes twinkling with their own joy. "That's not bad. We're stuck either way. Might as well enjoy it."

"My thoughts exactly."

"You sound like you don't get many vacations."

Kaia shook her head. "It's been years. Lots of them. You come on the force and you get a little time, but you don't want to use it because you're a rookie. Then you don't want to because you want a promotion, then you're the new guy again. Next thing you know it's been five years."

"I haven't had to think like that in a long time. Money was always good in my business."

"I still can't believe you deal drugs. How did that happen?"

"They're everywhere where I lived. If you know anyone you have a connection."

"But why deal?" Kaia asked.

Adrienne shrugged and looked out to the water. "I guess I started to fit in, to be cool. I was pissed off and poor and wanted friends and respect. After a while, I knew all the right people, had a lot of regular buyers, almost never ran into trouble. Then when I met Gianna I didn't even have to deal with my own problems when they did happen. It was rare for anyone to try to rip me off, but when they did she took care of it. We had plenty of money and we did whatever we wanted."

"Sounds nice," Kaia admitted.

"It was at first. Eventually, Gianna was too jealous to let me work. She didn't like me on the corners talking to all those people. She said she was worried about me, but she was screaming at me every day about someone she thought I was flirting with. That's what it was really about. The Wild AKs were trying to make a name for themselves anyway and I had the connections to get bigger quantities than they could find. I just couldn't sell it all myself."

"So you became the WAKs' dealer. You found the big quantities for them, they broke it down and handled it on the street level, and Gianna got to hide you away in the house."

"You got it. That's when it all started going really sideways, though, when the WAKs started wanting more and more. And Gianna was so tight with all of them, they all look up to her. Next thing you know the gang has keys to your house. They come and go whenever they want, and there's always some kind of emergency. I could have used a vacation from that."

"How did you really get so mixed up with Gianna?" Kaia asked. "Was she always like that? I know you said the gang felt normal to you, but what about the abuse?"

"She was always tough, hard, but no, she wasn't always abusive. I was shocked the first time she hit me."

"What happened?"

"We were having a party. She was drunk. She was treating me like a servant, asking for drinks, yelling at me for not taking people's coats. She was being an ass, but I thought she was just trying to impress her friends, that we'd talk about it later. I tried to pick up a glass, but it was wet from condensation. It slipped out of my hand and broke. She slapped me."

"What did you do?"

"It was like the whole room froze," Adrienne said. "We all just stared at her. She asked what I was waiting for and told me to clean it up. She didn't even remember the next day so I told myself she was blackout drunk and had no idea what she was doing. But she started drinking more and needing less to get to that point. Pretty soon it was too late."

"I wanted to kill her that day I first saw you. If I had known who she was and what she'd done to you when I was chasing her..." she trailed off, not sure how to finish. "I don't know. I just wish I'd known."

"Don't say that."

"You know I don't mean it like that. I would never hurt someone I didn't have to and hide behind my badge."

"What did you mean, then?"

"I don't know, it just twists my stomach that I was nice to her. I was just having a normal conversation with her, oblivious to the fact she'd just hit you. That doesn't feel good."

"But you got her," Adrienne said. "That's all that matters. Things got out of hand enough without you picking a fight."

"I don't think it would have mattered who it was or how they acted. She hates cops on sight."

"If she'd had better experiences with law enforcement it might not be that way."

"I just don't understand these 'bad experiences.' The cops I work with are professional, maybe cold but not hateful. And we're under more scrutiny than ever. Everyone thinks we can just do whatever we want, but we absolutely can't. We have to wear body cams, every little complaint gets investigated even though it's the nature of the job to piss people off. Everyone is looking to get out of trouble. I've seen plenty of times an officer should have tazed or shot someone for their own safety but put themselves in danger instead."

"I believe what you've seen, Kaia, and I think you're a great person. There's just another side and you have to hear it. You have to believe I'm not lying either. I've been a drug dealer for a long time. Do you know how many times I've seen cops pocket someone's stash or money instead of arresting them? Or how many times I've seen a cop lie about what happened and everyone just nods and backs them up? Isn't it cop gospel that they can't rat each other out?"

Kaia sighed. "Yes, it is, in theory, but I've never had to lie for someone. I've never had to do anything that made me feel dirty or corrupt or crooked."

"I'm glad," Adrienne said. "But that Kitchen guy Davis likes is as crooked as they come. And I saw cops beat Gianna when she was unarmed and cooperative. I saw it with my own eyes. And can you honestly tell me you think they won't beat her or worse when they find her for what she did to you? No matter how Gianna acts?"

Kaia squinted into the sunlight, the beams shined from behind Adrienne, blinding her.

"I don't know," she said. "It's possible."

Adrienne touched her hand. "That's all I want. Just don't be blind. Don't defend them before you hear the story. I know loyalty is important to you, but if you want to be believed you have to be unbiased. You have to want the truth. Otherwise you really are just another gang flying blue, taking payoffs, and killing rats."

"Do you think we'll ever get past this cop thing?"

"Who, the country? Or you and me?"

"Us."

Adrienne cocked her head. "We're already past it. I may never love it, but I know you're still you."

Kaia smiled and leaned back on the rock, letting the sun rays warm her face and the day melt by.

Chapter Sixteen

The cop's car wasn't in the parking lot. Gianna was on her third hour and was getting stiff and annoyed. She needed to see Adrienne. Waking up without her and not being able to talk to her was driving her crazy. The rage of what had happened was wearing off, and now all she felt was the emptiness left behind.

Adrienne's phone was shut off. None of the crew had seen her anywhere. Gianna was starting to be afraid she left town. She'd thought Adrienne would come right back like she always had, that she just wanted to stay away until things cooled off. She knew it was different when Adrienne surfaced with the cop, but even then she'd had hope Adrienne would come to her senses, that she just needed to try Blondie on for a night and she'd come right home. Adrienne with a cop just didn't fit. Adrienne might not have become Wild, but she was a midlevel drug dealer in her own right. How could she possibly think she was going to find a life with a police officer?

"Oh my God, this is so boring," Anna said.

"That's why I brought you, stupid."

"Can we please do something else?"

Anna didn't understand that the anxiety had her. She couldn't think, couldn't move on. She felt like she was imploding every second that passed that she couldn't find Adrienne. Waves of panic and distress came like hurricanes, and she nearly lost control during them.

"If she's not here, where is she?"

"Fuck if I know," Anna said. "All I know is you have the whole city looking for you, and we've been sitting in a cop's parking lot for three hours like we miss jail."

"You have a better idea?"

"Yeah, literally anything else."

"Marco said to handle her, and I don't know where else to look."

"They're obviously not here and they're probably not coming back. They're not stupid. They know you're going to look here."

"All right, we can drive around town then."

"Let's just pay Kitchen a visit and ask him," Anna said. "Adrienne knows he's on the payroll. He needs us to find her before she talks as much as we do."

"I don't want him to know that. It'll make us look bad and it'll make him think about abandoning ship."

"Okay, I have a better idea." Anna started texting someone, then gave Gianna directions. "I have a friend who knows a cop. She owes me a favor, just cashed it in for this dude's address."

"Sounds solid." Gianna hoped the sarcasm hit hard.

"Christina bribes cops all the time. She says it's easy."

"Okay, and we're just going to hope this random dude you don't know is willing to sell out another cop? Are you stupid?"

"Sell out Adrienne, not the cop. And Christina says they're all crooked for the right price."

"Well, yeah."

"Okay, so it'll work."

"If it doesn't we go to jail."

"If it doesn't, we kill him. Or we don't do this at all. How bad do you want to find Adrienne?"

Gianna followed the directions to the house. When they knocked on the door a short but beefy guy in his thirties answered.

"Doug?" Anna asked.

"Yeah?"

"Could we come in a minute? We have some of the same friends. They said you might like an offer we have for you."

"What kind of offer?"

"The discuss inside type," Gianna said.

"I don't know what you're talking about. What friend? Who have you been talking to?"

"You're Chicago PD, right?"

"Oh fuck off." He tried to close the door, but Anna put her foot in the way and took a stack of cash from her pocket.

"You don't even want to hear the offer? It's very hands off."

He glanced at the cash. "I could arrest you right now for bribing an officer and take that if I wanted, but I'm not like that. Now, get off my porch."

Gianna raised her chin, drawing his attention to her WAK tattoo. His eyes locked on to it and reflected recognition. "It's rude not to even hear the offer, Doug. You don't want to be rude. Look, there are a few bills in it for you just for listening. How fair is that? Just let us inside."

Doug glanced from Gianna to the money in Anna's hand and back. He finally stepped aside and let them in. They followed him to an oak dining table and sat down. There was clutter stacked on the end of the table and on some of the chairs. The room looked feminine in design but like a bachelor pad in practice.

"All right, what do you want?"

"Adrienne Contreras. She dropped off the planet."

"So file a missing person report. Jesus, what is this?"

"I want you to tell me where she is. She's with a cop, so I know you can find her."

"No idea who you're talking about."

"I know that, but we need you to find out."

"No. I don't know who told you I do this type of thing, but I don't."

"Fifty thousand dollars." Anna slapped the stack of bills on the table. "She's being hidden by you guys. We just need to know where. It'll be easy to find out. All you have to do is tell us where Officer Kaia Sorano has her squirreled away."

"Adrienne is my girlfriend," Gianna said. "Nothing bad is going to happen to her. She just needs help."

"She's in hiding with an officer but she needs help?" Doug pointedly raised an eyebrow at each of them. "I don't think so. Your story doesn't make sense. I'm not going to give you protected information."

"Seventy-five K."

"It's not—"

"One hundred thousand."

"Deal."

It happened so fast Gianna had to blink a few times to catch up.

Doug leaned forward. "Fifty now, fifty after. Nothing happens to the cop."

"Deal." Gianna nodded at Anna, and she slid the fifty thousand across the table.

He rested his hand on top of the money before taking it. He looked Gianna in the eye. "Nothing happens to the cop, or you see a side of me you don't want to see."

She nodded. She wasn't afraid of him, and he had to know her word was useless, but if it helped him sleep at night, that was fine.

"When will you know?"

"Depends on how buried it is, and on opportunity. I'm not getting fired over this, but I'll find it."

"Sooner is better," Gianna said.

"Always is."

They shook hands.

Kaia was sitting on the floor. Carpet. The space was too small for her and there was scattered, noisy clutter that would give her away if she moved. She barely allowed herself to breathe as she slowly leaned close enough to the closet door to see through the slats.

Ted was standing by the bed. His jeans were tight, a button-down shirt was half tucked in, half falling out. He had one leg propped on the bed frame, his elbows on his knee.

"Take off your clothes," he said. Kaia strained to hear. Surely he hadn't said that. Adrienne was a statue, stiff, pale, an ancient Roman piece of art, frozen with a hint of grief forever captured.

"Now, Adrienne," he said sternly, like he was telling her to clean her room. It struck Kaia as a particularly heinous abuse of his authority to dare to use his dad voice.

"I don't feel good. My tummy hurts." Adrienne reverted to younger language. It perplexed and somehow revolted her.

"Don't make me say it again."

Adrienne sheepishly maneuvered out of her shirt, covering herself with her hands. He got on the bed on his knees, grabbed her wrists, and pinned them over her head. Kaia could feel Adrienne's self-consciousness. Ted kissed her neck, her chest, he bit her nipple and Adrienne flinched and whimpered. She tried to pull away. He shoved her down in an unnecessarily strong motion. Kaia looked away. She felt frozen. She was sweating. She heard a struggle and Adrienne say "ow." She forced herself to look again. Adrienne was naked. He was unzipping his pants with one hand, holding Adrienne down with the other. Kaia's eyes flashed around the closet. Suddenly, she had a bat in her hand. She opened the door. He looked at her, eyes wide.

"Whoa there," he said, but she'd already started her swing. The bat connected with his face. Blood flew through the air and he fell over backwards to the floor. Adrienne's scream rang through her head, but instead of stopping it got louder and louder until it hurt and she saw white.

She was pulling a trigger. She was firing in rapid succession. A person in blue was in front of her, bandana covering most of the face so that only the determined eyes showed. She heard bullets whizzing past her ears. She shot. A fountain of blood erupted from the person's chest and their rifle veered off to the sky, still firing. She shot another Wild AK, and another. They kept flooding out of the Escalade, but they couldn't hit her. She shot them all, hitting each with perfect accuracy, punching holes through their bodies like butter.

Finally, they'd all fallen. Kaia came out from behind the wall. There were so many. The thrill of survival faded into horror, and she ran to the bodies, splashing through blood. They were all still bleeding. It came from every gunshot hole, their mouths, their eyes, their ears. It poured in impossible quantities. She knelt by someone, pulled down their blue bandana to reveal a young girl struggling for breath.

"I'm sorry," Kaia said. She tried to cover the wound in the girl's chest, but it gushed over her fingers. When Kaia looked to her face, she was dead. She tried to check another who was writhing in pain. When she reached out to touch him, he died. Again and again, they died at her touch, but she couldn't stop herself from racing on to the next, and the next, trying to help.

"No," she said to herself. "Stop. Stop!" But she kept reaching for them.

Kaia was tossing in the bed. She was drenched in sweat and mumbling. Adrienne reached out and touched her arm. She was burning hot.

"Kaia." She tried to wake her gently, but Kaia kept muttering "no" and "stop." Adrienne touched her shoulder and gently shook her. "Kaia, you're dreaming, honey. Wake up." She shook her harder. Kaia finally jumped awake. Her eyes raced around the room. She was obviously confused about where she was.

"You're okay," Adrienne said.

Kaia was breathing hard. She touched her shirt, realizing she was soaked in sweat. Finally, her eyes found Adrienne and she started crying.

Adrienne wrapped her arms around Kaia and pulled her close. She'd never seen Kaia fall apart, but she was comfortable handling it. She ran her fingers through her hair and held her. When her crying quieted she whispered, "You okay?"

"I kept killing them. Ted and those recruits, and then just everyone. When they shot at me I wanted to kill them. I wanted to kill them desperately, but when they died I just wanted them back."

Adrienne squeezed her again. She felt fragile. Adrienne hated herself for ever doubting who Kaia was, for harassing her about police corruption. She wasn't some robotic killer, she was the same sweet Kaia, and she was horrified by taking life.

How could she have been with ruthless Gianna, overlooked her remorseless violence for power, but have reservations about Kaia just because she had a badge?

"I'm so sorry, Kaia."

Kaia leaned back to the bed but kept her arms wrapped around Adrienne, nestled close. Adrienne closed her eyes and breathed her in, letting herself transport back to the nights they fell asleep this way when they were sixteen and their worlds were so simply each other. She should have never let go of that. They should have run away together. They should have been together.

Chapter Seventeen

A nna had a hard time convincing Gianna not to go to the funeral. It was understandable she wanted to be there, but gang funerals often got violent, which gave the police an excuse to monitor them. They'd be here today for sure. It was getting harder and harder to convince her old friend to make careful choices, which was concerning and out of character.

Marco had convinced the recruit's family to let the Wild AKs control most of the funeral planning. They hadn't wanted to, but Marco promised the funeral would be ruined entirely if they didn't, so they'd been able to fill the room with their blue WAK banners and include rap lyrics in the memorial.

Anna found Christina and Celeste, along with an East Side WAK with mocha skin and young, boyish features. When she walked up, they fell quiet.

"What?" she asked. They shifted uncomfortably. "Come on, what?"

"We were talking about Gianna," Celeste said.

"What about her?"

"We think it's weird she's not here."

"You know she can't be."

"Fuck that," the East-Sider said. "I'd be here no matter what."

Anna looked from one face to the next. She expected this, but never from her own circle. Why were Celeste and Christina humoring this? Even engaging it?

"What's your name again?" Anna asked the East-Sider.

"Carlos."

"Gianna has to stay away. She didn't want to, but this was a recruit, not a member, and she's dead. Gianna can't change it, and she's going to prison for a long time if the cops pick her up. It would be stupid of her to show up, and the second she did they'd be crashing this place and ruining the whole thing."

"The recruit had a name, yo. Karina. And Gianna got her killed. Just because she was a recruit doesn't mean she don't matter. All she ever wanted was to fly blue, be Wild, and roll with you and Gianna. Now Gianna can't even be bothered to show up and you don't know her name."

"Wanting to be a Wild AK isn't enough to be one. You have to prove yourself. That shit is dangerous. Not everyone makes it and she knew that. If she wanted in so bad then she respected it."

"Yeah, whatever. Fuck you both. Neither of you are real."

"You sure you know who I am, homie?" Anna took her knife from her pocket and flipped it open.

Carlos paled even as he tried valiantly to stay hard. "You killing members now?"

"Nobody disrespects me. You think I'm going to stand here and let you call me fake and question my loyalty? No way, baby boy, especially not from some skinny little bitch that probably got jumped in last month. You think you're going to just walk in here, start talking trash about two original members, and then walk away? You need to shut your mouth before you get hurt."

His cheeks flushed. "Look, my bad. I didn't mean any disrespect. She was just a friend of mine and emotions are up, you know? Trust me, I got nothing but respect for you. And I know you were in the car too and *you're* here."

"I wasn't ID'd. It's not the same."

"Yeah, I know. Look, I'm sorry, for real. I'm actually excited to see you take things over with Gianna on the low."

Anna was much better at disguising her adrenaline than he was. She'd had much more practice, been in much worse situations. He would never know her heart was racing too. She had been aware Gianna was taking heat for the shooting going wrong, but she couldn't believe they were openly bashing her. Until Carlos, all Anna had received for her involvement in that night was praise for guts of steel. In fact, members had started calling her for advice. They looked at her differently. It didn't make sense to her; they'd been caught up in shootings before. She could never guess what was going to travel and what was going to get buried. Marco had even given her point on the drug game while Gianna hid, which was no small task with Adrienne no longer supplying them.

She knew she was taking Gianna's place, and it made her both ecstatic and sick. Gianna had led their escapades since they were kids. She'd never minded following Gianna's lead. She liked being her backup, the one person with enough guts to keep up. Now that the opportunity to lead had presented itself, she realized she did want it, but she didn't know how Gianna would take it.

"How long you been Wild, Carlos?" she asked.

"Six months."

"Okay," she said. "You're still new so let me explain something to you. Gi has been hustling these streets for fifteen years. She's as Wild as they come. She doesn't need to prove shit to you. She bleeds blue."

"That's cool," he said. "I feel you."

"You have to think big picture, kid. You know what Gi going to prison for most of her life does to this gang? And over what? A formality? Ceremony? Trust me, she's torn up about Karina, but this shit happens. It's about what's best for the gang. Always."

The staff asked everyone to sit for the ceremony. Carlos was more than happy for a reason to break away. Anna glared at Celeste and Christina.

"What the fuck was that? You were humoring that crap?" She walked away without waiting for a response. She'd deal with it later.

A coffin sat at the head of the room, a podium for the reverend was center. The reverend looked scared stiff when he came in, but once he started reading his passages it was like any other funeral. When he finished, a recruit that had joined up with Karina draped blue blankets over the coffin.

A small, squat, Hispanic woman in the front row stood in a rage and ripped it off. She pointed at the recruit, yelling at him in Spanish. Anna couldn't understand a word, but she was enraptured by the display.

The recruit ripped the blanket from her hands and put it back. The woman ripped it off again, threw it to the ground, and spat on it. Half the room stood up in a fury. The recruit reared back to slap her, but a member stopped him.

"Not her mom! Not at a funeral."

Another voice chimed in. "She spit on our flag."

The room erupted. The staff hurried out and the cops rushed in. Most scattered for the doors. Anna felt hands on her wrist.

"You're under arrest, Fields."

"Fuck you, I didn't do shit."

"In relation to the attempt on Officer Sorano's life."

Anna spun and head butted the officer. His head flew back and his hands cupped his nose. She ran for the back door. She heard the officer screaming into his radio that she was headed out the back, but she had no choice. She'd have to blend into the chaos. She burst out the back door and ran beside a group of members, splitting off as the cops cut in for them. She made it out of the cluster and ran down a side street. Most of the cops were distracted by the others, but there was one on her heels still. She led him down an alley, pulling him away from his cover.

She hadn't brought a gun. She didn't want one on her in case cops did crash the funeral, but she hadn't known she was wanted for attempted murder.

"Stop!" the cop screamed. It occurred to her he might shoot her in the back. She *was* wanted for trying to kill a cop. But she was thirty feet ahead, and she couldn't bring herself to stop. She had him. She rounded into an alley and stopped at the corner. She grabbed a piece of wood by the dumpster. When he came around the corner, she swung at his head. He managed to get his arms up, but it still dazed him. She hit him again and he stumbled. She tried to kick him, but he grabbed her leg and slammed her to the ground hard. She scrambled away before he could get his weight on top of her. She took off again. She must have hurt him because he had a harder time keeping up now.

She turned out of sight as fast as possible and stripped down to her tank top. She was about to toss the blue shirt into the bushes when Celeste pulled up at the end of the street. Anna kept the shirt and sprinted to the car. She jumped in and Celeste squealed away before the cop was visible again. Anna breathed in relief that he hadn't spotted Celeste's car. That was the last thing they needed.

"Shit!" Anna screamed.

"I got you," Celeste said and turned away from the flashing lights ahead.

Anna completely forgot her hard feelings about the discussion at the funeral, now as mad as everyone else at Gianna. Anna fist bumped Celeste. "Thank you, girl. They're going to try to box us in. We need to get out fast."

"Scanner."

Anna turned the scanner on her phone on. It wasn't perfect, but it was better than nothing. "Try Seventy-first."

"We can't get stuck at the tracks right now," Celeste said.

"I know. If it's stacked up we'll find a way around."

Celeste took the turn. Anna held her breath until they were over the train tracks and well out of the area. When she was confident they were in the clear she fished for her phone. She got Gianna on the line.

"Gi, your fucking girlfriend is snitching. It's official. They just tried to pick me up on the shooting. She must have told them I was there."

"Fuck," Gianna said. "Where—"

"Fucking handle your bitch, Gianna!" Anna hung up and threw her phone at the floor of the car.

CHAPTER EIGHTEEN

Kaia was on her phone in the other room. Adrienne didn't understand why she always crept so carefully out of bed just to talk too loudly in the next room anyway, but it made her laugh. They'd spent another chaste night in the same bed. It was becoming easier now that they'd done it a couple times, but Adrienne still felt the pull of Kaia's gravity in the quiet moments before sleep. Adrienne forced herself away from the warmth of the bed. Kaia hung up just as Adrienne walked in the room.

"They tried to pick Anna up. She got away." Kaia nervously tousled her own hair. Her blue T-shirt pulled out the striking color of her eyes and made Adrienne's head swim. She struggled back down to the low those words deserved.

"So now they know I snitched and they're both still free."

"I'm sorry, Adrienne. But we're safe here. They'll find them."

Adrienne was shocked by her own calmness. All of the Wild AKs would be after her now, not just Gianna, but she almost felt relief.

"We should be out there."

"What? No."

"They know they're wanted. Your people are never going to find them. They're not going to come out. The only thing they'll risk that for now is me."

"You want to be bait?"

"I want this to be over. I don't want to be afraid of her the rest of my life, and if we don't get her soon she'll disappear."

"It could go so wrong."

"Call your cop friends," Adrienne said. "Do it smart. Set her up."

"But we can't control when she shows up."

"We show up in WAK territory. They'll see us. They'll tell her."

"What if they don't? We're probably both shoot on sight."

"Gianna wants me. Probably you too. She'll have word out she's claimed us."

"I don't know, Adrienne. That's a huge gamble."

"Yeah," she said. "But it's how we catch her."

She watched Kaia weigh it all out. This was a risk to her life too, but Adrienne knew that wasn't her hesitation. Finally, she nodded. "You're sure?"

"I'm sure."

Kaia got back on the phone and gave the plan to Davis. It seemed to take less convincing than she'd expected. Soon they were in Kaia's Taurus heading back to town.

They'd agreed to go to the patio across from the site of Reid's attack. Since then it'd become a popular WAK hangout, a symbol of defiance. They were sure to be seen.

"This is going to be an obvious move," Kaia said.

"Yeah, and that'll piss her off," Adrienne said. "She'll know we're calling her out, but she still won't be able to resist."

"And you're sure they won't move on us without her?"

"As sure as I can be."

"I should do this alone," Kaia said. "They want me worse than you. I killed one of them."

"No, they hate you, but they can respect a shootout. I'm a snitch. They hate me more. And I'm Gianna's ex so she has a more valid claim on me that they're more likely to respect. If anything *I* should do this alone."

"No way in hell."

"So we'll do it together."

When they pulled up, Kaia checked her gun and shoved extra magazines into her pockets. She verified backup was ready, then looked to Adrienne. "Ready?"

Adrienne grabbed and squeezed Kaia's hand. "Ready."

They found seats on the patio in plain sight. The familiar smell of piss soaked alleys that seemed to crawl all over Chicago was particularly damp and noticeable after being at the secluded safe house for a few days, yet it was also somehow comforting and familiar. Adrienne's heart raced as she swept the crowd for blue. She didn't see any.

"Someone will see," Kaia said, reading her thoughts. "They have hired eyes at these businesses."

Adrienne nodded. All she could focus on was looking over Kaia's shoulder, making sure no one snuck up on her. A half hour had passed when Kaia's phone rang. She answered.

"Yeah?" She listened. Kaia looked completely relaxed at a glance, lounging in the deep patio chair. The way her eyes stayed trained on Adrienne told her her mind was anything but.

"They have Christina watching near the Laundromat," Kaia said. "They're ready to grab her if they have to. She's on the phone."

Adrienne grabbed Kaia's hand. She leaned across the table and gently kissed Kaia on the lips. She felt Kaia tense in surprise, but Adrienne knew she'd catch on. It was a tactic, a show, all business, but Kaia's warm smell made her dizzy and she felt like she was falling. She hooked her fingers behind Kaia's neck, pulling her intimately closer. Kaia's soft lips responded, accepting the bold strategy. When they parted, Kaia's phone rang again. She hung up without saying anything.

"Good," she said. "Let's go."

Adrienne's heart hammered as they went back to Kaia's car. They went directly to the gang unit and were quickly shuffled inside.

"Ladies," Davis greeted them. "Want to tell me what that was about?"

"Christina is part of Gianna's inner group," Adrienne said. "She'll report that straight to Gianna. The more personally offended Gianna is the more rash she'll get."

"We want this to be Gianna's fight," Kaia said.

"Well, I think it worked," Davis said. "Whoever Christina called it looked like she got hung up on. Hopefully by a pissed off Hernandez."

"Perfect," Kaia said.

"Now what?" Adrienne asked.

"We're upping our surveillance on members in hopes she reaches out. As far as you two, I recommend you get back to the safe house."

"If we drop off again so will she," Adrienne said.

"What do you want to do? Stay in the Sixty-Second Street house?"

Adrienne glanced at Kaia.

"Absolutely not," Davis snapped. "That wasn't a real suggestion."

"No, that's too dangerous," Kaia said. "But we can stay in a hotel. Close to WAK territory but not in it. Street visibility. We need to look like we're hiding but not be."

"I know a place," Davis said. "Easy to monitor, about a mile north of the WAK border. We used to do drug stings there."

"Perfect."

Gianna closed her phone and punched the dashboard. Anna stared at her from the passenger seat.

"Fucking bitch!" Gianna's pulse thundered in her ears. She turned to Anna. "Adrienne just showed up in the square with the cop."

"What?"

"That was Christina," Gianna said. "They're sucking face in the square." She started the car.

"Whoa," Anna said and grabbed the wheel. "They'll be gone by the time we're there. Let's finish what we're doing."

"I've been looking for her for days. I have to get them now."

"They'll be gone."

"I'll have Christina tail them."

"Gianna, if we don't kill this judge, Marco will freak. If Adrienne thinks they can hang out in the square they either think we left town or they want to be found. Either way, we'll find them later."

Gianna punched the dash again. "Fucking whore snitch mother-fucker."

"We'll deal with her after we do this," Anna said. "But right now we need to get back in Marco's good graces."

Gianna grit her teeth. Anna wasn't even in his bad graces. Anna thought she was being nice by acting like they were in the same situation, but it just pissed her off. She was the only one taking the heat for things going wrong lately.

"We can do this any time," Gianna said. "Adrienne could drop off again."

"We can't do this any time. Marco's court date is coming up."

"Fine." Gianna put her gun in her waistband.

"Gi."

"I said fine. Let's kill the motherfucker and go. How long does it really take to shoot someone?" Gianna opened the car door and ran to the side of the house. Anna followed in a more careful crouch. Gianna powered ahead and punched out the window.

"Damn, Gianna, look inside first!"

"You coming or what?"

She crawled in the window. Anna followed. The lights were out. The place was immaculate, sparsely decorated and easy to navigate even in the dark. Gianna pointed to the stairs. When she started up them a voice startled her.

"I'm armed! Don't come up here!" the voice came from the other side of a doorframe that was on the left side of the hallway at the top of the stairs. "The police are on their way. I suggest you run now."

"Shit," Anna said.

Gianna ignored him and ran up the stairs, gun drawn. A full sounding bang rippled through the air. He *was* armed. Maybe a shotgun. A warning shot.

"Fuck!" Anna yelled, backing away. "Gianna!" Gianna ducked at the sound, hesitated, but then charged up the stairs.

She rounded the corner the shot came from. Another huge blast sounded as she lunged to the side. A chunk of wood was dislodged from the doorframe, exploding into the air. She rushed the last of the space to him and pushed him over, pinning the shotgun safely to his chest. She punched him, then ripped the gun away.

"Who are you?" he asked. "What do you want?" Gianna hit him again. "I have money."

"Shut up." She wrapped her hands around his neck. A surge of strength from him surprised her. Adrienne used to surprise her too. People were always stronger when they were afraid, but he was old, somewhere around seventy and obviously sick. She overpowered him, squeezed harder. She pressed her weight on his throat, stopping the air and the blood. His hands clawed for her face but couldn't reach. His eyes were wide and frantic.

It all stopped suddenly. His hands fell, his eyes stopped searching the room. She let a good while pass before she let go. She turned. Anna was watching, frozen.

"The fuck are you looking at, pussy?"

"Let's go."

Gianna took a picture of him and followed Anna out to the car. They rode away in silence. When Anna pulled into the square it was deserted.

"Shit. I told you we were going to lose them."

"They'll be back, Gi."

Gianna dialed Doug, the cop they'd bribed. He picked up.

"What do you have for me?" Gianna asked.

"Nothing."

"What the fuck do you mean, nothing? I throw down that kind of cash I want results."

"I found your safe house, but it's useless to you now. They moved back out today."

"Why?"

"I don't know. That information wasn't part of the deal. They were there, now they're not, and I have to go back to square one and find them again."

"I need that address."

"Trust me, I don't want to do twice the work any more than you want to wait for it."

Gianna hung up on him. "Useless." She turned to Anna. "I want these streets scoured. They have to be in town."

"I'll spread the word."

"Anna."

"What?"

"Never tell me what to do again."

"What are you talking about?"

"I told you we needed to go get Adrienne and I let you talk me into killing that judge first instead. Now she's gone just like I said. We tried it your way, but there's a reason I take lead."

"Oh, fuck you. We did the right thing."

"Fuck me? You aren't shit without me."

"You're pussy whipped on Adrienne and it's making you a fucking embarrassment. Marco said get the judge so we got the judge. I don't care about your girl situation."

"She snitched on you, stupid. You're the one who said 'handle your bitch, Gianna.' What happened to that, tough guy? You think this is all about pussy? Marco said get the snitch. He said get them both, and we could have had them both *and* the cop all tonight."

"Please, Marco doesn't care about her. He told me. He just wanted to shut you up and keep you cooperative."

"Oh, you're tight with Marco now?"

"That's right," Anna said.

"You're a boss now, huh?"

"Who do you think he gave your crew to when you had to go dark?"

"You're dark now too, stupid. That's why we should be finding Adrienne. What don't you understand?"

"We will, but Marco cares more about the judge. What don't *you* understand?"

"Shut up, Anna, quit acting like hot shit. You wanted to bitch out when you heard the gun, and I saw you get squeamish when I strangled him. You can't do what I do so stop acting like somebody."

"I didn't even have to go with you to that," Anna said. "Marco gave you that hit because you fucked up, not me. And don't act like you don't know about my body count, man. I'm no bitch. I'm Wild, hundred percent."

"Pulling a trigger ain't nothing."

"What do you want, a medal for strangling an old man? That ain't nothing either."

"You better get out of my car before you become a body count, bitch."

"Fuck you, Gi. You're letting this girl make you stupid."

"Out."

"Fucking cry baby." Anna got out of the car and slammed the door. Gianna left her on the curb and sped off in search of the blue Taurus.

Chapter Nineteen

Kaia and Adrienne unpacked in the hotel room. It felt strange being with Adrienne in a third place together in just a handful of days.

Kaia's lips still tingled where Adrienne had kissed her. She couldn't help but wonder if the kiss had been necessary, but she couldn't deny it had done its job. Was that all it was?

"I'm ordering pizza," Adrienne said. "What do you want?"

"Hawaiian."

Kaia double-checked the doors and windows while Adrienne ordered. They were the end unit on the second level of the strip motel. There was a sliding door that led to a small balcony that hung over the end of the building. The parking lot had a direct view of both the balcony and the front door. The wall opposite the front door was all floor-to-ceiling glass windows, but it faced the brick building next door with only a couple feet between the buildings and didn't concern her. Kaia spotted the undercover cars watching over them from the permanently shut small window on the front wall. They were well disguised, but she felt like a sitting duck. Surveillance was boring. What if they fell asleep? What if they were distracted by a phone call? Adrienne and her life could depend on them. Not to say she hadn't brought guns. She had plenty.

Adrienne touched her side. A shiver went through her body. "You okay?"

"Yeah," Kaia said. "You?"

"I'm great, actually. I know it's more dangerous, but I feel so much better doing something."

Adrienne's lips were distracting. Kaia kept flashing back to their times in bed together so long ago. Their first time. Kaia had been terrified to make a move, afraid she'd read everything wrong and would destroy their friendship. Adrienne had been the one to advance, and she made it seem effortless. She'd taken off Kaia's shirt and teased her nipples until Kaia thought she would come. She'd licked and sucked until Kaia begged to be fucked, but the lovemaking had been gentle, the timid explorations of virgins. Now Kaia wanted to rip Adrienne's clothes off and fuck her against the wall until her legs were Jell-O.

"Are you sure you're okay?" Adrienne asked. "We don't have to do this if it's too much."

"No, it's fine. You were right. It's a good idea."

"Thank you for this, Kaia. I've given you such a hard time, but I've never even thanked you. You risked your life for me even when I was being impossible."

"You're very welcome," Kaia said. Adrienne was standing close. Her eyes lingered like she wanted more. It was like she was begging Kaia to talk, but she didn't know what to say.

"I've always cared about you, Adrienne. Always will. I pretended I stopped thinking about you, but I never really did."

"Me either. I knew we'd meet up again one day. Even when it didn't happen that time at the bar I still knew it would eventually."

"Adrienne, that kiss…"

"Should I not have?"

Kaia stepped closer. "You just need to know I can only resist so much."

"I don't recall asking you to resist."

Kaia leaned in and touched Adrienne's lips with her own. She pulled Adrienne close and let her tongue caress hers, rhythmically dancing in and out of her mouth. Adrienne wrapped her arms around Kaia's neck and pushed herself against Kaia, begging to be touched. Kaia slid her hand over Adrienne's skin, up her shirt, gently brushing her nipple with her thumb. Adrienne moaned quietly in response and pressed her breast into Kaia's hand.

Kaia teased her nipples, bit her gently on the neck. Adrienne's body responded eagerly. Kaia backed her onto the bed and centered herself on top, pressing herself between Adrienne's legs. Adrienne gasped and bunched Kaia's shirt in fists. The thrill of Adrienne's pleasure shot through her, making her desire almost unbearable.

Kaia's phone rang, her work phone with the ring she'd designated to the officers watching their hotel. They looked at one another, slow and drugged by desire. Finally, they processed it and jumped up. Kaia grabbed her gun and answered the phone.

"You got something?"

"Someone in a pizza uniform at your door in five seconds. You want us to grab him?"

"No." Kaia stifled the laugh she knew they wouldn't appreciate. "No, he's okay. Sorry."

Kaia mouthed "pizza" at Adrienne just as the knock came at the door. Adrienne covered her mouth and giggled.

"That's the kind of thing you warn us about, Sorano. Otherwise we end up making some kid shit himself and give ourselves away."

"I know. I'm sorry."

She hung up as Adrienne collected the pizza and carried the boxes to the bed. Adrienne's hair was a gorgeous brunette, wavy and tousled from their kissing. She looked at Kaia mischievously as Kaia joined her on the bed.

"I guess we're supposed to be treating this like work, huh?" she asked.

"This is a damn good job if we are."

Adrienne smiled. "We can't forget this is dangerous, though. Not on vacation anymore."

"You're right," Kaia said. "It would be awkward trying to put on clothes and run after Gianna at the same time."

Adrienne giggled. "Naked super cop."

"And her naked sidekick."

"I guess we'll have to resist after all."

Kaia didn't mind. She could play this game with Adrienne forever.

"At least there's pizza."

❖

Gianna went through Marco's back door, greeted again by the same security guard. He barely acknowledged her, just nodded at the stairs.

Marco was shirtless, lifting weights though his extremely thin frame gave no indication it was a habit.

"Well?" he asked.

"The judge is handled."

Marco set down the weights and walked over, shining with sweat. "Really?"

Gianna handed him her phone with the picture of the dead man.

"Strangled? Suffocated?"

"Strangled."

"With?"

Gianna held up her hands and wiggled her fingers. He raised an eyebrow. "Impressive. You stage it as natural then?"

"Couldn't. He had a shotgun, blasted the shit out of the walls."

Marco raised an eyebrow again, then shook her hand. "Shotgun, huh? Glad to see you in one piece, then. I sometimes forget how good you are. I'll remember this one."

"Appreciate that."

"I have something for you," he said. Gianna waited as he searched his pocket. He produced a piece of paper and handed it to her. She expected a name, a new identity, but instead found an address.

"What's this?"

"It's your little friend. It's a setup, though. It's guarded."

"This is where Adrienne is?"

"Yeah. My eyes spotted them, but they sat on it. Good thing too. It's surrounded. I don't know how you're going to get to her, but she's there."

"Thank you, Marco."

He nodded. "Anna is mad about all this. She's mad your girl ratted. She's mad about something you two got into."

"Anna can go fuck herself. She's letting my laying low go to her head. Thinks she's some hotshot now, but she's a pussy without me."

"I don't really care," Marco said. "I just need to know if it's going to be a problem."

"No," Gianna said. Sometimes she and Anna needed a good fistfight, but they'd never go further than that.

Gianna held up the paper. "Thanks for this."

She called Doug from her car.

The annoyance in his voice was clear the moment he answered. "Hernandez, get out of my ass, I'm working on it."

"Forget it. You're too slow. I have what I need."

"Oh, okay then."

"I'll be by to pick up my fifty K."

"What? No, half is paid up front for a reason," he said. "I already took risks. I get paid to take risks."

"No, you get paid to produce results. You didn't. You think I'm going to pay you fifty thousand dollars for nothing?"

"You paid me to get involved in this shit. And now you're paying me for silence."

"I can think of a cheaper way to shut you up."

"Don't threaten me, punk. I told you there's another side of me."

"I will be there in an hour. You can give me my money or I can take it. I don't give a shit which." She hung up.

When she pulled onto his block there were three cop cars parked outside.

"Shit." She turned around and crept off. "Little crooked ass bitches."

She wanted to call the crew and come light the place up, but that was the last thing anyone wanted to hear from her right now. She'd have to deal with it another way. Every time she knocked someone off her kill list someone new made it on.

Anna had never been alone with Marco. He didn't let many people know where he lived. Most saw him at a party once or twice, but he rarely had a real conversation with anyone. Now she was here and had no idea why.

"I heard you had a falling out with Gianna," he said.

"It was nothing," she said. "It happens."

"Tell me, Anna. Would you describe Gianna as stable?"

Anna shifted. She couldn't imagine this was going anywhere good. "What do you mean?"

"Gianna is loyal and ruthless, but she's rash. Didn't used to be, but these days she's bordering on uncontrollable, wouldn't you say?"

"It's just this Adrienne thing. She'll be herself again after this."

"But if a girlfriend does this to her, when is the next time she loses it?"

Anna couldn't answer. She felt sick. A film of cold sweat covered her and she wanted to sit, but hadn't been invited to do so.

"Just tell me what you honestly think," he said. He spoke quietly, as if that could make her miss the hungry look in his eyes. "She says you're a pussy. Says you have no nerve without her, that you're a dumb order-taker who just wants to be her."

Anna's ears burned, her palms tingled. "She said that?" Anna couldn't believe Gianna would say those things to Marco. To Anna, maybe, when she was mad, but Marco? Her chest hurt. "She has a temper," Anna said. "When she loses it she does what she wants. No one else matters."

"I haven't said much about those recruits that were shot. Gave her a good brass knuckled punch for each and she thinks that's it, but I don't forget these things."

"Gianna is loyal. She just killed a judge for you. She's crazy sometimes, but she'll kill for this gang. Or die for it."

"And you?"

"Of course. Why do I suddenly have to prove myself? Just because Gianna was pissed and ran her mouth a little? There's nothing Gianna's done that I haven't. I've spilled blood, done time, everything she has."

"Relax, Anna. I'm just trying to figure out what to do with the two of you."

"What is that supposed to mean? We fight every now and then, but you don't have to *do* anything. It's not a big deal."

"It's not that."

"What then?"

"Kitchen isn't happy about all this attention. He wants me to turn you guys over. Says the cops need to catch at least one of you or he'll never be able to make it blow over."

"So what, you're trying to decide which one of us to keep around? You're going to listen to that shit? He's a stupid crooked undercover cop, Marco. We're members."

"Calm down," Marco snapped. "Of course I'm not going to turn either of you over, but Gianna *is* a problem right now. Shooting at a cop, losing a recruit, it all attracts a lot of eyes, and Kitchen can't do what he does with too many eyes on him. And without Kitchen telling them our hands are clean in the gun game, life gets a lot more complicated for all of us. Worse, he's getting nervous he's going to be at risk of exposure, and the way Gianna is acting is making me think he's right. He's not the type to take that sitting down. I'm worried he might try to grab you or Gianna on his own, be the big hero, get clear of any suspicion he thinks is meandering his way."

"He has to know what will happen if he moves on us."

"He does, but he's got his whole gang behind him. The Hijos de la Santa Muerte have a lot to lose if the detectives figure out Kitchen flipped. He's more than a resource for them now, he's high enough in the ranks they'll spill blood to protect him."

"They'd go to war over a cop?"

"He hasn't been a real cop in a long time. He was for sale even before he went undercover with the Hijos."

"They still can't possibly think they can trust him," Anna said. "He'll do whatever he has to to save his ass. The second shit gets real he'll try to crawl back to the protection of the police department."

"Look, I don't know their inner workings. He's obviously done something convincing for them. The point is they're at risk of exposure and if it happens they'll blame Gianna and all of us will have to answer for it."

"I don't know what you want me to say about it. What happened happened, and if we go to war, we do. Since when are we afraid to spill blood? Gianna would do that for any one of us if it was the other way around."

"I need to know what Adrienne knows."

"What?" Anna resisted the urge to wipe the sweat from her palms. "What do you mean?"

"Gianna said Adrienne doesn't know anything she shouldn't, yet she's acting like a rabid dog about finding her. Sitting in plain sight in a cop's parking lot, driving by the police station, stupid stuff, the kind of thing you do when you're scared someone is going to keep talking. Sure, she could be lovesick, but does that really sound like Gianna to you? She's either lost her fucking mind or there's a much more urgent reason to find Adrienne than she's admitting." Marco was average height and very thin, yet he had the presence of anyone with power, the ability to make her uncomfortable, to make her heart race under the pressure of his heated gaze.

"Adrienne betrayed her," Anna said. "She left Gianna for a cop and then she told them I was in the car the night of the shootout. Isn't that enough?"

"To be pissed off? Sure. To order a hit? Absolutely. To personally stalk a cop while every cop in the city is trying to pick her up? Doesn't make sense. Look, Anna, I need to know. How bad can Adrienne hurt us? What is Gianna trying to stop?"

Anna was well aware Adrienne did know Kitchen was on the payroll and that Gianna was trying to conceal that, but with Adrienne actively snitching the way she was, in all likelihood Kitchen was already exposed. Anna had always trusted Marco, but if Gianna had lied to him about what Adrienne knew, revealing otherwise would get Gianna in even deeper trouble. If Kitchen really went down because of Adrienne and it got back to Los Hijos de la Santa Muerte, it might even get her killed.

"If Gianna said Adrienne doesn't know anything else, then she doesn't. She's not a liar." Anna could barely breathe. Her whole life had been about loyalty, but what was loyalty now? She had to lie to the gang's founder or betray her best friend, endanger the whole gang or put Gianna directly in the line of fire.

"Don't make me look like an idiot, Anna," Marco said. "If there's something I need to know, you need to tell me."

"Gianna loves this gang," Anna said. "She can be a little wild, but she would never do wrong by us. This thing with Adrienne is personal, but it's also serious. She named me, Marco. She told them I shot at a cop. Who knows who else she'll name. I'll talk to Gianna. I'll tell her to be more careful, but we can't sit on this Adrienne thing, either. She needs to be killed."

Marco nodded. "I gave Gianna the address today. She knows where to find Adrienne. Let her handle it."

"I'll help."

"No. I don't want you anywhere near it. There are cops surveilling the place." Marco held up his hand when Anna started to protest. "She knows that and she's a smart girl. She needs to clean up her own mess. I don't want her putting anyone else at risk. Like you said, Adrienne named you. You're wanted for crimes that will put you away for life, and that's if they don't just shoot you. That's Gianna's fault. That might not be how you see it, but it's how I see it and it's how the rest of the gang sees it, so you need to let her fix this if you want to see her come out of this with a shred of respect."

Anna sighed and nodded. Gianna did need to redeem herself. The angry chatter at the funeral couldn't be ignored. Even Celeste and Christina had doubts, and that was dangerous. Not to mention Anna wasn't thrilled with Gianna at the moment anyway. She hadn't taken their fight that seriously at the time, but it hurt to think Gianna had really said those things about her to Marco. She almost couldn't even believe it was true, but she recognized Gianna's style of speech as he'd relayed it. Yet Anna had still lied for her. She owed Gianna a good sock in the jaw the next time she saw her.

CHAPTER TWENTY

Adrienne rested her feet on the railing of the balcony outside their hotel. She scanned the property line, the bushes, the streets. For the first time since leaving, she had to admit she missed Gianna. She knew she could never go back, knew it had been years since Gianna was the person she missed now, but she couldn't help the dull ache, the longing for the familiarity of Gianna.

In some ways, she and Kaia went back so far she felt like family. In others, she was a stranger. Gianna had been a steady presence in her life for years.

"You okay?" Kaia opened the door and stuck her head out. Adrienne could read everything on her face. She knew something was wrong, was trying to give her space, but wasn't comfortable with Adrienne being outside alone.

"Come on out," she said.

Kaia sank into the lawn chair beside her and took her hand. "What's wrong?"

Adrienne wanted to tell her, but she didn't want to hurt her. She knew it sounded insane to outsiders. She knew she couldn't explain how she could love someone who had hurt her so much. And she couldn't deny she knew Kaia had feelings for her. She wasn't sure what Kaia wanted, if it was their years apart or their years together that were pulling them to one another now, but in any case she wouldn't want to hear Adrienne still had feelings for Gianna of any kind, even if Kaia did know on some level that five years couldn't possibly just vanish overnight. When she looked at Kaia, her eyes were warm and compassionate, like she already knew everything.

"Gianna will come here," Adrienne said. "This will work."

"Scared?" Kaia asked the words, but Adrienne knew she knew that wasn't it.

"I just feel like I'm ruining her life. I know I have to, but it's still hard."

"If there was another way, I'd help you," Kaia said. "If you could be safe, I'd find another way."

"I just don't understand how it all went so wrong. How we ended up such different people. Who will we be in five years, Kaia? She was nothing but loving for so long. How do I trust again knowing what that can turn into?"

Kaia squeezed her hand. "I can't promise we won't change, but I can promise I will never, ever hit you."

Adrienne smiled weakly. That should be a given, but it wasn't anymore. Promises felt so empty. How many times had she heard Gianna swear she'd never put her hands on her again? How many times had her mother said her love was unconditional when it really wasn't? She felt betrayed even by herself. How many times had she told herself she deserved better only to chicken out at the threshold? And now, after all the promises of undying love and loyalty to Gianna, after all her words of scorn toward the idea of being a rat, her pledged alliance with the Wild AKs, what were even her own words worth?

Nothing was permanent. What she'd meant with all her heart then felt like a sham now. How could she expect Kaia or anyone else to hold true? Why was everyone so intent on commitment and forever when all life wanted to do was tear it all apart? Everyone was hunting for the one love that would be strong enough to be exempt from the dominating condition of life that is change.

She remembered Kaia's hand in her own and looked down. Kaia's hand in hers after all these years. The same hand that had traveled under her comforter and found her skin, pulled her closer. The same hand that had touched her face with infinitely gentle love. The same hand that had smoothed back her hair when she cried. Now that hand had touched others, it had pulled a trigger and ended a life, it had put handcuffs on Gianna. After all that, it was back in Adrienne's hand.

Kaia had changed. She'd become her own person, and her beliefs and desires had taken turns they might not have if Adrienne had been by her side this entire time. But Kaia had never become a bad person, and Adrienne couldn't believe she ever would. She just didn't know if she could trust herself to be a good person too. She'd followed Gianna places Kaia would have never gone. She'd fallen into traps of naiveté and anger and resentment. She'd let her surroundings mold her. She'd hated police, she'd enjoyed crime, she'd accepted abuse, she'd hurt others in the name of loyalty. Where had her loyalty to herself been? She'd soaked up a mentality she should have rejected, and now she felt weak.

"I should go to jail too," she said.

Kaia shook her head. "No, honey. You can't control someone else. What Gianna did wasn't—"

"I was in the car the night Gianna and Anna shot at that cop car."

Kaia was plainly confused and just waited.

"The gold Corolla. It was ours. Gianna switched the plates, but it was us. I was the driver. I was with them."

"Why?"

"They asked me to and I said yes."

"You had to."

"No," Adrienne said, tears coming to her eyes. "I tell myself that, but I didn't. I could have said no, but I knew she wanted me to. I was thinking about joining the Wild AKs. Even after you showed up, I still considered it." She could barely breathe. She waited for Kaia to pull her hand back. To storm away, but she just sat.

"I just drove," Adrienne said. "I didn't go inside. I don't even know what happened in there. They went to get money from someone and came back with thousands of dollars. The cop pulled up behind us and they told me go, so I went. I couldn't lose him. I kept trying but I couldn't, so Anna shot at him. That's when he stopped."

"Anna was the shooter?"

"Yes. Gianna was in the front with me. Anna shot from the back window."

Kaia squeezed her hand again. "She didn't hit him. He's fine."

"I know, but what if he hadn't been? I'm no better than they are, Kaia. I don't know why you want me."

"You are better."

"How can you say that? I'm telling you I did it because I wanted to. I bought into their loyalty and family bullshit. I was a heartbeat away from jumping in."

"Why didn't you?"

"Because." Adrienne's tears spilled over. "Because I thought about you. About if it had been you in the car, if she'd shot you, and I couldn't handle it." Adrienne wrapped her arms around Kaia and held her tight, as if she was still afraid Kaia was hurt. Kaia held her, rocking her slightly.

"That makes you different," she said.

"No, it doesn't. It just makes me lucky. If I'd grown up like Gianna I would have ended up the same. I was only in that neighborhood a few months when I started dealing. Imagine if that had been my whole life."

"And if I had gone through what you did I probably would have ended up the same," Kaia said. "It's not about judging them, Adrienne, it's just about stopping them. I can't let them hurt you."

She touched Kaia's face. "And I can't let them hurt you."

CHAPTER TWENTY-ONE

Gianna was staying east of WAK territory in South Shore in a shithole that didn't care if you lived, died, or shit in the hallway as long as you paid rent. It was a normal rate, and the only people who would pay it were people like Gianna, people who paid with dirty money and wouldn't answer questions.

Anna went down the back steps and waded through beer bottles and thousands of aluminum cans. She pounded on the rotting door.

"Yo, open up."

Celeste opened the door.

Anna craned her neck. "She here?"

"She's here. Christina too." Celeste let her inside. "I need to talk to you all."

"I know, I got your message. We have business first."

"Anna, wait."

Gianna walked around the corner and held her arms up. "What, bitch? I'm right here."

Anna charged her and shoved her into the wall. Christina leapt from the couch to get out of the way. Anna swung, connecting with Gianna's face. Gianna hit back, going for the body, working her solar plexus and organs. Anna shoved her head into the wall and elbowed her in the mouth. Gianna dug her foot into the floor and pushed her, sending her several feet back. Anna had felt Gianna's strength many times, but she refused to be intimidated by it.

It was much better to go down swinging than back down. Her refusal to show fear had always won Gianna's respect and she needed it again.

"Guys, wait!" Celeste yelled.

"You told Marco I'm a nerveless pussy?" Anna yelled over Celeste. Christina was starting toward them to help break it up but put her hands up and spun the other direction when she heard that.

"Yeah, I did," Gianna said. "Because you are."

Anna punched again, throwing her weight at Gianna. She shoved her toward the furniture, trying to take it to the ground, but Gianna was a brick wall. She whipped Anna around and pushed her back again.

"No matter how pissed I am at you I always have your back," Anna yelled. "Even when he told me about you."

"That makes you stupid."

"No, it makes you a double-crossing bitch. See how far that gets you. I'll tell them all they can't trust you, see what happens to you when no one cares anymore. See how you do alone."

"I'm already alone, punk. I've been alone!" Gianna landed a punch to Anna's jaw. "I take the big risks, I take the heat when it doesn't work out, and I handled that judge alone while you hid. The fuck you want me to call you? You're a pussy."

"Bitch, I didn't go anywhere. Just because I didn't run in there like some stupid ass bull. That's not tough, it's dumb. No one wants to follow you anymore because you keep running at gun barrels face-first like a moron. You're going to get people killed."

Gianna swung at Anna and grazed her ear, making it ring. "It's not my fault that recruit got popped. You all act like that's never happened before, like I did some horrible thing when all I did was go after someone who was coming for us. I was there too. I was shooting too. I could have died too. I'm there to handle myself, not to be some bulletproof vest for newbies. I don't have time for bitches. You're down or you ain't."

"I've been down since we were nine years old," Anna yelled. "How dare you question me. How dare you act like you've ever had to do anything without me." Anna backed her into the wall again and hit as hard and fast as she could, holding nothing back.

Gianna's arms wrapped around the backs of her legs, lifted her, and slammed her to her back on the ground. She straightened over Anna and punched. Anna grabbed a decorative statue from the table and swung at Gianna's face. It connected and sent her reeling backward.

"Guys! Stop!" Celeste screamed. "It's Marco!"

Gianna wiped blood from her mouth, moving sluggishly. Anna struggled to get her breath back from the slam. They looked at each other, deciding if they were finished. Anna could tell the statue had rocked Gianna. She offered her a hand. Gianna stared at it, then accepted and pulled Anna in for a hug.

"Crazy bitch," she said.

Anna laughed. "Big brute."

"Motherfuckers, can you not hear me?" Celeste yelled.

"God damn, what?" Gianna laughed.

"I have to talk to you. Sit your immature asses down."

They each settled on the couch, touching their burning wounds, checking for blood. Christina walked back to the couch and sat beside them, always calm and unfazed.

"You guys know Ron?" Celeste asked. "Marco's security?"

"Black guy? Mans the door?" Gianna asked.

"Yeah. He told me some shit you need to hear."

"Girl, why are you talking to Ron?" Anna asked.

"Don't worry about that. It's not important." She blushed.

"Oh God, you're hooking up?" Christina laughed.

"Shh!"

"It's just us here, you know," Anna teased her.

"Fine, yes, we are. But that is so far from the point. This is serious. Can we please focus?"

"How is he?" Anna asked.

"Marco is setting Gianna up."

"What?" Gianna stood up but was dizzy and sat back down, holding her head.

"Ron heard him talking to Kitchen. Kitchen says the detectives are really pressuring him to turn some information over, pushing harder than usual. He thinks it's because they know or at least suspect he's not one of theirs anymore. He thinks someone snitched and it must have gotten back to him that it was Adrienne. He wants Marco to take you out of the picture. He thinks it's your fault."

"My fault?"

Celeste nodded gravely. "Marco agreed."

"No way," Christina said, shaking her head in immediate dismissal.

"Out of the picture how?" Gianna asked.

"Prison. That's how Marco found Adrienne's address for you. Kitchen gave it to him. He's trying to deliver you to the cops. Kitchen gets to convince the Gang Unit he's still a real cop and Marco gets to have you deal drugs in prison."

"I can't believe this shit," Gianna said. "If Adrienne really did tell them Kitchen is dirty what good is turning me in going to do? It's already over."

"Probably thinks he can claim it was all part of his cover," Celeste said. "Or maybe just rely on his word as a cop and call Adrienne a liar."

"Marco did tell me Kitchen wants one of us," Anna said. "Said Kitchen can't get the heat off himself until he turns something big over. Marco told me he wasn't going to do it, though."

"When was that?" Celeste asked.

"Yesterday."

"Ron heard this today."

Gianna let out a heavy breath and shook her head. "This can't be right. He warned me there were cops on Adrienne. Why would he do that if he wanted me to get caught?"

Celeste shrugged. "Maybe he doesn't want it to be obvious he's doing this? I don't know. But he wants you gone and he wants Anna to take your place."

"Shit," Anna said. "He did forbid me from helping you with Adrienne. Said you need to earn your respect back alone. I bet he knew I wouldn't stay away, though. That explains why he told me what you said, Gi. He wants us to fight."

"He thinks I'm emotional enough about Adrienne to do something stupid even if I know cops are there," Gianna said, a thousand-yard stare taking over her eyes. "Thought he could warn me and still get it done. Then he gets to look innocent. He probably thinks I'll try to observe, not knowing Kitchen told them what kind of car I'm in."

"Wait, guys," Christina said. "What if Marco is playing Kitchen? He told you where Adrienne was like Kitchen wanted so that he can look like he's holding up his end, but he also warns you it's a trap so they won't actually catch you?"

"And what's the play after that?" Gianna asked. "Kitchen will keep trying to set me up until they get me. Marco's just going to keep sabotaging it? And if that's what he's doing, why not just shoot straight with me about it? Why try to make us fight? Keep Anna away?"

Anna stared at the ground. Marco was their founder. She'd never been his best friend the way she was with Gianna, but she'd trusted him. It went against everything she knew about him, all the things he claimed to believe in when he made the Wild AKs, but she was out of other explanations. "So what do we do now?"

"I still need to take care of Adrienne," Gianna said. "A rat is a rat. The cops can have Kitchen. And we need to take care of Marco."

"Are you insane?" Celeste asked.

"If he'd been a man and talked to me it'd be different, but instead he defected. He wants to put me in prison as a favor to a fucking cop? I don't care if Kitchen does have the Hijos behind him. We don't betray our own people for cops or for another gang or for money or guns or anything. Membership is sacred. That's the whole point. He should have told them to shove it."

"Fuck yeah, he should have," Christina said.

"But Marco isn't some dumb recruit," Celeste said. "He's the founder."

"He's not fit to lead anymore. Time to evolve. You guys got me?"

Anna nodded. "You know I do."

Christina nodded.

Celeste hesitated. "I mean, I got you, but I don't know how this is going to work."

"Leadership changes happen," Anna said. "It's not that crazy."

"But what about the retaliation?"

"From who? We're taking out a snitch and a traitor. And no one knows Marco, really. He stays locked up at his pad. Members know us, respect us. We got this."

Celeste finally nodded. "All right, let's do it."

Chapter Twenty-two

K aia was in the shower when her phone went off. It rang twice, then the swishing sounds that meant text messages started coming in. On the third one, she got nervous even though it wasn't the surveillance team's ring tone.

"Adrienne?" she called out.

Adrienne opened the bathroom door a crack. Kaia realized she'd have to come inside to get the phone, which made her tingle with nervousness, but the shower had frosted glass and was steamy.

"Can you look at my phone? Just in case? It's blowing up."

"Sure." Adrienne came inside, pausing as she entered and glancing Kaia's way before she grabbed the phone.

"Password?"

"Sixty-nine sixty-nine."

"Really, Kaia?" She laughed.

"Easy to remember."

Adrienne shook her head and clicked into her messages. "Oh my God, Kaia!"

"What?"

"Reid woke up!"

Kaia opened the shower door a crack and stuck her head out. "Really? You're sure?"

Adrienne turned the phone around for her to read. Kaia felt like she was going to explode with joy. "I knew he would. I'm going to hurry up and get out of here and we'll go to the hospital."

"Of course. I'll get dressed."

Gianna noticed the hospital parking lot was full of cop cars and pulled in. It had to mean one of two things, the cop she'd beaten senseless was either better or dead. She pulled into the back of the lot and parked. Either way, Blondie would come. If she was lucky Adrienne would be with her. This was her chance to catch them out of the guarded hotel.

Anna would be furious with her for sitting in a lot full of cops. This was the kind of thing she kept throwing in Gianna's face when she called her reckless. But Anna wasn't here. A split was happening between them that Gianna couldn't reverse. Anna was committed, a fighter, Gianna's throbbing head could attest to that. She'd been wrong to call her a pussy. Anna would charge headfirst into battle to back Gianna up. That didn't change the fact that given the choice, Anna preferred peace to war, caution to boldness.

Ever since Adrienne left, Gianna wanted chaos. She wanted blood and danger. She wanted it messy. Even now as she sat in the back of the lot, safely concealed by dark windows, part of her hoped a cop would approach her. Part of her wanted to fight her way out.

The blue Taurus pulled in, followed by two black undercover SUVs. She smiled. Finally.

The whole way to the hospital Kaia felt like she was going to explode. She couldn't stand the drive time separating them. They jogged through the parking lot up to his room. A gathering was assembling, a horde of officers with fresh flowers and banners. Sergeant Cruz was already there and greeted her with a warm hug.

"Go on in."

Adrienne hung back with the officers and nodded reassuringly at her to go ahead.

"I got her," Cruz said. Kaia felt like she should do more to make sure Adrienne was situated, but she trusted Cruz and she was dying to see Reid's smiling face.

She rushed into the room, beaming. Reid looked a thousand times better. His caramel skin wasn't discolored any longer, the swelling on his face had gone down, the tubes were gone.

"Look what the cat finally coughed up," Reid said with a wide smile. Kaia walked over and carefully found safe places to hug him.

"What are you talking about, finally? I came straight over."

"Yeah, but you were supposed to be crying by my bed."

She gently punched his arm. "Oh, I did, fucker."

"I know, they told me. You okay?"

"Me? Forget that, are *you* okay?"

"I think I will be. I was out for the worst of it. Shit, you probably know more about it than I do. I hear I had four surgeries?"

"You did," Kaia said. "They all went as planned. You've been out for two weeks."

"Doesn't feel like it. It's so strange, makes me feel like maybe dying isn't so bad, you know? You're just gone."

"I couldn't handle it if you died. I barely handled this. You're my family, Reid."

He reached out and squeezed her hand.

"Do you remember what happened?" she asked.

"Yeah. Wish I didn't. I was driving around the north end of South Side and felt something dragging under the car. It wasn't shaking loose, so I pulled over to get it out. I didn't call anything out. I thought it was going to be quick and simple. I was in the square, it was well lit, hadn't seen anything suspicious. But when I leaned over to see what it was, all of a sudden there were all these hands on me. They grabbed my arms, someone took my gun, my radio, everything. Hernandez came out and started hitting me. There were people everywhere, walking right by. No one would look."

"Fuck, Reid. I'm sorry."

"There was nothing that could have changed it. It was an ambush, obviously well planned. It was the way they got my arms. I couldn't do anything. I struggled hard and I just couldn't get a hand free. I thought there was no way they could keep me from tapping my emergency button, but they did. It really wakes you up. You think this shit can't happen. You think you'll figure it out if you have to, but I couldn't."

"Did she say anything?"

"Called me crooked. Threatened you too. That's what really drove me nuts. I knew she was going to come for you and I wouldn't be able to warn you."

Kaia shook with anger picturing Gianna beating Reid. She'd known it was her, but it was still different hearing it from him.

"She's still out there, Reid. I'm so sorry. We have the warrants, but we haven't been able to find her. We should have her by now."

"Don't apologize. They told me you knew before they did, that you about socked her in the square." He chuckled. "There you go biting off more than you can chew, crazy girl."

"They shouldn't have told you that. And I think I could have won." She laughed. "After what she did to you I don't think she could have stopped me."

"Well, I'm glad you didn't. I don't want you getting fired over me. I know you did everything you could."

"We're still going to get her, Reid. Adrienne is with us now, gave us plenty to put her away. Gianna's just been slippery, but we'll find her. I won't stop until we do." Kaia rested her hand on his shoulder. "Oh, did they tell you Hernandez tried to kill me too?"

His eyes went wide. "No. What happened?"

"Oh, saddle up for this shit."

Adrienne couldn't stop watching Kaia and smiling at her joy, at the way she interacted with Reid. It was like getting a glimpse at all the years she'd missed.

"Sergeant Cruz," he introduced himself. "Feel free to call me Cruz."

"Adrienne."

"Oh, I know," he said. "You're famous."

"Jeez."

He laughed. "No, don't worry about it, nothing bad. Most of the guys are just jealous you're with Sorano. Don't ever let men tell you they don't gossip."

Adrienne laughed. "I'm not even sure I'd really say we are together."

"You look more together than we've ever seen her look."

"Interesting."

"That's beside the point. Not our business. I just want to tell you what you're doing, helping us get your ex, it's very brave. I'm sure it's complicated for you. I don't know if anyone has acknowledged that part of this, but I want you to know we know."

Adrienne was taken aback by his sincerity. "Thank you, that's very kind. You don't owe me anything though. You've all helped me just as much. You got me out of that situation, gave me the opportunity to help you when you could have just thrown me in jail."

"Aw, we're not too keen on arresting people that don't need to be. Helping people out of a bad spot might not always be action-packed, but eventually you figure out it's the best part of the job."

"Well, you helped me out of a real bad spot."

"Glad to hear it."

"Adrienne." Kaia leaned out the door. "Come say hi."

Adrienne was terrified to show her face to the man Gianna had almost killed, but Kaia was so warm and excited. She met Adrienne at the door, grabbed her hand, and led her inside.

"Adrienne, this is my best friend, Reid."

Reid extended his hand with a genuine smile. "Nice to meet you, Adrienne. You been taking care of this one while I've been out?" He elbowed Kaia.

"I've been trying, but I think it's been more the other way around."

"That's not what I heard."

"I'm so sorry about what happened to you."

"Back at you," Reid said. "Sounds like we've all been in the path of destruction."

The nurse came in and nodded at them. "Sorry to interrupt. We're going to have to take care of some things and let him get some sleep."

"Bathroom stuff," Reid said in a mock whisper. Kaia laughed and gave him a long, tight hug.

"All right, we'll leave you alone for now."

"Yeah, get out of here and have yourselves a date night or something." Reid squeezed Adrienne's hand and winked. Adrienne followed Kaia out. Kaia was beside herself with joy, and Adrienne couldn't stop her own joy just seeing her so happy. She'd forgotten what that kind of happiness felt like.

Kaia looked over each shoulder as she went through the hospital doors into the parking lot. "Looks like our security team is straggling," she said.

"They were right behind us a second ago. I think they're just wrapping up a conversation." Adrienne turned and checked over her shoulder too. The atmosphere in Reid's room had been so light, so happy, they'd let their situation slip their mind and wandered off alone.

"I'm sure they'll be along in a minute." Kaia said the words casually, but Adrienne could see her color draining as she looked around the lot.

"You okay?"

"Yeah, just weird, being here again."

Adrienne followed Kaia's gaze and saw the chipped pavement and walls where bullets had shredded concrete.

"This is where it happened?" she asked.

Kaia nodded. Her eyes were glassy, and she looked far away. There was a sheen of sweat across her skin. Adrienne remembered the way Kaia had woken from her nightmare about that very night, the way she'd cried and trembled and fallen apart. She couldn't stand the pain in Kaia's distant, haunted eyes.

"Let's just go," Adrienne said. "The hotel isn't far and there are still two cars posted there. We'll be there in no time."

Kaia nodded like she hadn't really heard, and they got into the Taurus. Once they pulled out of the lot, Adrienne saw Kaia's color return as she slowly relaxed again. Adrienne reached out and squeezed her hand.

"You should talk to someone, you know? A professional."

"I know," Kaia said. "I have to. The department makes you after something like that."

Adrienne squeezed her hand again gently. "You should for you, though, Kaia. Not just because you have to."

She could see Kaia wasn't comfortable admitting how affected she was, but she smiled weakly and nodded.

"I know. I will," she said. Kaia shook herself and smiled again. A genuine warmth finally returned to her face, and she changed the subject. "God that was nice. I've missed Reid so much. I don't really talk to anyone else like him."

"Your mom?"

"She hates hearing cop stuff, makes her worry. Dating stuff has always been kind of awkward. She's fine with me being with girls, but there's still just that invisible barrier about it. I love her to death, but our conversations stay pretty shallow."

"Your brother?"

"He's great, but he's in Australia. The time difference makes calling hard and he's just always busy."

"I see. Sounds lonely."

"Sometimes. Not as much lately." Kaia smiled at her.

The gas light sounded and lit up. "Crap," Kaia said. She pulled up to the next gas station. It was only seven, but the sun was already setting. Kaia jumped out and started filling up.

"Hey, I'm going to run to the bathroom," Adrienne said.

"Okay."

Adrienne walked into the convenience store and to the front counter. The register was manned by a middle-aged woman with hair that looked wet but was really just over-gelled. She was staring at a sudoku book, copying the puzzle over to paper so she wouldn't have to buy the book.

"Do you have a restroom?"

The woman grabbed a key from behind the counter and slid it toward Adrienne, barely glancing at her. "Around back. It's on this side of the building." She pointed a thumb over her own shoulder at the back wall.

"Thanks." Adrienne went back outside and circled the building. They were single bathrooms, one marked men and the other women, though there was only one key that fit both. She opened the door and went inside. Like most gas stations, it was bordering on disgusting. She should have gone at the hospital, but she hated those restrooms too.

When she opened the door, Gianna's frame filled the space. She tried to slam the door shut again, but she'd reacted a second too late and Gianna blasted the door open with her palm and pushed Adrienne back.

"Ka—"

Gianna rushed forward and clapped her hand over Adrienne's mouth. She'd thought too slow again, paralyzed by the shock of

Gianna's face. Gianna kicked the door closed and locked it. She pushed Adrienne against the wall.

"I told you I'd find you. I told you a hundred times if you ever ran I would find you. I told you!" Gianna screamed in her face. "And still you ran."

Adrienne pushed Gianna away. She let Adrienne free, amused by it now that Adrienne was trapped with her in the locked bathroom.

"I told you snitches lose their skins. I told you they're the lowest of the low. And still you snitched."

"You did this to yourself, Gianna. They caught you without me. You took off your mask."

"I told you if you cheated I would kill the bitch you were with, and still you cheated."

"I didn't cheat, I left."

"I didn't tell you you could leave."

"That's not up to you."

"Yeah? We'll see." Gianna swung at Adrienne's head. Adrienne ducked and sprang for the door. Gianna grabbed her by her hair and pulled her back.

"Kaia!" Adrienne screamed at the top of her lungs, but she had little hope Kaia could hear from the other side of the building.

"Next time your girlfriend sees you you'll be a corpse, bitch. And then I'm going to kill her too. Believe that."

Gianna shoved Adrienne backward, grabbed her head and smashed it into the tiled wall, then slung her to the ground. Adrienne kicked, hitting Gianna's legs, trying to knock out her knees. Gianna sidestepped and kicked her in the side. She stomped Adrienne's stomach, curling her into a ball of pain.

"Gianna, stop. Please just stop."

"Fuck you. You betrayed me! Don't you say my name now. Don't you ask me for mercy. You did this!"

Gianna stomped her again.

"Kaia!" She tried again. Gianna knelt and punched her. She grabbed her throat and pressed, sinking her weight on Adrienne's neck. "This isn't how I wanted to do it," she said. "But since you can't seem to shut up."

Adrienne scratched Gianna's face. She tried to reach her eyes but couldn't. She couldn't die in here, not with Kaia fifty feet away pumping gas on the happiest night she'd had in years. She couldn't let this happen. She reached over and banged on the door, again trying to attract attention, anyone's. Gianna grabbed her arm and pinned it beneath her knee. Even the second it took her to do that gave Adrienne a decent breath. She leaned forward with all her strength, clawing for anything to hurt. She reached Gianna's breast, grabbed her nipple and squeezed as hard as she could, twisted, determined to rip the skin. It felt ridiculous, but it was all she could manage, and Gianna yelled in shock and pain.

She pulled Adrienne up by her shirt, then slammed her down hard, making the back of her head hit the ground. The thunk of impact scared her. It knocked her dizzy and her hearing felt dull and far away. The pressure was back on her throat.

"Stupid bitch," Gianna growled. "Just die."

The tank had been full for a while. Kaia was getting uncomfortable with how long Adrienne was taking. It felt obnoxious to bother her, but she couldn't keep herself from it. She walked around to the bathrooms and knocked on the door.

"Adrienne? You okay?"

No answer. Kaia's pulse rose with that alone. She told herself she was being crazy, but she knocked again.

"Adrienne?"

She heard a thud and the sound of something sliding.

"Kaia!"

Her heart leapt into her throat, and she drew her gun. She kicked the door as hard as she could. It shook but didn't open.

"Kaia!" Adrienne's voice was desperate. Kaia couldn't breathe. She kicked again. She heard another crash inside. She didn't want to shoot the door and risk hitting Adrienne. She couldn't tell where she was inside. She had to kick through. She summoned all her strength, envisioned the door opening, and kicked with all she had. The door gave behind her foot, breaking almost through. She could see the light from inside now. She threw her body against the door and it finally flew inward.

Gianna flung herself at Kaia's gun, using her whole body to control Kaia's arm, trying to wrestle the gun away. Kaia tightened her grip and tried to bend her wrist so the gun pointed at Gianna, but Gianna was prying her fingers away, using her considerable frame to control the barrel. Kaia head butted Gianna with the crown of her skull as hard as she could. Pain reverberated through her head and Gianna recoiled, but neither lost their grip of the gun.

Adrienne was on the ground. Kaia could barely spare a glance, but she was unconscious. Kaia pulled back on the gun as hard as she could. They both lost their grip and it fell to the ground. Gianna dove for it. Kaia kneed her in the face as she dove, then stepped on the gun and kicked it behind her, out of the bathroom. Gianna tried again to lunge after it, but Kaia wrapped her arm around Gianna's neck from behind and squeezed with all her strength. Gianna grabbed Kaia's forearm and bicep and curled forward, lifting Kaia off her feet and flipping her over Gianna's shoulder as if her weight was nothing. Kaia landed hard on her back. Gianna tried to hold her down, but Kaia maneuvered out and back to her feet.

Gianna shoved her backward into the sink, then stepped back and took a knife from her pocket, hitting the button that made it flip and snap open. The five-inch blade flashed in the cold bathroom light.

"I've been waiting for this, Blondie. Ready to bleed?"

"Put it away, Hernandez. You don't want it the easy way."

Gianna's eyes flashed and a smile crept across her face. "Smart, Officer, but no go. I'm going to have a look at your guts."

"Coward."

"Fight back, Blondie. Let's see how dirty you really are."

Kaia dodged the first jab and pushed Gianna into the wall, using all her strength to smother her, to take the room Gianna needed to use the knife effectively. She pinned Gianna's knife hand to the wall as hard as she could, but Gianna was too strong. She gathered herself and pushed Kaia off, swiping at the air again. She felt the blade bite into her arm and pulled away. She had to get to her gun, but it was outside now and Gianna was blocking the way.

Adrienne moved like she was dreaming, enough for Kaia to know she was alive, but she wasn't awake enough to help. It was like she was trying to wake up but couldn't. Kaia made a move for the gun, but Gianna rushed her again and pinned her against the side wall. She was closer to the gun, but not close enough, and Gianna had the blade to her neck. Kaia grabbed Gianna's wrist and met her push with all the resistance she had. Her arms burned, but if she let go, if she slipped, all Gianna's strength would send the knife deep into her throat. Gianna's eyes glowed with excitement as she sensed Kaia's failing strength. Kaia saw movement from the corner of her eye. Adrienne stood up behind Gianna silently. She grabbed the porcelain lid from the toilet tank. Gianna heard the rattle as Adrienne picked it up, but she was already swinging. As Gianna turned it connected with the side of her head. A thick thud and slight ring sounded with the impact and Gianna went down. Adrienne's eyes were wild when they met Kaia's.

Kaia kicked Gianna's knife away and retrieved her gun to be safe, expecting Gianna to spring back up any second. They both stared at Gianna, unsure what they were waiting for. There was a square red mark on the side of her face, marking where the lid had hit. Her eyes were closed.

Slowly, red gathered and seeped out from under her head. It spread in an oblong oval, crawling farther and farther out.

"Oh God," Adrienne said. Kaia took the tank lid from her and set it down. Adrienne knelt and touched Gianna carefully on the shoulder, then pulled back in horror.

"Oh God. Oh God. Her skull is cracked. Kaia, her skull. I think I can see…"

Kaia pulled Adrienne to her and held her head to her shoulder, shielding her eyes. "Don't look."

"She's dead. She'd dead. Oh God, I killed her, didn't I?"

"I don't know," Kaia said.

"Look. Please look and tell me if I saw that."

Kaia gently let her go and knelt. Gianna's hair was soaked with blood. A two-inch indentation told Kaia the blow had indeed broken the skull. There was a split in the skin where she saw what Adrienne saw. There was a piece of white skull visible and thick globs oozing from it that might be brain.

She stood, trying to keep a straight face, to be strong for Adrienne. She simply shook her head. Gianna was dead. Adrienne gasped and fell into tears. Kaia rubbed Adrienne's back gently.

"I'll call help."

Adrienne clung to her. "No," she said. "No! Don't. You can't."

"It was self-defense, Adrienne. You saved my life. It'll be okay."

"Not with the Wild AKs, it won't be."

"What?"

"If we call the cops everyone will know we did this. They'll never stop until they kill us."

"What are you saying? What choice do we have?" Kaia watched Adrienne's thoughts move a mile a minute.

"They can't know, Kaia. This is Gianna. The revenge for this…" She grabbed Kaia's hand. "We will never be safe. People will die."

"You can't be saying what I think you are."

"No one can know. You can't call it in."

"Adrienne, no. This is a bad idea. If we get caught—"

"Then we won't. You're a cop, what do we do?"

"We fucking call it in is what we do! Do you know how many ways there are to get caught? If we hide this and they find out it's game over. And we have motive to kill her. It will not look good."

"If the Wild AKs find out it's game over. Kaia, how hard are they really going to look into this? Won't they just be glad?"

"They'll still investigate."

"If the gang finds out, they will shoot all of us," Adrienne said. "Me, you, our families, cops, everyone. Anna will be savage."

Kaia dragged her hand down her face. "Fuck, Adrienne, I don't know. This is such a bad idea."

"I know you know how to do this. Please, Kaia. I just want it to be over."

Kaia saw the calm desperation in Adrienne. There was fear, but not panic. She meant what she was saying. It wasn't an impulse.

"Trust me, Kaia. Please. We have to do this."

"Start wiping prints."

Adrienne grabbed a paper towel, wet it, and wiped down every surface she could find. Kaia did the same. They cleaned the sink, doorknobs, the tank lid, the toilet seat, the handle to flush, sink knobs, railings, towel dispensers, everything.

Kaia cleaned her footprint from the door where she'd kicked it in, cleaned the knife, terrified to leave it after it had cut her, but also unwilling to have it in her possession.

"Who else would have done this?" Kaia asked.

"God, no one. Everyone knows not to mess with Gianna." Adrienne sighed and ran her hand down her face. She met Kaia's eyes. "Los Hijos de la Santa Muerte, maybe. They're allies with the Wild, but things can always go wrong. We're in their territory. If it was anyone it would be them. If they thought Gianna was dealing out of bounds, if she got in an argument with one of them…"

"How would they claim this?"

"Kaia, we can't do that. People will die. You don't understand, the retaliation for this is going to break the streets."

"If we don't make the answer obvious they'll dig more. It could come back to us."

"Won't they think other gangs anyway? Isn't that what they always think when a gang member turns up dead? If we frame them, the deaths are our fault."

Kaia sighed. She knew the deaths would probably happen either way, but she understood. "Okay, we'll risk it. Go move the car. It's been there too long. It's getting suspicious. I'll finish up here. I just have to get the floors."

"What about cameras?"

"There aren't any. I've been here before on a shoplifter."

"What do we do with…" Adrienne paused. "Her?"

"Nothing."

"What?" Adrienne hissed.

"Nothing. We can't do anything."

"We have to do something."

"No. We don't want our DNA on her. We definitely don't want her DNA in my car."

"But, Kaia." Adrienne's eyes watered again. "She's on a bathroom floor."

"We can still call it in."

Adrienne shook her head again, seeming to understand. "We can't."

"Okay, then. Get the car."

"I still have the bathroom key."

"Shit."

"Should I keep it?"

"No, that puts you here last."

"What then?"

"Give it back."

"Are you fucking crazy?" Adrienne asked. "I can't show my face in there. They'll question her."

"She's already seen you. It just makes it worse if she says you never came back. Just throw it on the counter when she's doing something else. Not many people come back here. As long as she doesn't come looking for you, it could be hours before anyone else comes by. Who knows when they'll notice. By then there will be a lot more people who have come through the area and you'll be less fresh on her mind. You need to seem normal. You used the bathroom; you left."

Adrienne looked petrified, but she agreed and left the bathroom. Kaia did clean the floor, but she also cleaned Gianna, something she didn't know how Adrienne would handle. She cleaned under Gianna's nails thoroughly and checked the rest of her for stray drops of blood from Kaia or Adrienne. The blood from the cut on Kaia's arm was making her nervous, but it didn't look like it had dripped.

Adrienne was probably right. How hard would they really look into someone like Gianna? She had lots of enemies. She was a gang member, a lifelong criminal, an extremely wanted suspect who was a danger to society and law enforcement with attempts on two officers' lives under her belt. Would they really care? Another gang was the go-to answer because it was usually true.

Kaia still couldn't take chances. If they did look, if they did find, it could ruin them both. Kaia's heart pounded through every step. She couldn't believe what she was doing. If anyone walked by, if she missed a hair, a drop of blood, if someone recognized her car, it was impossible to be perfect. She just had to be very good and count on a quick wrap on the investigation.

She glanced at Gianna. She was white as a ghost now, all her blood had either seeped onto the floor or stopped circulating and pooled where gravity took it. A morbid fascination drew her eyes back to Gianna's head and the goo dripping out, but when she looked she felt like she was going to be sick and turned away. Just moments ago, Gianna had been an inch from severing Kaia's carotid. A few minutes before that, she'd been trying to strangle Adrienne. And now, gone.

Had it even crossed her mind it could go that way? Had she even seen this as a risk to her life? Had she felt the blow to her head? Had she known Adrienne dealt her a deathblow? Had she known when she was living her final seconds?

Adrienne pulled up outside the bathroom door in the Taurus. Kaia took one last look at the scene, went over every inch with her eyes, careful not to step in the blood, then nodded and got in the car. Adrienne took off in silence. Kaia couldn't imagine what she was thinking or how she'd recover. They were committed now. The window to do this clean was closed.

Chapter Twenty-three

The drive to the hotel was silent. Adrienne felt hypnotized by the lines passing under them on the street. Kaia drove. She seemed calm, but Adrienne knew she wasn't. She hadn't wanted to do this; she did it for Adrienne. They nodded to the surveillance team in the lot. There were fewer than usual, but someone watched at all times, even when they weren't there in case Gianna came by or tried to sneak in. The others were probably still at the hospital or driving back, oblivious to what had happened. It felt stupid now, but they had to continue this charade until Gianna was found. How long would it take? She guessed longer was better, but it was agonizing waiting.

Kaia ushered Adrienne into the hotel and locked the door. Kaia slumped into a chair, sighing heavily and running her hands through her hair.

"I didn't mean to kill her," Adrienne said.

Kaia looked up abruptly. "I know that. Of course you didn't."

"She had a knife to your throat. She—"

Kaia stood up and walked over. "I know, Adrienne. You did nothing wrong. You had to. She tried to kill us. She *would* have killed us."

"You told me you didn't mean to hurt Ted so bad with that bat." Adrienne lowered her head. "It wasn't that I didn't believe you, I don't want you to think that. But I guess I didn't really get it, either. Not like I do now. I—" She choked up and Kaia held her. "I just wanted to knock her out. I wanted to be sure it would knock her out."

"I know, Adrienne. I know."

"What do we do now?"

"We act normal until we hear the news."

"And then?"

"Then this is over, I guess."

"So this is probably our last night together?" Adrienne asked.

"Do you want it to be?"

"No."

"Me either."

"I thought you might after I got you into this. After what I made you do."

Kaia touched her face, deep in thought. "I agreed to it. I'm scared, but if I didn't see your point, if I didn't think we could, I wouldn't have."

"I feel like I've been nothing but trouble for you, even when we were kids."

Kaia smiled. "Well, you did talk me into sneaking out of freshman homecoming to get wasted."

Adrienne tried not to laugh but couldn't help it. "And got you to smoke weed for the first time."

"And got me busted for cheating out of the teacher's manual."

Adrienne burst out laughing. "I thought you knew not to get them *all* right."

"Well, I didn't. I was a good kid. You corrupted me." Kaia's smile was stunning, warming Adrienne's frozen chest.

"You corrupted me plenty too," Adrienne said.

"We had lots of firsts to discover, that's all."

Kaia went to the kitchen and poured them wine. She came back to the couch and handed Adrienne a glass.

"I would have done anything with you," Adrienne said.

"So would I."

Adrienne leaned against Kaia, pulling her arm around her shoulder. "Is it bad I'm relieved? I'm sad, but I might be even more relieved."

"You've been afraid for your life for years. This is probably the first night you can relax in a long time."

"If we get caught I'll say it was all me."

"Shh. I would never let you do that, but we won't get caught."

"Okay." Adrienne stood and walked to the window. The light of the city creeping through between the buildings somehow calmed her.

Knowing the world was still going, all those people out there were still moving.

Kaia's hands wrapped around her hips. Her body formed to Adrienne's back. Kaia's breath tickled at her ear, her lips parted and pressed Adrienne's neck.

Adrienne reached behind her and grabbed Kaia's thighs, encouraging her to press harder. Kaia's teeth ran across her shoulder, then bit. A rush shot down her spine and a moan escaped. She tightened her fists around Kaia's jeans and pulled Kaia against her. Kaia pressed Adrienne against the glass window and traced kisses along her neck, pressing herself against Adrienne in a subtle, gentle rhythm.

Finally, Kaia turned Adrienne around to face her and kissed her deeply, slowly, but with desperate hunger. Adrienne pulled Kaia closer, wanting to disappear into her, to be swallowed by her love. She threaded her fingers through Kaia's hair with one hand and grabbed her ass with the other.

Kaia pulled Adrienne's shirt up, breaking their kiss long enough to remove it, then crashed back into her. She wasted no time reaching for Adrienne's bra clasp and undoing it. She cupped Adrienne's breasts and let her kisses travel down her neck, eventually taking a nipple in her mouth and making Adrienne's knees buckle with need.

Adrienne clawed at Kaia's shirt, eager for skin. Kaia reached for Adrienne's pants, deftly undoing the button and pulling them down. Kaia stood and picked her up in one motion. Adrienne wrapped her legs around her and chased her kisses. Kaia's tongue teased her, dancing in and out of her mouth while she pressed between her legs.

"Kaia," she whispered in her ear. Kaia made space for her hand and ran her fingers over Adrienne's underwear, feeling her wetness. She ran her fingers gently over her clit, making Adrienne moan again and push herself against Kaia, pleading for contact. Kaia held her with one arm while crushing her against the cold glass. Kaia's kisses were searing hot against Adrienne's aching skin, her sweet smelling hair soft against her face. She caressed Adrienne's inner thighs, driving her crazy.

"Fuck me, Kaia. Please."

Kaia slid Adrienne's underwear aside and touched her, gentle at first, then plunging inside. Adrienne arched off the glass with the explosion of pleasure, gripping Kaia's shoulder with one hand and her hair with the other. Kaia pulled slightly back, then went deeper still, holding Adrienne tight as she bucked in ecstasy.

Adrienne pushed her hips into Kaia, meeting her thrusts with aggressive desire. Kaia went slow and deep, in no hurry yet bringing her to the edge of orgasm with her steady rhythm. When she sped up just a fraction, Adrienne couldn't wait any longer. She threw her head back and let the waves of her climax take her.

"Oh God, Kaia." She gripped her, holding her as close as she could, like she'd die without her. Kaia kissed Adrienne's chest, gently lowering her to her feet. Adrienne's legs could barely support her, but she couldn't wait another second. She pushed Kaia down on the couch, undid her pants, and pulled them off, taking her underwear with them.

She knelt in front of the couch between Kaia's legs and pressed herself against her. She moaned at the simplest touch. Adrienne kissed her stomach, trailing up her long waist with her hands until she found Kaia's nipples and squeezed. Kaia arched off the couch and weaved her fingers through Adrienne's hair. Adrienne licked and nibbled her hips, down to her thighs. She breathed over Kaia's clit, relishing the way her hips shifted.

"Oh, Adrienne."

Adrienne gently licked, letting her hot breath drive Kaia crazy. Kaia's fingers tightened in Adrienne's hair in a hungry plea. Adrienne pressed her mouth against her, tasted her, and slipped her fingers inside. Kaia's moan tingled down Adrienne's spine and made her head spin.

She grabbed Kaia's hip with her free hand, absorbing the rhythm Kaia wanted and matching it with her tongue and fingers, alternating between fast and hard and slow and deep. Kaia's fingers tightened in Adrienne's hair again as she came. Adrienne felt her tightening around her fingers, pulsing in her mouth. She waited for the shocks to fade, then gently pulled away.

Adrienne crawled onto the couch and snuggled into Kaia's embrace. She breathed in her smell and kissed her neck.

"I love you, Kaia."

"I love you too." Kaia squeezed her closer. "Always have."

❖

Kaia woke with Adrienne sleeping on her shoulder. They were both still naked. The night came back to her backwards, Adrienne, Gianna, Reid. She felt the highs and lows pinballing through her body. Adrienne slowly emerged from sleep and smiled up at her.

"Morning."

Kaia kissed her. "Morning."

A knock came at the door. Their eyes locked.

"Who's that?"

"They must have found her."

Adrienne looked petrified.

"It's okay," Kaia said. "Get in the shower. I'll deal with it."

Adrienne quickly disappeared into the bathroom while Kaia got dressed. She hurried to the door and checked the peephole. Davis. Oh yeah, they knew. She took a deep breath and opened the door.

"What're you doing here?" she asked.

"Sorry if I scared you," he said. "I need to talk to you."

Kaia waved him in. He looked around the room. "Adrienne?"

"Shower."

He nodded. "Maybe that's best. I don't know how she'll take this. I'll let you break it."

Kaia was confident her acting was coming across genuine, but it made her feel awful. "What is it?"

"Hernandez is dead," he said it in a near whisper, making every effort to spare Adrienne the cold cop reading of the information. "She ran into someone who wasn't happy with her. Blunt force to the head."

"Jesus," Kaia said.

"Why don't you come down to the scene? Have a look."

"Me? Do you need me? I have to fill Adrienne in and she'll probably need me."

"Take your time, but I'd like you to come down at some point. This is your investigation as much as it is any of ours. You risked your life for it."

Kaia nodded. "Okay. After."

"Right, we're out at Sixth and River," he said. Kaia nodded. "And, Sorano," he held out his hand for her to shake. She accepted it. "Good and bad day," he said. "I don't want to be insensitive to the uniqueness of this, but I'm glad to have you safe again."

"Me too."

Adrienne came out of the bathroom as soon as the door closed. She searched Kaia's face for answers.

"They want me to go investigate the scene."

"What?" Adrienne looked horrified.

"It's okay. It's good, actually. Gives my DNA a reason to be there if it does turn up. Yours too, through me since we're living together."

"It's that sensitive?"

"Can be. One of your hairs gets on my shirt, I investigate the scene, it falls off, you're tied to the murder." Adrienne looked pale. "It's okay," Kaia said. "Like I said, it's good. Now we can explain that if it happens."

"What if the attendant recognizes you?"

"Doubt she'll still be there."

"But what if she is?"

"Maybe I should just tell them we got gas there."

"Won't that raise flags?"

"It's not ideal, but if I don't say so and they find out later it'll raise more. I paid with my credit card and the clerk saw you. I don't want to put us in jeopardy of having to change our story. That's never good."

"Shit, this is already a mess."

"It's basically impossible not to leave evidence behind. That's why I didn't want to do this. But you're right, they're not going to tear the city apart investigating this one. I'll tell them we went to the gas station on our way back. They'll assume she was following us, which she was. By doing that she was led out of her territory where a rival gang member saw her out of bounds and moved on her."

Adrienne nodded. "Okay. That makes sense. Just please be careful."

"I will."

Kaia took her time getting to the gas station. She focused on centering herself, on being calm, but her heart jumped when she pulled up. There were several cars and a lab team just arriving. Kaia found Cruz immediately.

"I didn't realize it happened at this station. Adrienne and I stopped here for gas on our way home from the hospital last night."

Cruz raised an eyebrow. "Really? That's interesting. You didn't see her?"

"No."

"Must have been trying to tail you to the hotel," Cruz said.

"Something stopped her."

"WAK territory doesn't start until well south of here."

"Yeah," he said. "That's why we put you two where we did. You think it's just a turf thing, then? Blue in the wrong part of town?"

"I don't know. It wouldn't be the first time."

He shook his head. "I hate that she was so close to you after all the precautions we took. It's a shame to think we ended up with another gang to thank for keeping you safe."

She shrugged. "As long as we're safe I don't think it matters much."

"True enough. Come on, have a look." He handed her a pair of gloves and walked into the bathroom. Kaia took a breath and followed him back into the room where she and Adrienne had almost been killed.

CHAPTER TWENTY-FOUR

Anna answered the door. Celeste and Christina stood outside, stiff, with puffy red faces.

"Who is it?" she asked. She knew someone was dead. It was part of street life. She hated this moment in between knowing something awful happened but not knowing what or who. Celeste's tears started to fall down her face.

"Anna." She looked at her through broken eyes. "Anna, Gianna's dead."

Anna felt a wave of heat and nausea circulate through her. "Are you sure?"

They both nodded.

"That can't be right." Nothing, no one, could kill Gianna. She'd survived a childhood of starvation and beatings. She'd survived drug corners from the age of nine. She'd survived getting jumped, fistfights, knife fights, cop fights. She'd even survived being shot. No one could hurt Gianna.

"No," she said. "That can't be right. She's just in jail, or faking it. She's not—"

"She's dead, Anna."

"Don't fucking say that!" She punched the door, turned inside, and raked everything off her counter with a swing of her arm. Celeste and Christina watched, eyes and cheeks turning red with fresh tears. She'd never seen them like this, even when people died. She knew it had to be true.

"What happened?"

"They found her in a gas station bathroom. Someone hit her in the head with something. It broke her skull."

Anna heard her own ragged breathing, but she couldn't feel it. Celeste reached out and touched her arm, but she pulled away.

"Who did it?"

"Cops said they don't know yet."

"Of course they don't. Crooked pigs, they're not even trying. They don't care. It was probably them." Anna flexed her muscles until they burned.

"It was down and dirty," Christina said. "They said it was a scrap to the end, maybe a fight that went too far. No gunshots. Not really cop style."

"Who then?" Anna asked. "Who do you know that Gianna would lose a fight to?"

Celeste cocked her head and looked at her knowingly, catching up to her suspicion, "Marco?"

"Maybe someone he hired," Anna said. "Maybe one of the Hijos. Or Kitchen. They wanted her out."

"Out, yeah, but killed?" Celeste asked.

"Whoa, hold up," Christina said. "Weird shit happens in fights sometimes. Marco would never do this. We should look at the Hijos. It happened on their streets."

"What the hell was she doing up there?" Anna asked. "She knew they were up to something. Why would she go there?"

"Don't know."

"She didn't tell anyone about anything on that side of town?"

They both shook their heads. "She would have told you if she was going to tell anyone."

"Where is she?" Anna asked.

"Still at the gas station, I think," Celeste said.

"They got her just rotting on some nasty gas station floor? These fucking cops." Anna grabbed her gun. "I'm going up there."

"What? No!" Celeste and Christina blocked the door.

"They're letting her get all nasty out there because they don't care, not even investigating anything I bet, just scratching their asses."

"Your warrants," Celeste said.

"I don't care."

"You can't get the fucker who did this if you're arrested," Christina said. "This is your kill, so let's figure it out and handle it."

"Fine, let's handle it." Anna nodded. "We start with Marco. He did it or he knows who did. He green-lighted this send Gianna to jail project. It has to have something to do with that."

"Fuck, all right," Christina said.

"Let's go."

"What? Now?"

"Yes, now. You want to wait until Christmas? Get the car."

Celeste and Christina looked around the room like they'd find a way out of this, but they couldn't. They gave in and followed Anna to her car.

Anna rode shotgun. She checked her gun a thousand times and pictured herself walking in and blowing Marco away immediately, even though she knew she couldn't do it that way. Celeste drove to the back of his house and parked.

"Your man will let us in?" Anna asked.

She nodded, pale.

"Are we sure about this?" Christina asked.

"He knows something, Christina. This didn't just fall out of the sky. Gianna wanted to waste him anyway, remember? We already agreed to this." They nodded and followed her. Celeste texted Ron and he opened the back door quietly, doubt clear on his face.

Anna patted his chest in gratitude and crept up the stairs, gun drawn. She'd never done something like this without Gianna. It made her heart hurt to feel her vulnerability without her best friend. There was a giant hole on her left where Gianna should be. Anna turned the corner with her gun raised.

Marco was leaned over his coffee table snorting a line when they walked in. A Hispanic man sat next to him. He spotted them and yelled, reaching for his gun. Anna shot him in the face without hesitation. Marco and the girls all jumped. The Hispanic man slumped down the couch, his mouth hung open, a trail of blood dripped down his face from the bullet hole in his cheek. Anna let her arm fall back to her side.

"What the fuck do you think you're doing?" Marco screamed. "Do you have any idea who that is?"

"One of your buddies from Los Hijos de la Santa Muerte? He the one you hired to kill Gianna?"

Marco's face lit with shock and fear. "What the fuck are you talking about?"

"You told me Gianna was a problem, that Kitchen wanted one of us. Now she's dead."

"Anna, I had nothing to do with that." Marco stood up, claiming some of the power his presence usually held, but it was diminished by the way his eyes kept flashing to Anna's pistol. "Gianna is one of my best people," he said. "I meant it when I said we would figure something out. I was trying to keep her safe, not kill her."

"You made a deal with Kitchen," Anna said. "You set her up to go to prison. You're lying, Marco, and I want to know why right now."

"Where did you hear that?"

"They wanted her gone and you said yes. You betrayed your own because you're scared of some other gang? Of some cop? You chose a pig over us?"

"I didn't do this! We were trying to come up with something. The heat was too much around here. I didn't know what to do, but I would never do this!"

"You wanted her in jail?"

Marco shifted. "It came up."

Anna took aim. His hands shot into the air. "No! That's what Kitchen wanted, but I was going to talk to her about it."

"Oh, bullshit. You had your chance to tell her, you didn't."

"Killing her wouldn't help anyone, not even Kitchen! Wait!"

"Shut up, Marco, you're full of shit. I don't know what your plan was and I don't care. You betrayed her. Gianna knew what you did. She was going to kill you anyway, so this is for her."

She fired the rest of her magazine into his chest. He looked down in shock, unable to speak. He struggled for breath, blood trickled from his mouth. He slumped next to the other body, dead.

Anna turned. Celeste and Christina were trying to cover their shock but were failing. Ron slowly came up the stairs and peeked around the corner.

"Well, damn, guess I'm out of a job."

"You should be, shouldn't you?" Anna said. "What kind of security lets people sneak right in?"

"Anna," Celeste said.

"What? You helped me out and everything, but you'll never guard my people."

"He did it because we're together," Celeste said.

"That's great for now, but look at Gianna. All this started over Adrienne. Those two were together for five years and now Gi's dead. Love is weak."

"Can we talk about a plan, please?" Christina said. "You just killed our founder and God knows who from Los Hijos."

"The plan is I'm in charge," Anna said. "You two are with me and the rest of our crew is with us. The others will come on board. It's just like Gianna said, no one was tight with Marco. And these Hijos cats can come at us if they want, but as far as I'm concerned, they got one of ours, we got one of theirs. Bet this idiot was their hit man and Marco was the brains."

"But they have heavy artillery, Anna, and they give us ours," Celeste said. "They're not going to now."

"There are plenty of people who sell guns. We're fine."

"Marco was right, though. Why would they want her dead? Kitchen wanted to turn her in. Now he can't prove himself."

"I don't know," Anna admitted. "We'll keep digging, but Marco had to go. He was a traitor."

"What about the cops? They're still looking for you."

"I don't give a fuck anymore. Anyone who wants to come at me can come, but I'll be shooting."

Adrienne opened the door of the creaky house on Sixty-Second. It felt like years had passed since she'd escaped out the back door with Gianna on her heels promising to kill her. She knew Kaia wouldn't want her here alone, but she wanted the moment of quiet, one last moment alone with her past, with Gianna.

The house was in even worse disrepair than she remembered. She felt the sickness of the relationship she'd left, the misery she'd grown numb to. The walls were punched through, trash littered the floor, drug residue dusted every surface, graffiti marked the walls. She timidly walked into the kitchen, listening for signs of anyone crashing here. There was still a splatter of blood dried to the floor from when Adrienne had cut Gianna. She knelt down and touched it, tears welling in her eyes. She couldn't fathom how everything had gone so wrong. Gianna had been her first and only ray of happiness since the day her mother dragged her out of Kaia's arms. She'd thought she'd never breathe again, and Gianna made her smile. Had she changed or had Adrienne just been blind?

Adrienne went to the bedroom and into the safe. The money was gone, but the pistol remained. She put it in her waistband, but it felt wrong and she took it back out. She gathered the things she couldn't bring herself to leave, pictures, a few clothes, her laptop.

She heard the front door open. She stood, pistol ready, unsure how the gang would react to her now that Gianna wasn't around to hunt her. She contemplated hiding or sneaking out, but she could tell it was only one person and she knew it wasn't Anna by the soft walk. She went into the living room. Celeste was on the couch with her face in her palms. She looked up when Adrienne entered. Their eyes locked. Finally, Celeste stood up. Her eyes were red and swollen. She walked over and hugged Adrienne. Adrienne hugged her back tightly, surprising herself with how badly she wanted it. She needed to hold someone who loved Gianna, who didn't just see the criminal who beat Adrienne, someone who wasn't secretly trying to hide relief and even happiness.

Celeste shook with sobs, and Adrienne felt herself losing her hold on the emotions she'd felt the need to suppress. She'd felt so conflicted around Kaia. She needed to mourn Gianna, but through no fault of her own, Kaia made it impossible. When she looked at Kaia, Adrienne hated Gianna for nearly killing her. She saw all the gentleness Gianna could never give her. With Celeste, she remembered Gianna's fierce loyalty, her laugh, her protectiveness, the way Gianna had made her feel so alive. They finally released each other and sat on the couch. The broken frame sank to the floor.

"I'm glad you came," Celeste said. "I would understand if you didn't, but I'm glad you did."

"I'm glad it's you I ran into."

"Christina misses you too."

"Anna not so much," Adrienne guessed.

"Not so much. She hasn't said much about you, but she's dangerous right now. For anyone."

"Is she okay?" Adrienne never liked Anna, but she didn't want anyone to hurt the way she knew Anna must be now. She and Gianna had been friends their entire lives. In many ways only they understood one another. It was a relationship that used to make Adrienne jealous. Even though she knew there was nothing romantic there, Anna saw parts of Gianna even she wasn't allowed to.

"I don't know," Celeste said. "Not really. Things have gotten…" she paused. "I probably shouldn't tell you, should I?"

"You don't have to if you don't want to."

"She's gotten scary. It's like she absorbed Gianna. She's twice as ruthless as she's ever been. I never realized how much they balanced each other."

"You be careful then."

"I'm trying," Celeste said. "What about you? Are you okay? Are you better?"

"I think so. Just sad."

"I won't tell them I saw you."

"Do they still want to kill me?"

"It's come up."

Adrienne couldn't help but laugh at the bluntness. What else could she expect? Snitches sometimes fell to the back burner, but they were never forgotten.

"Anna probably wants to for Gianna," Celeste said. "Honestly, I think they have bigger issues right now, though."

Adrienne embraced her again. "I better get out of here."

"Take care of yourself."

"You too."

Adrienne went down the porch steps, took one last look at the house. She knew she'd never come back. Part of her mourned it, felt the need to honor it with a moment of reflection, but the rest couldn't wait to put as much distance as possible between herself and the hell that had happened there.

❖

Adrienne moved the few belongings she was keeping to Kaia's apartment and let herself in with the spare key. She felt out of place being there alone. It was one thing staying in a hotel with Kaia while they were in hiding, but this felt like moving in, which was crazy. She hadn't had time to think about realities like her new need for a job and a place to live. Even if she wanted to go back to drug dealing, the streets were no place for her now. She was too hated.

The pressures bubbled up, making her anxious and agitated. As much as she needed to focus on those things, Gianna was still consuming her. She couldn't stop worrying about being caught and replaying the whole thing, searching for things they might have missed. It had been hours since Kaia left for the gas station and Adrienne checked out of the hotel. How long could it take?

She couldn't stop herself from looking around the apartment. There were a few pieces of art, but no pictures. It was clean and simple and spoke of no attachments. It seemed to match the way Kaia described her life, but it was still surprising. Kaia was so warm and charismatic. It was hard to believe no one had made their way into her life in a meaningful way. Surely they'd tried.

Kaia finally showed up after ten at night. She hurried in, setting things down as she went, looking for Adrienne and finding her in the bedroom.

"Marco is dead."

"What?" Adrienne bolted upright.

"Him and some other guy. An Hijo de la Santa Muerte."

"What does that mean?"

"Consensus is leaning toward retaliation for Gianna."

"Do you think that's true?" Adrienne's heart hurt at the thought of having caused this.

Kaia shrugged. "Not sure. Could be. I don't have a better answer."

"But why would they think Marco did it? He's one of them."

"Don't know. Maybe something to do with the other guy who was there."

"Wow," Adrienne said. "So we really did this. We're in the clear?"

Kaia came and sat next to her on the bed. "I think so, yeah."

"Is it just me or was that too easy?"

"I'm not complaining. If they jumped to Marco there must have been something going on to make them suspicious. Wonder who's in charge now."

Adrienne hadn't thought of that. "It would be Anna."

"What's that going to look like?"

"Not good. Celeste said she's losing it."

"Celeste?" Kaia's face filled with concern.

"I got some things from the house. Don't be mad. I have nothing of my own anymore. I had to go."

"I could have gone with you. Anna could have been there."

"It was fine."

She knew Kaia wanted to argue, but it had already happened, so she didn't.

"Kaia, I don't know who I am now. I have no job, no experience, no home, no stuff, no money, no friends."

Kaia's eyebrows softened and she rested her hand on Adrienne's leg. "We'll figure it out. I can help you with a lot of those. Give yourself time. You've been through hell."

"That's already feeling like a cop-out."

"You haven't had time yet."

"I shouldn't be staying here. I should be able to take care of myself."

"Adrienne, you will get on your feet. And I don't mind that you're here."

"Are you sure?"

"Oh, I'm sure." Kaia leaned over and kissed her. It was soft at first, but they both quickly tumbled into the sensation. Adrienne felt swallowed by her feelings, powerless against the force of her desire. She pushed Kaia to her back and got on top of her, spreading Kaia's legs with her knee and pressing against her with her thigh. Kaia's hands were under Adrienne's shirt, moving up her back and pulling her closer. Adrienne pushed harder. She smiled as Kaia arched and kissed her exposed neck. Kaia breathed into her ear; a gentle moan made Adrienne tremble. She unbuttoned Kaia's pants and pulled them down enough that she could fit her hand inside. Kaia's breath caught as Adrienne pushed inside her. Kaia's nails raked down her back and Adrienne pressed deeper, letting her own moan escape.

Kaia flipped Adrienne on her back and straddled her, never letting Adrienne's fingers escape, grinding slowly against her, stealing the control. Adrienne smiled and gently pressed her hips into Kaia's rhythm, watching her intently as she took what she wanted.

Soon Adrienne was surprised to find herself on the verge of coming. She sat up, seeking more contact, feeling Kaia's body against her chest and stomach.

"Come with me," she whispered.

Kaia pressed against her harder and faster. She spun her fingers through Adrienne's hair and kissed her with abandon. Adrienne pulled Kaia's hips closer, desperate for release but waiting. Kaia's body tensed in the first waves of orgasm. Adrienne tightened her grip, pulled her closer, and joined Kaia's climax.

Kaia's skin was hot and glistening. Adrienne wrapped her arms around her and rested her head on Kaia's chest, listening to her racing heart. She gently lowered Kaia to the bed, holding her tight to her body as she drifted to sleep.

CHAPTER TWENTY-FIVE

Anna was used to being paranoid about being followed. Cops had followed her many times. Sometimes they got her, usually they didn't. With the kinds of warrants she had right now, she knew if they spotted her they would pursue her no matter how many cars she smashed or lives she endangered. If it was an undercover unit, the black Escape that had been behind her for five miles should have lit her up by now, or at least called in a second car, but it hadn't.

She led him to Christina's house, taking the long way while she called Christina and told her to get people together and ready. She expected it to drop off when she pulled into the neighborhood, but it didn't waver in following her all the way to the driveway. She threw her car into park and got out. She pointed her gun at their windshield, but it was too dark to see inside. Christina and five other members she'd rounded up came out the front door of the house. The Escape idled.

Christina came down next to Anna, shotgun in hand. "You got a problem or what?" She leveled the shotgun at the vehicle. All four doors opened at the same time and the driver eased casually out. He halfheartedly raised his hands.

"Easy," he said. It was Kitchen. He wore all black except for his silver chains. His hair was jet-black, slicked back. Everything about him seemed exceptionally clean and neat. Three others in similar clothing got out, each armed but guns pointed down.

"I like your style." He pointed at Christina, who still had the shotgun aimed. "You the one that killed my boy?"

"I'll kill all your boys if you don't back the fuck off."

He whistled. "You trying to make me fall in love? Look, I just want to talk to whoever's in charge around here, no need for things to get messy."

"What do you want?" Anna asked.

"You the boss?"

"Yes."

"I'm Kitchen. This is my crew." He gestured at the others.

"I know who you are."

"Good, we're old friends then."

"We're not friends."

"That seems to be the case these days," he said. "I don't know why you took out Marco, but I don't see why it has to bring our business relationship to an end."

"Excuse me?"

"We give you guns, you give us money, it's been working out, I thought. For both of us."

"Are you fucking serious? You killed Gianna. If you think we can still work together you don't understand who she was."

"I'm familiar with the infamous Gianna. She and I got along fine. I asked Marco not to send her to pickups anymore since she carried a high chance of being followed. It was a common sense decision to protect our secrets. I don't see why it's being taken personally."

"You wanted to arrest her to pick up a gold star from your detective friends," Anna said. "Then she turns up murdered. Then I walk in on Marco having a secret meeting with one of your boys. Explain that."

"Made good sense. She was heading to prison one way or another with those warrants, might as well get myself in the clear and both our businesses back on track in the process. You have to understand that. But like you said, I wanted to take her in, not kill her. If Marco took out a hit, I don't know why and it had nothing to do with us. We didn't want cops at our door, and that's the end of it. Why should I care who he has in his crew?"

"Because you saw her as a risk. Because of what she knew."

"Gianna was well known for her ability to stay quiet. Renowned for being uncooperative with police. I had no concerns about what she knew reaching the wrong ears. I know it was her girlfriend that mouthed off. I still have people who believe I'm loyal. They tipped me off."

"Revenge for Adrienne snitching, then," Anna said. "Blamed Gianna."

"That made her a good target for arrest, sure, but a body doesn't help me."

"Then what was your guy doing with Marco?"

"Dropping off your new identity," Kitchen said. "So you could run the show when Gianna was in jail without getting picked up."

Anna felt truth in the easy way he answered, but she didn't want to. It felt like being pumped full of cold chemicals; a sick chill crawled through her skin.

"Yeah, the way I see it, it's actually your people that did *us* wrong."

"Why would you want to work with us then?"

Kitchen leaned forward. "Money, of course. What you did was wrong and we have to deal with that, you and I, but I understand what happened and I'm a reasonable enough man. I'm sure we can work something out that will keep us rich and you dangerous."

"You still double-crossed us with that wack ass plan."

"I worked it out with your leader, that's not double-crossing. Your issue is with Marco and I see you've handled it."

Anna had to admit he was making sense. "What do you mean deal with it?"

"If I may have a word with you alone."

"Like hell," Christina said. Anna scanned him again. He was calm, but that didn't mean anything. She'd seen Marco shoot people with hardly a pause in conversation.

"Just me and you," he said. "We'll both leave our guns and we'll stay in sight."

"Fine." She felt Christina look over in shock but didn't acknowledge it. She had to make these decisions and she did still want the guns.

They both put down their weapons and Anna followed Kitchen down the street, out of earshot.

"All right," Anna said. "What is it?"

"You killed one of my people unjustly," Kitchen said. Now that he was closer, she realized how tall and built he was. "I meant it when I said I want to keep working with you, but I can't let that slide unanswered."

"Fuck you, you're just a dirty cop," Anna said. "I'm not afraid of you."

"You're going to have to let the cop thing go. I'm the leader of Los Hijos de la Santa Muerte now. My affiliation with the Chicago PD is being used to all our benefits, and when that's no longer possible I'll be going dark."

"How can I believe that?"

"I made real friends, family, out of this gang. I could no more betray them than my own kids. The detectives put me too deep and they lost me. Sure, it started with a little extra side money, but that's not it anymore. I found love, loyalty, riches, and power. You think I could have climbed the ranks if I hadn't filled my people in a long time ago? If they weren't absolutely certain I was one of them?"

"How'd you convince them? There's nothing you could do that—"

"I killed an officer," Kitchen said. "It came down to them or my members and I chose. I don't tell many people that, but I want you to trust me and I want to work together. We can make this right."

"What do you want?"

"A Wild, of course."

"You want me to kill one of my own people?"

"Of course not," he said. The light reflected off his slicked back hair and he smiled. "We'll kill them. I want your agreement that this is fair and your word there will be no retaliation. No war."

"I can't do that."

"Let me be clear, we *will* kill one of your people either way."

"Fuck you. You do that we're taking all of you out."

"You can try, but we're both going to lose a lot of people that way. My way has us one for one."

"I'm sorry about your member, but it was a misunderstanding. I went to Marco's house. I went to talk to *my* people and he raised his gun. He shouldn't have drawn on me. We had good reason to think he killed Gianna, and then that. Wrong place, wrong time, this shit happens in the streets."

"Maybe, but that doesn't bring him back."

Anna's ears burned. She couldn't deny his proposal made a brutal kind of sense, but how could she give him the okay to kill one of her friends? Maybe if he'd just done it she could muster a pardon, but giving the go-ahead was too much. Had she not just killed Marco over consenting to a similar agreement?

"We can all go to battle," Kitchen said. "Both of us will lose people, come out weaker and poorer. Or you can make this right and no one else gets hurt. I'll even let you pick the member. You can protect those important to you, like my favorite back there with the shotgun. Rumor tells me you have dozens of members. Do you even know them all?"

"That's not the point. You join the Wild AKs, you're protected, we'll die for you. This is about family. And you want me to give a life away."

"Maybe it will help you see what it means to take a life."

"Fuck you, you think I don't know what it means to kill someone? I don't take life lightly."

"An innocent dead man begs to differ."

She did take his member's life lightly. She'd been torn up over Gianna, bordering on rage, and he'd given her the opportunity she wanted. Anna didn't want Kitchen to see her stress, but she knew she wasn't hiding it well.

"You know this is the right thing," he said. "I asked you alone so you wouldn't have to agree in front of your people. You don't have to tell them. You just have to see they understand they are not to retaliate. And I'll even sweeten the deal."

"How?"

"I'll tell you what I know about how Gianna really died."

"You know how she died and you haven't said anything?" Anna's blood ran hot. Now she wanted to kill this son of a bitch. "I ought to blast all your people away and torture it out of you."

He clicked his tongue. "That's not very diplomatic. I know you're new to leadership so let me help you out. I don't owe you anything other than swift and violent vengeance, yet I offer you a peaceful way out. I offer you information you can't find any other way. You should be kissing my feet, not throwing a tantrum."

"You're about to see more than a tantrum if you keep talking to me like a child."

"All right, you're testing my patience now. Do you want the deal or not?"

Anna wanted the information on Gianna more than anything. She would burn the city down if she had to to avenge Gianna.

"I pick the member?" She wished she could just give Adrienne's name, but she wasn't a member and Kitchen had been around long enough to know that.

Kitchen smiled. "That's right."

"Take Kendra. She lives on Lincoln. Orange pickup outside."

Kitchen held out his hand. Anna reluctantly shook it. "Gianna?"

"One of my guys knows the employee that worked at the gas station that night. She'll never talk to cops or you, just Eduardo."

"And?"

"Said she never saw Gianna, but she gave me a list of everyone she remembers coming through. I don't know who all Gianna had problems with so the list means nothing to me, but you do and I'd be willing to guess your guy is on her list."

"How the fuck does that help me? I have to look at some list, hope her memory was good enough to describe this person in enough detail I know who she means? And that's if she even saw them, which she probably didn't just like she didn't see Gianna."

"I didn't say I know who killed her. I said I'll tell you what I know. And seeing how you currently don't know anything at all I'd say that isn't so bad."

"Fine. Let's see this list."

Kitchen took a slip of paper from his pocket and handed it over. Anna glanced at it, immediately concluding the vague descriptions would be of no use.

"I'm going to need to talk to her to do anything with this. I need to ask specifics."

"There's an idea. Tell you what, you take a look at that list for now, narrow it down. We're going to handle the rest of our business and when I see you're holding up your side, we'll talk about a sit-down with her."

When they went back, everyone was watching anxiously. Anna nodded at Christina and saw her relax. Kitchen got in the driver's seat of the Escape and they took off. Only Anna knew they were on their way to kill the newest and least experienced Wild AK.

CHAPTER TWENTY-SIX

"A guy is in a coma for a couple weeks and everything changes," Reid said.

Kaia looked over to him in the passenger seat and smiled. "What do you mean?"

"You get in a shootout, you're Davis's favorite, you have a girlfriend. Was I holding you back, Sorano?"

Kaia laughed. "I prefer not to be in shootouts, you're the one who got me in with Davis, and Adrienne," she thought it over, "Adrienne is a force I can't fight."

Reid beamed. "Oh Lord, pigs must be flying. You didn't try to tell me she's not your girlfriend."

Kaia blushed. "Since you mentioned it, I guess we haven't talked about it. And it is pretty fast."

"No!" Reid said. "That was not an invitation for you to start your usual shit. Don't you dare tell me you're just having fun."

"No, it's definitely not just fun. I think I might be the one on the other side for once."

"You don't think she's serious about you?"

"That's not how I'd put it. I just mean she might not love the girlfriend word. She's been through a lot. I'm not sure what she really wants for herself now. I'm not sure she knows either. You don't just forget five years with someone. Gianna was nothing like me. Her life has been nothing like mine. I hope she wants to be with me, but I wouldn't be surprised if she just wants to start fresh and cut ties with this whole life."

"I think you're making it harder than it is. I saw the way she looked at you."

Kaia pulled into her parking lot. They were having a get-together to celebrate Reid getting out of the hospital in the evening, but Reid wanted to come get situated first. Moving around wasn't easy and left him grumpy and hurting. He needed time to recover from that before he would be ready to entertain.

"I hope you're right," she said, aching inside just at the thought Adrienne might take off when things settled. She knew she wouldn't be able to ask Adrienne to stay if it came to that. She deserved a fresh start, and if it made her safer, how could Kaia argue?

She went around the car and set up Reid's wheelchair, then helped him into it. His upper body was still strong, but his legs and hips were injured badly, and while he could walk, it was going to take time for him to get back to normal. For now he could only manage a few steps at a time.

"Is Adrienne sad she can't go to the funeral?" he asked.

"She doesn't talk about it." Kaia felt guilty she hadn't tried harder to encourage it. She wouldn't blame Adrienne for mourning, but she didn't trust herself to hide her contempt for Gianna, and she knew that wasn't what Adrienne needed.

She hated Gianna for more reasons than she could count, including the way she'd put Adrienne in the position that led to her killing Gianna. She couldn't imagine how it must feel to kill someone she'd been with for five years. She hated how deeply that must have scarred Adrienne, and she had a hard time not blaming both Gianna and herself for not finding a way to take that decision out of Adrienne's hands.

When they got upstairs, Adrienne had cleaned everything; it was immaculate. She had set up banners and snacks and had upbeat music playing lightly. The weather was cool and overcast, and Adrienne had the windows open to let the crisp breeze through.

"Wow," Kaia said.

Adrienne smiled and came over. She wrapped her arms around Reid. "Welcome back to the real world. I'm so glad you're doing better."

Reid hugged her back. There was a sensitivity to Reid; his emotions were always on his sleeve, and the deeply touched look in his eyes made Kaia feel a rush of love for both him and Adrienne.

Adrienne walked over and kissed Kaia. Her smile was so warm and genuine Kaia realized she had to stop seeing Adrienne as a victim. She was strong and staggeringly resilient. Kaia smiled and had to kiss her again.

She turned her attention to Reid. "Do you want to stay in the wheelchair or do you want help onto the couch?"

"Will you…" he paused, looking embarrassed. "I'd like to try to walk to the couch. Will you help me?"

"Of course," they said in unison, smiling at each other.

"I have physical therapy and all that, but I never feel like it's enough. They said I can start trying to walk short distances as long as I have help."

Kaia and Adrienne each took one of his arms and lifted him. He stood, shaky but supporting himself almost entirely. He took a timid step forward, leaning heavily onto Kaia. She knew more than anything he wanted his independence back, and while she wouldn't let him fall, she refused to let herself baby him when he didn't want it.

It took several minutes for him to make it across the room. Adrienne said nothing about his grunts and pain, seeming to pick up on his needs the same way Kaia had. He finally sat on the couch and slumped back. He was sweating and out of breath, whether from pain or exertion Kaia couldn't tell.

"Shit," he said. "Who knew walking ten feet could be such a bitch." He tried to laugh but was transparently discouraged.

Adrienne pulled up a chair next to him and held his hand. "That was amazing, Reid. How many breaks do you have?"

"It wasn't that—"

"How many?"

"Six."

"Six fucking breaks. Six places your bones were not attached to themselves and you are walking on those motherfuckers."

Reid's infectious smile crept back onto his face. "Well, shucks."

"That's right. And that was more like twenty feet. After two weeks? I'd say you're a badass. You think your physical therapy isn't enough because you're a beast."

"I love her," Reid said to Kaia with a bright smile.

"Yeah, she rocks," Kaia said. "And she's right. You're killing it. Don't beat yourself up, and do *not* injure yourself trying to get back to normal in a day."

The doorbell rang. When Kaia answered, a whole slew of people filed in, shouting hellos and congratulations at Reid. Kaia laughed and ushered them inside. Davis and his wife were among them, along with Cruz.

They gathered around the table in the living room, hitting the apartment like a hurricane of loud fun. Kaia tended to the drinks, contentedly watching Cruz tell the group, but most directly Adrienne, a story about Reid.

"I'm in my office trying to do some paperwork, right?" he said. "I have my radio turned up, but pretty much all I'm asking for is an hour or two where nothing ridiculous happens. Not with this kid on the streets."

Reid laughed and covered his face. "It's not my fault! Crazy shit loves me."

"I'm sitting in my office and I hear this lunatic start screaming for emergent cover. I mean screaming, thought the kid was dying. I'm grabbing my keys and running through the parking lot. I get to him and he and the guys have three naked dudes in handcuffs. Reid tells me they were trying to dance with him and hug him. That's his emergency."

"Hey, three naked dicks is a lot to deal with!"

Adrienne laughed. "Try being a woman. Your whole life is about guys trying to force naked dicks on you."

Cruz laughed. "See, Castillo? She could have handled it."

"I don't doubt it," Reid said. "Women are just better at some stuff."

"That why we partnered you with Sorano?"

"Shit, probably." He laughed.

"I did not sign up for naked dicks," Kaia said, moving into the dining room with them.

"But you're one of the best at dealing with it." Cruz tipped his beer at her.

"Thanks?"

Davis stood up. "On that note, I'd like to say a few words. Sorano, you really are one of the best. I've been talking to your friends, sergeants, coworkers, and all I've heard over and over is that they feel safe with you, that they know you have their backs, and that you are always the first there when they need help, that you'll chase an armed suspect without hesitation, that you'll fight when you have to, but that it's rare because you make people feel heard and handle yourself professionally and with empathy. Recently, we've seen you take on a sensitive and personal investigation without a single issue of conflict of interest coming up. I know you will keep yourself and your fellow detectives safe and on point."

Kaia's heart jumped. "My fellow detectives?"

"Welcome to the Gang Enforcement Unit."

Reid whooped and slapped the table. Cruz smiled and held out his hand. "It was hard to let you go, but I still gave you a pretty good reference." He winked. Kaia ignored his hand and hugged him.

Reid leaned over and hugged her next. "Congratulations, love. Kick ass."

Adrienne waited sheepishly for the cops to finish and let her go, then made her way over. She kissed Kaia on the cheek and smiled. "Congratulations."

Kaia felt her reservations. She waited until everyone had fallen back into conversation and snuck off to her room, pretending she was going to the bathroom. The hum of them laughing in the other room was comforting, but she had a pit in her stomach about how Adrienne was really taking it.

She was still afraid this was simply not the life Adrienne wanted. She knew it was absurd to let that make her doubt something she'd worked so hard for, but she couldn't help it. This meant that to be part of her life, Adrienne would always have to worry about her, that gangs would always be dancing by the outer fringes of her life, and that cops would become part of her inner circle. She didn't know if Adrienne was up for it, and while she didn't believe in letting a significant other alter the pursuit of her dreams, she couldn't help but ask herself if she wanted to be a detective bad enough to let Adrienne walk out of her life.

She wasn't sure what to do, but she knew she didn't want her ecstatic friends to witness her being anything but happy. She'd only been in her room a couple of minutes when the door opened and Adrienne stepped in.

"You okay?"

"Yeah," she said. She wasn't prepared to put a mask back on yet. She tried, but Adrienne saw right through her. She came and sat next to her on the foot of the bed.

"Why don't you look happy?" Adrienne asked. "They said amazing things about you. You got the job."

Kaia forced herself to look Adrienne in the eye. "I feel like I'm really good at something you think only assholes are good at."

Adrienne's eyes softened. "Oh, Kaia, that's not true. I was in a very different place when I said those things. I had limited experience with cops and it wasn't a great collection, but it wasn't a full representation either. I know that now. I love you and I love your friends."

"I don't want to lose you because you hate my job."

Adrienne kissed her softly. "I know you've wanted this for a long time. Don't you dare throw that away for me. You shouldn't, even if it did mean losing me. You deserve to be loved for who you are and to live your dreams. Don't feel guilty about that."

"It's still just a job. It's not worth…" Kaia couldn't finish. She was crazy giving Adrienne this much power over her. What she'd told Reid was true; she couldn't even confidently say they were together. Their history was making her fall fast and hard. She already loved Adrienne when she first saw her with Gianna. Adrienne kissed her again, seeking more, dragging her out of her sadness.

"You don't have to give up anything to be with me," she said. "I want you to have everything you ever wanted." She kissed down Kaia's neck. "Detective."

Kaia couldn't help but laugh. She gave in and finally returned Adrienne's kisses. Adrienne's tongue teased hers.

"We should get back out there," Kaia said. Adrienne put her arms on either side of Kaia on the edge of the bed, caging her.

"They seem fine to me."

Cruz was in the middle of another story that had the group in a loud roar of laughter. Adrienne reached for Kaia's pants and undid them.

"You're bad," Kaia whispered.

"Yes. You can punish me later." She slipped her fingers inside Kaia, making her gasp. "Shh," Adrienne whispered in her ear, then bit and tugged her earlobe. Kaia wrapped her arms around Adrienne's warm, tan shoulders and let her deeper, smothering a small moan in her neck.

Kaia met the thrusts of Adrienne's hand with her hips. She weaved her fingers into Adrienne's dark, silky hair and pulled until she'd exposed her neck. She breathed along her neck and gently bit, determined to make silence just as challenging for Adrienne.

Adrienne's thrusts were deep and maddening. Kaia was lost in her commanding touch. She ran her hands up Adrienne's perfect stomach and over her tight breasts, finding her nipples and squeezing. Adrienne let out the softest moan, only for Kaia's ears.

Adrienne's free hand made its way to Kaia's neck and pulled her into a deep kiss as she fucked faster and harder. Kaia's body tensed and she held Adrienne tight as she silently felt her orgasm flow through her body. Adrienne's fingers slowed as Kaia came, then stopped. She kissed Kaia's neck as she slowly removed them.

"You're so sexy," Adrienne whispered.

Kaia smiled and made a half-hearted effort to return Adrienne's tousled sex hair to order, but it was too gorgeous to mess with much.

"You are." Kaia kissed her again.

Adrienne smiled. "You're not getting rid of me, especially not over a promotion, silly."

"I like your style of reassurance."

"Anytime. *Now* we better get back out there." She winked.

CHAPTER TWENTY-SEVEN

Anna sat at the kitchen table with Kitchen's list in front of her. Some of it was as specific as a car's make, model, and number of occupants, some as vague as "two guys in their twenties."

"You going to tell me what happened?" Christina was pacing. Her jeans were slung low, and she had fresh ink on her forearm. Anna knew Christina was power hungry, that she wanted to move up the ranks, and now was the prime time to do it. She was trying to look and act harder, whether she was conscious of it or not.

"We worked it out," Anna said.

"How? You killed one of his guys."

"He gets what happened. He's not happy, but he's not going to torch our business over it. He makes too much money with us."

"That's it?" Christina asked. "I thought he was some vicious big shot."

"Marco may have exaggerated. Wanted to look badder than he was."

"Why the secrecy then?"

"He doesn't want his people knowing he let it go so easy."

"What a weak piece of shit. I don't like this guy."

"We don't have to like him. He has guns and a hookup with the only person who might have seen something the night Gianna was killed."

"But if it's his person how do we know she's telling the truth? Isn't that a little convenient? Maybe it really was him and Marco that killed her and that's why he wants it swept under the rug. I don't get why we're just dropping this. You were sure enough to kill Marco and that dude and now what? He says it wasn't him and you're like okay, my bad?"

"His story about the new identity makes sense. Marco did owe me one."

"That doesn't mean he didn't kill Gianna too."

"Well, if he did then we already got him."

"But—"

"I don't know, Christina! What do you want me to say? I don't know who killed Gianna and it makes me fucking sick. Right now this stupid list is what I have to work with so I'm working with it. If he turns out to be full of shit we'll waste him, but in the meantime, we need guns and I need somewhere to start. That okay with you?"

Christina nodded and sat next to her. "All right, I get it. So what's on the list?"

"Two white guys in their twenties, older businessman, a red Honda, a white Tahoe, group of black teens, someone in all red, blue four-door little car, thin girl with dark hair, fat guy in a blue shirt off the bus, a dude with a kid. Shit like that." Anna got irritated with reading it and tossed it on the table.

"Wow, great."

"Yeah. If we can narrow it down we can meet with her and ask more."

"You think he'll really help us with that?"

"Fuck him," Anna said. "I'll grab the bitch myself. He says she won't talk to outsiders, but I think she can be persuaded if need be."

"Won't that cause problems with them?"

"I won't kill her, but he needs to know I'm not going to let him run me."

"You want to ask about the guy in red? Sounds like one of the Forty-fours. He could have had a problem with her."

"Yeah, but I'm more interested in blue and the girls."

"Really?" Christina leaned over the list. "Who you thinking?"

"One of ours."

"What? No way."

"It happens. Gianna wasn't liked by a lot of members at the end. Things changed after those recruits got shot. A lot of people blamed her. If it really wasn't Kitchen that's my next bet."

"Maybe family of one of the recruits? And that Carlos kid was kind of mad."

"Maybe. Do me a favor, get as many pictures together as you can and we'll take a trip over."

Christina's phone beeped with a text message.

"Shit," she said. "Something happened at Kendra's. They got shot up."

Anna's heart raced. "They okay?"

Christina's phone beeped again, and she looked up slowly. "No, man. Kendra's dead. She got shot in the head."

More messages flooded in, and Anna heard her phone starting to go off too, but she didn't look.

"Everyone else is fine," Christina said. "They didn't see anyone."

"What do you mean?" Anna asked. "How could they not see something?"

"Came through the window. Someone fucking sniped them. Who does that?"

Anna's surprise was genuine. She would have never predicted the style of it. "They saw nothing?"

Christina's fingers raced across her phone as she texted back. "Nothing. We should go over there."

"I can't. Cops."

"Right. God, this has to be those fucking Hijos. They have the beef; they have the guns."

"No, we squashed it."

"Who else, Anna? These guys are bad news. We have to hit back."

"No."

"What?" Christina snapped.

"I said no!" Anna stood up in a rage. "It wasn't them, and even if it was that means it's done now. We're even. I am not interested in warring with these guys. I want the guns, I want the intel, and I want to go talk to this girl at the gas station and figure out what happened to Gianna. That was our best friend and until that's handled I don't give a fuck about anything else. Shootouts mean people die and people go to jail, and I'm not doing either of those until I find out who killed Gianna and make that motherfucker suffer to death. Now get the fucking pictures and let's go, or put 'em up."

Christina's shock was plain. "I'm not going to fight you, Anna."

"Good."

"But you could have told me you gave Kendra up."

Anna's cheeks burned. She didn't know whether to lie or come clean. She wanted to lie, but Christina was confident and she didn't think there was any fooling her. Lying would just make her look like even more of an ass. Her history with cops gave her the instinct to never come clean about anything, to keep that shred of doubt intact no matter how small it may be, but Christina wasn't a cop.

"I'll get some pictures." Christina sighed. "I have a lot on my computer."

"Christina."

"Yeah?"

"I was Gianna's right hand. She could tell me anything. I had her back no matter what she got into, no matter how dangerous or dirty it was."

"I know."

"If you want to know this shit, I'll tell you, but that's what I expect back."

Christina turned back around. "Gianna got pissed at you sometimes. You even fought sometimes, but people still always knew you were not to be messed with unless they wanted to face her too and all the heat she had. They knew she'd go down swinging for you if she had to. I expect *that* back."

Anna nodded. "Of course."

Christina came over and hugged her. "All right, what really happened with Kendra?"

"He was going to kill one of us no matter what. Everything I just said was true. I don't want to go to war. We did owe him a life, and by doing it this way I could make sure it wasn't yours, or Celeste's. I still would have said no under normal circumstances, but he offered the info on Gianna and…" She paused. "Christina, I have to know and I have to kill them. Then we can hit them back. You know I'd die for you guys."

Christina nodded. "Our people can never know."

"They won't."

"Let's go chat with your clerk." Christina grabbed her laptop and brought the whole thing with.

They parked in front of the gas station. Anna spotted the clerk looking nervous and dialing the phone.

"Must be her," Christina said. "She knows who we are."

"Good."

Christina tucked her gun in her waistband and got out. Anna led the way inside. The clerk was probably in her forties, older than Anna expected, short and plump. She was radiating nervous energy. Anna leaned on the counter.

"No need to be alarmed," she said. "We're not going to hurt you."

"What do you want?"

"Did Kitchen or Eduardo tell you why they needed to know who came through here? Did they tell you they gave it to me?"

"They said it was for you, but I wasn't expecting you."

"We're friends with them. Don't worry. Honest."

"What do you want?"

"I have some pictures for you to look at. I just want to know if you recognize anyone, if they were here that night."

"I don't know," she said. "We should wait for Eduardo."

"The girl who was killed in your bathroom was my best friend. I just want to know what happened. No tricks."

"But there are so many gangs around here," the clerk said. "I get left alone because I don't talk."

"You want to keep your peaceful little life here you need to cooperate," Christina said.

"We're asking about our own members," Anna jumped in before she got too spooked. "There's no war, no blowback. This isn't even our part of town. Help me and we're out."

The woman was still hesitant. "I don't even remember much. I already gave you all I know."

Christina opened the laptop and clicked into the pictures. "Just try your best." She pulled up a picture of Celeste.

The clerk shook her head. "No."

Christina clicked through the members; some were in groups of three, some alone. She kept urging the clerk to look carefully, but she kept shaking her head. Christina pulled up a group picture from a party with at least fifteen people, many of them repeats from other pictures. The clerk shook her head again. "No."

"You're sure?" Anna asked. "There are a lot of faces there. Look carefully. Please."

The clerk's eyes pulled away to someone trying to approach the counter to make a purchase.

"We're busy," Anna said.

"Come on," he whined in exasperation. He was a young, clean-cut white guy.

Christina lifted her shirt to expose her gun. "Hey, she said fuck off." He stumbled backward and hurried out of the store.

The clerk leaned forward and studied the picture. "Wait."

Anna's heart jumped. She desperately wanted to know, but she also hated this idea that it could be one of her own friends.

"Maybe this one."

"Who?" Anna and Christina both leaned forward.

"I'm not positive," she said.

"Who?" Anna fought down the urge to get angry.

"This one." She pointed. "But I don't know. Don't hurt her unless you find something else, please. I wasn't paying that close of attention."

Anna looked where she pointed. Christina glanced at her. "Adrienne?"

"Was she alone?"

"No, she was with someone, but only she came in the store. Didn't get a look at the other one."

"They were in a car?" Christina asked.

"Yeah. It's on the list."

"Which one?"

"The blue one."

"What kind?" Anna asked.

"I don't know cars," the woman said. "Small, blue, unmemorable."

"Definitely blue?"

"Yes."

"Definitely four doors?"

"I think, but not definitely. Definitely blue."

"What time did they come by?"

"I don't know."

"Think," Anna said.

"I don't fucking know," the clerk snapped. "I just work at a shitty gas station. I play games and text all night. I barely look up."

"All right, all right."

"Look at another picture," Christina said and pulled up another shot of Adrienne, this one with Gianna. Anna felt sick to her stomach seeing Gianna's face, seeing her arm wrapped around Adrienne, who may very well have ended her life.

The clerk nodded and quietly muttered, "I think so."

Anna dropped a hundred on the counter and headed for the door. Christina was on her heels.

"Of course," Anna said. "Adrienne. Of fucking course. How did we miss it?"

Christina hurried to keep up. "Because she's a stick who's probably never fought a day in her life and Gianna was a beast. She couldn't have pulled that off, could she? No gunshots. It was a brawl."

"Maybe whoever was with her then."

"The cop?"

"Bet money."

"Why is it unsolved, then? Cops have license to kill. She would shoot her and say she was attacked."

"I don't know," Anna said. "But Gianna was after Adrienne for snitching. Come to think of it, I don't know what else could have lured her up here with everything that's been going down. Shit, I can't believe I didn't think of it. I never thought Adrienne could or would put up much of a fight, but obviously she did. Or her bitch did."

"Now what?"

"I know where the cop lives."

"Okay," Christina said, full of doubt. "And?"

"We look for the blue car. Make sure they have one. I know the cop drove one at one point, but she was in a different car every day for a while. Let's see what she has now."

"And if we find it?"

"Then we handle them."

"The cop too?"

"Yes."

CHAPTER TWENTY-EIGHT

K aia crossed the parking lot. She could tell from a distance her car had been broken into. It didn't happen often in this area, but it wasn't unheard of either. She was irritated more than anything. She knew better than to leave valuables in it and the car itself hadn't been taken. Her door was open a crack. She looked inside. The steering column looked fine. Her glove compartment was open, the papers inside had obviously been rifled through. She also knew better than to leave the registration or anything with too much personal information on it inside. All they could have seen were car repair and oil change receipts. They had her name on them, but nothing sensitive.

She considered calling out the lab to take fingerprints, but it was her first day as a detective and she didn't want to be late. She drove in to work and asked the officer at the desk to call them out, then hurried on to roll call.

"Hey, there she is," Davis greeted her. When the room filled, he made her get up. "Everyone, I know you already know Sorano, but it's official now. Let's all welcome her to the team."

They clapped and whooped enthusiastically. Kaia playfully bowed and took a seat.

"With no further ado, Kaia, I have you partnered with Detective Jack Collins over here."

Kaia found the man who raised his hand and nodded at him with a smile. He was in his thirties, had light brown hair and a round face that had a shiny quality to it like he'd been in the sun too long.

"Kaia, Jack, I've got you on the WAKs still. There's plenty yet to be done. Seems like we're still dealing with the aftereffects of Hernandez's homicide. We've got another body. Kendra Wilkes."

"Suspects?" Collins asked.

"None as usual. Family says they didn't see anything. Might be true this time. They said they were sniped."

A chuckle went around the room.

"Yeah, not something you hear every day, but it's actually lining up with the scene, so take a look at that."

Kaia started flipping through the file she'd been handed while Davis moved on to other assignments for the rest of the detectives, giving out some new ones and simply getting updates on others. The first photo in Kaia's file was of Kendra Wilkes, alive and well. The next was of her lying facedown on the floor with a bullet entry wound in the back of her head. It was an accurate and deadly shot. She would have died instantly. Kaia always got the creeps when she thought too long about an instant death, the idea of life as usual one moment and then gone forever the next, with no inkling it ever happened.

When the meeting let out Jack made his way over to her and shook her hand.

"Glad to have you," he said. "I've seen you around working on this, but it's nice to be official."

"Glad to be here. I've wanted this for a long time."

"Great. Let's go check this place out. We'll chat on the way."

Kaia loved getting straight to business. Jack seemed nice enough, but she already knew she wasn't going to click with him the way she had with Reid. They'd been instant friends, and Jack had near impossible shoes to fill. She realized she was probably filling someone's shoes too, and that he might not be thrilled either. She resolved to give him a fair chance. It wasn't necessary to be friends with her partner, but it certainly made things easier and often downright fun.

"So it's Kendra's family's house," Kaia said, reading the details in the file while Jack drove. Men loved to be the drivers, and while many female officers resisted the stereotype, Kaia enjoyed reading through the calls and being the one to bail out and chase if someone took off on foot.

"Mom?"

"Yeah, mom and two little brothers."

"That's too bad. They were there?"

"Yeah."

Jack pulled up to the house and parked. It was a small brick house. The front yard was littered with sports equipment and Halloween decorations. Kaia led the way to the door and knocked. A woman in her forties answered with tear stains down her face.

"Ms. Wilkes, I'm Detective Sorano. We're investigating the incident that happened here yesterday. May we come in?"

She silently opened the door wider and walked away. It was hardly friendly, but it was an invitation. Jack went straight to examining the window that'd been shot through.

"We're here to find out who did this," Kaia said. "Did you see anything that might be helpful?"

"No. No one."

"Did Kendra have enemies?"

"Of course she did. She was a gang member. That's all they do is make enemies." She fished a cigarette out of a crushed pack and put it between her lips while she searched for a lighter.

"Anyone specific?"

"She didn't tell me her business. She knew I hated it."

"Did she mention anyone—"

"No."

"Ms. Wilkes, I realize this is hard, but even small details can turn out to be very helpful. Do you remember any names that stood out? People she talked about a lot? Even just a first name or a street name?"

"No."

"Detective Sorano." Collins waved her over. She found him crouched over bloodstains. They'd been cleaned but the outline of them was still visible.

"What's up?"

"Just figuring out the angle of this," he said and turned to look back through the window. Kaia followed his gaze. There weren't many vantage points someone could realistically use. There was a square building a ways off, maybe an office building.

"You think he shot from that roof?"

"I think so, and it's a good half mile away at least. Davis is right. This looks like a legit sniper."

"That matches retaliation for the body we found at Marco's."

"Does it?"

"Hijos are the big gun guys. Makes sense they have sniper rifles. That's not something your average dealer carries."

"Doesn't mean they have the skills for this," Collins said. "That's a hell of a shot."

"I suppose that's true."

"Retaliation is as good a place to start as any. Let's get out of here and see if we can track down some Hijos de la Santa Muerte."

"What about the brothers?"

Jack shrugged. "They're not going to tell us anything. Why make them relive it?"

"All right, let's go."

They each left a card with Kendra's uncooperative mother and headed for the car.

"Where do we find these guys?" Kaia asked.

"Beats me. They're ghosts lately."

"Any idea why?"

"My guess is because of the mess with Kitchen," he said.

Kaia felt her cheeks flush. Adrienne's tip about Kitchen being crooked had been upsetting. She couldn't imagine how the people who actually worked with him felt. It had been a good thing Adrienne told them, and it certainly wasn't her fault Kitchen was dirty, but the mention of him made Kaia feel guilty and disliked.

"How so?" she asked. "You think he tipped them to lay low?"

"I'm not sure I believe he's dirty," Collins said. "I do think all the extra surveillance we've put on him trying to figure it out has probably spooked them all into laying low."

"What do you mean you don't believe it? We know he's dirty. Adrienne was inside. She told us so."

"Yeah, but Kitchen is a cop. And a friend."

"I can understand that, but Adrienne isn't a liar, and even if she was, why would she lie about that? How would she even know he was an undercover if he hadn't turned?"

"Calm down, I'm not calling her a liar. I'm just saying sometimes shit goes sideways undercover. Maybe he had to do some things to stay alive. All I'm saying is we haven't heard his side. It's all just rumor right now. Davis is leaving him in the field trying to get proof, and I'm not going to think the worst of a friend without even hearing him out."

"Fair enough." Kaia wanted to be amiable, but she had a hard time swallowing his denial of reality. Kitchen was lying to the department. It was clear where his loyalties were now. They wouldn't arrest Kitchen until they were positive they could prove everything. He still represented a threat, and Kaia couldn't see him as a detective anymore, let alone a friend. She knew it would be an unpopular position. Cop loyalty ran deep. Many would protect Kitchen even if they did believe he'd gone sideways. They'd assume it all amounted to an indiscretion or two for a little extra pocket money, something many of them had done. They wouldn't easily believe he'd abandoned the force entirely.

"It has to be connected to what happened at Marco's." Collins got back on topic.

"All just a gun deal gone sideways?"

"Maybe. Deal goes bad, sour feelings, someone takes advantage of Gianna being alone on the wrong street. WAKs get the Hijo for revenge, but why Marco? And then why Kendra?"

"I don't know," Kaia said. She felt horrible concealing what had happened to Gianna. She knew she was misleading the entire investigation, and she couldn't help but wonder if Gianna was going to taint her entire career in the Gang Unit. How long would it follow her? How many more times would she have to lie about it?

"I think we have to go rattle some cages to shake something loose," she said. Even if she knew damn well Gianna wasn't killed by Hijos, she had no explanation for Kendra or Marco. The investigation wasn't a complete sham. She could still do worthwhile detective work.

She was terrified that Adrienne's worst fear was exactly true, that their cover-up was causing a gang war, that they were the ones responsible for all the bloodshed. Kaia would do it all again for Adrienne if she had to, but that didn't make her okay with innocent people dying over it.

"I'm all for rattling cages," Collins said. "But we can't find Anna Fields, we have no idea where the Hijos are holed up. Who do we rattle?"

"There's still Celeste Romero and Christina Vickers."

"Will they even know anything? Are they big enough players?"

"I bet they are now. The big players are gone. I wouldn't be surprised if the shuffle to fill those shoes has somehow contributed to all the bloodshed."

"There's a thought. And I do have addresses for them."

"Let's do it."

"Bold move, Sorano. They're not exactly friendly."

"You're telling me."

❖

"We have company," Christina said. Anna sat up and looked through the blinds.

"Oh, you have got to be kidding me."

"It's your cop friend."

Anna reached for the AK-47. Christina cut her off. "You have to hide."

"Bullshit. She's here, I'm taking her out."

"What about the guy? She has a partner with her. If you kill her now that will be it. You'll get shot or arrested or at the very least you won't know where to find Adrienne anymore. You wanted Adrienne."

"I'll find a way."

"We will, but this isn't it. You can't die or get arrested until it's done, remember?"

They knocked on the door. Christina hated cop knocks. They were over-the-top, too hard and demanding, like they thought they could bully people through the door. The part she hated most was that it often worked. People let themselves be intimidated into giving up all kinds of rights.

"Chicago PD."

"Christina, I have to take her out," Anna said. "She's right fucking there. You don't even have to open the door."

"If that's what you want to do, Anna, but you know it's not the right move. We'll have an extra cop to deal with, two bodies on my doorstep, and no idea where Adrienne is. We can get them both and we can do it clean."

Anna pulled the gun to her chest. "I'm going upstairs. I'm taking this. Get rid of them. If they search the house I *will* shoot them." Anna walked quietly up the stairs. Christina gave her plenty of time, ignoring several more knocks. She knew they wouldn't leave. They knew she was here. Her car was parked out front, the lights were on, music was playing. She waited for the next hard bang on the door and finally opened it.

"What do you want, pigs?"

"We need to talk to you."

Christina didn't recognize the guy. She always made an effort to commit their faces to memory in case she came across them in plainclothes, but right now she couldn't focus on anything but the woman. Gianna had called her Blondie. Adrienne's former lover. Adrienne's new lover. The dirty blond hair barely held Christina's attention next to the way she carried herself. She had a quiet confidence that was disconcerting. Christina couldn't figure out if it was real or if it was just a trick of her imagination sprouting from the knowledge that this woman had played some part in Gianna's death. Gianna had been invincible to Christina. The idea that anyone could chase her down or outfight her or survive a shootout with her was intimidating, though she hated herself for letting that thought manifest.

"What do you want to talk about?" Christina asked. "The reason you all are useless when someone from the streets dies? I have three dead friends. What have you told us? Nothing."

"Makes it pretty difficult to investigate when no one close to the victim will talk to us," the blonde said.

"What was your name again?" Christina asked.

"Detective Sorano."

"Detective, huh? I thought you were a uniform."

"I was."

"What'd you get promoted for? You haven't solved shit."

Sorano glanced around the house like the question hadn't fazed her. "Who had a problem with Kendra?"

"What are you talking about?"

"I want to find you your answers, but you have to give me some information to work with."

Christina laughed. "Right, so I'm supposed to believe you're here to help me? You're here to provide a civil service, huh?"

"Yes."

"Has nothing to do with you looking for Anna?"

"You know I can't ignore it if we find her here," Sorano said. "But no, that's not why we came."

"Jesus, you're all the same. How do they train you people? They just make you memorize a list of ways to manipulate people?"

"I wasn't—"

"Who killed Gianna?" Christina looked Sorano in the eye, daring her to answer. She searched for guilt, for doubt, for a sixth sense that Christina knew. "Who killed her?" She raised her voice. "You've had days. What have you found out? Are you even trying?" Blondie still didn't answer. "You're not trying because you don't fucking care. You're here pretending like you care when really all you want to do is pump me for information and throw us all in jail. You don't give a shit about justice. You hated Gianna, just admit it and ask me what you came here to ask me so I can tell you to go fuck yourself and we can all get back to our days."

"All right, I have a question for you," Sorano said.

"What?"

"Why are you only asking about Gianna? Why not Marco? Why not Kendra? Marco was your founder. Kendra was someone you recruited yourself. Why not ask about them?"

"Fuck you. Gianna was my best friend."

"No, Gianna was Anna's best friend. There was nothing exceptional about your relationship," Sorano said. "I think you're not asking about the others because you already know what happened to them."

Christina felt her face twitch with contempt. Anna was right, they should have just shot her.

"You do know, don't you?" Sorano stepped closer. "Were you there?"

"Get the fuck out of my house."

"Was it Los Hijos?"

"You tell me."

"Or did you do it? You trying to take over? Gianna dies, you see a path to the top so you take Marco out. Maybe Kendra found out and you had to take her out to keep it quiet."

"You have no idea how stupid you sound right now," Christina snapped.

"It's making sense to me," Sorano's partner jumped in.

"See how that holds up in court then."

"You'd be surprised," he said.

"So you're threatening me? If I don't talk you'll just make a bunch of shit up and throw me in jail? You call that investigating?"

"We're drawing the best conclusions available with the information we have," he said. "Thanks to you, that's not much. That's how mistakes happen." He stepped closer too. "You know who doesn't cooperate with investigations? People who don't really want the crime solved. You know who that is?"

"I told you to get out of my house, you arrogant, condescending shits."

"Guilty people. That's who."

"You bitches would know."

"Just tell us what you know," Sorano jumped back in.

"I know I'm real tired of this conversation. I know this is your job, not mine. I know if you're at my door it means you're not even close to figuring this out because I had absolutely nothing to do with it."

"Los Hijos de la Santa Muerte had something to do with all this. Tell us how to find them."

"What kind of stupid do you think I am?"

"Do you want the truth or not?" Sorano snapped.

"Please, if I talk to you about another gang I become a target, and call me crazy, but you two don't exactly make me feel safe and protected."

"We can offer you protection," the partner said.

"Right. And you're trustworthy."

"We'll get it in writing for you," Sorano said. "This is how we get to the bottom of this."

"You guys just don't get it," Christina said. "You really don't. You see all of us out here struggling in the streets as these violent, mindless criminals. We're the bad guys and you're all heroes trying to stop us. But the truth is there's not a gang out here that I wouldn't rather face than you. Y'all are the meanest, dirtiest gang on the streets. Y'all are so bad *all* of us out here had to put our differences aside when it comes to you and make a code that no matter how much we hate each other, we're together against the cold blues. It's the only way we stand a chance. You mistreat us, disrespect us, beat us, kill us, incarcerate us, frame us, forget us. And you get away with it. Shit, you get a pat on the back for it. You're not here to help me. You don't really care. So no, I will not tell you where to find Los Hijos." Christina leaned closer to Sorano. "Now get out of my house."

Christina was shaking when she finally locked the door after them. She watched them drive off through the peephole, then turned and rested against the door. She hadn't seen any guilt in Sorano's eyes. If she didn't already know the cop was involved she would have never guessed. Even with the upper hand she thought her knowledge gave her, Sorano had still very much gotten under her skin.

Anna walked down the stairs. Christina wasn't sure how much she'd heard, but she suspected quite a bit by her expression. Anna came over and hugged her.

"She'll pay. Everything you said." Anna paused. "You're right, and she's going to pay for all of it."

"What do we do?"

"I don't know, but we're going to do it clean, just like you said. We're going to get both of them. Adrienne *and* Sorano. They're not going to know what hit them and they're not going to have a shot in hell at getting help."

"I want them to know what hit them," Christina said. "I want them to suffer. I want them to know we know."

Anna smiled. "They will. I want to know which of them actually killed Gi, and I don't care if I have to peel their skin off an inch at a time to find out."

"You really think Christina did it?" Jack asked in the car.
"No, but I do think she knows who did."

"Agreed. I think your rise to power theory works. Two top dogs go down, someone's climbing the ladder."

"But who? Anna wouldn't have killed Gianna, everyone agrees on that, and she's the one who climbed the ladder."

Jack shook his head in frustration. "Well, our next bodies were Marco and the Hijo. We thought that was retaliation for Gianna."

"But who was the target and who was collateral damage?"

"If this is just a chain of retaliation, the Hijo would be the target and Marco would be collateral damage. Then the Hijos hit back by taking Kendra."

"But if this is just two gangs that don't like each other anymore, how did Marco end up dead?" Kaia asked. "It was his place and it would have been his crew. Who pulls that trigger?"

"Yeah, he throws a wrench in everything."

"And we still don't even know what started all this. These gangs were allies."

"That part doesn't bother me," Jack said. "Gangs turn on each other. It could have been anything, really. Someone looked at someone wrong and they took it as disrespect."

"I just can't make sense of the double kill. The bullets came from the same gun. Someone killed a member of each gang. That kills the gang war idea, doesn't it?"

Jack shrugged. "Maybe it was both. Revenge and climbing the ladder. Hijo for Gianna, Marco for ambition?"

"We need Anna. We have to figure out how to flush her out. She has to be pulling the strings."

"Maybe she wanted retaliation for Gianna and Marco wasn't on board. She took over to start the war."

"That's good," Kaia said, sitting forward. "Word is she's dangerous right now. Marco wanted to make peace, she wanted to raise hell."

"What does Contreras say about where Fields would be?"

"Adrienne? Nothing anymore. She had information at first, but she's been out of the loop too long already. They know she's with us. They're not going to use any channels she knows about." She didn't like him bringing up Adrienne. She didn't want them thinking Adrienne was a tool they could use whenever they needed her. Adrienne was trying to distance herself from this world as much as possible, and she needed to be allowed to do that.

"Finding new connections and places to stay can be tricky," Collins said. "They can't instantly re-create a decade's worth of setup just because Adrienne knows about them. That's part of why they're so hard on rats."

Kaia refused to admit he was right, but she knew she had to go back through the information Adrienne had given. She had to find Anna before more people died. She couldn't make sense of everything that was happening, but she knew Gianna's death started it all and she knew people were dying because of it. She had to stop it.

Chapter Twenty-nine

Adrienne read the stress on Kaia when she walked in. She came over to the couch and kissed Adrienne, then slumped into her arms and snuggled close.

"You okay?"

"Did you know Kendra Wilkes?"

"Sure, a little. She came to parties but never talked much. Why?"

"She was killed."

Adrienne tightened her grip on Kaia. "Oh, God. I should have listened to you, Kaia. We should have just told the truth. It was self-defense; we wouldn't have been in trouble. All these people wouldn't be dying if we had just told the truth."

"We can't know what would have happened. We would have definitely been looking over our shoulders forever. Maybe people wouldn't have died, but we don't know that. And who else would've gotten killed instead?"

"But it's my fault. I should have stepped up and dealt with it. I should just come clean. I can't stand people dying for something I did."

"You can't do that," Kaia said. "It's too late anyway. It wouldn't bring anyone back and it won't stop whatever is going on between these gangs. Once these things start they take on a life of their own."

"We have to do something."

"We have to find Anna."

Adrienne saw the quiet question in Kaia's eyes. She needed help, but she didn't want to ask. "What do you need?"

"I just need to know where to look," Kaia said sheepishly. The light was hitting her blue eyes in a way that made them glow and penetrate to Adrienne's core. "She knows better than to stay at her own house, but she has to be somewhere. She can't replace her family or her friends or her drug connects. There has to be something she can't avoid, somewhere she's eventually going to have to go."

Adrienne nodded. "I want to go with you."

"Absolutely not."

"I don't know where to find her, Kaia, but I can show you what they did. I can show you where they hung out, where their borders are, where their big deals happen."

"And you can write all that down."

"I have to be there," Adrienne said. "I'll know familiar cars that pass, what their signals mean, I'll know something out of place when I see it. I'll just know more. If you're going to be driving around those streets looking for trouble you need me there."

"I'll have cover."

"I can't possibly teach you every name, face, car, house, corner, sign, route, buyer, and enemy. I just can't, and I need you safe."

"I need *you* safe." Kaia reached out and squeezed her hand. "I have a gun and a vest and other officers."

"And I have you." Adrienne knew Kaia didn't have much of a choice, but she didn't want to make her feel that way, so she quietly waited for her to decide.

"All right, fine. We'll drive around together. But if we see anything we're waiting for cover, and you are staying in the car the whole time."

"Deal."

Adrienne settled into the passenger seat. Kaia put a pistol in the glove box.

"That's there for you," she said. "If I'm out of the car dealing with someone and shit goes sideways, it's ready to go. Just pull the trigger."

Adrienne nodded. She was used to being around guns and she knew her way around one, but she'd never felt truly comfortable with them.

"I have two radios." Kaia held one up. "This one is staying in the car. Hold this down to talk. If something goes wrong and I can't do it myself, you ask for help on that. Don't forget to tell them where we are, that's the most important thing. If you can only get one thing out, it needs to be our location. If you can't say anything at all, you hit the red button."

"You really think this is going to go bad, huh?"

"No, but I want to know you'll be okay if it does."

Adrienne nodded and kissed her. "We ready?"

"Where to?"

Adrienne directed Kaia down the alleys Gianna used to use when she was selling drugs or guns, places so notorious for violence, even Gianna often wouldn't let Adrienne go. They saw plenty of suspicious activity, but Kaia drove through, single-mindedly looking for Anna.

"What about them?" Kaia pointed out two guys wearing a lot of blue.

"They're members. Probably selling coke." Adrienne felt herself shrinking into the seat even though she knew Kaia's windows were dark enough to hide them.

"Odds they'll meet up with Anna?"

"Low."

Kaia pointed out several people Adrienne would have missed entirely, even an argument on the verge of becoming a fight. Adrienne felt like she'd been walking through life oblivious. She thought things generally didn't happen around her, but now she felt like she probably just hadn't noticed them. Kaia said it took a trained eye, but it made her feel on edge and vulnerable. She obsessively watched the street signs, realizing she also frequently couldn't say exactly where they were on a dime. She spent the first couple hours on high alert before she finally started relaxing and felt they probably wouldn't find Anna tonight.

They rolled by every house Adrienne could remember ever visiting searching for Anna's car. She owned an old Toyota Camry, but she stole vehicles the way many criminals shoplifted. It was a minor occurrence in the day for Anna, and there was really no telling what she'd be driving.

Kaia finally sighed and looked over at Adrienne around one in the morning. "You want to call it a night?"

Adrienne nodded. "We'll try again tomorrow."

Kaia reached across the car and rested her hand on Adrienne's leg. Adrienne leaned over and kissed her neck, then leaned back and closed her eyes while Kaia drove home. She had just started dozing when the speed bumps in their parking lot jostled her awake.

Kaia pulled into her spot and they sleepily gathered their things and got out of the car. They were halfway through the lot when Adrienne heard an engine revving. A van screeched through the parking lot straight at them. The back sliding door was open, and Adrienne saw at least four people with blue masks in the back, another two in the front.

"Look out!" Adrienne yelled.

Kaia already had her gun drawn. "Run, Adrienne."

Adrienne grabbed the back of Kaia's shirt, urging her to run too, but she had already taken aim and fired off four rounds. The people in masks jumped out of the open van door and ran straight for them, covered in body armor. Kaia fired again and one went down, but she had to pause to reload.

"Adrienne, run! Now!"

"Looking for us?" A female laughed as she ran at Kaia and swung at her. Kaia ducked the punch, grabbed her body, and they both slammed to the ground. Adrienne ran toward Kaia's car, trying to get back to the gun in the glove box and the radio. She heard feet pounding after her, and she knew she'd be lucky to have time to do one or the other. She had to decide. Shoot or get help on the way?

She opened the door and reached for the gun. She spun. The person pursuing was only feet away. She fired. The person grunted and grabbed the gun, trying to twist it from her grip. Adrienne struggled to point it back at them. She managed to muscle it back at their body and fire, but they didn't seem fazed. A second blue mask caught up to them and wrenched one of Adrienne's arms off the gun. The first person finally pried it from her hand, and she felt the cold hard slap of metal on her face. Her vision went blurry and she felt herself being dragged back to the van. She heard feet scuffing on the ground, grunts, cussing. She knew Kaia was still fighting.

She shook the blow away, eyes slowly focusing. Each of the people in masks had one of her arms and they were supporting her weight while her feet dragged over the pavement. She dug her feet in and pulled back. She freed one arm and pulled the other as hard as she could. She felt herself slipping through their grip, but the full weight of the first person crushed her to the ground. Her face hit asphalt and she couldn't breathe.

She saw Kaia on the ground too with two people on top of her. They had her pinned. When they tried to drag her to the van, she swung and kicked at them, keeping their progress at a standstill, but she couldn't escape.

The driver jumped out of the van with rope and headed toward Adrienne. She recognized Anna despite her covered face. Anna circled Adrienne's wrists with the thick rope several times over while the other two held her arms behind her back. Once she was tied, Anna grabbed Adrienne and pulled her to the van by her hair. Adrienne tried to pull away, but Anna spun and punched her in the face. Unable to raise her hands, Adrienne took the full force of the blow. Anna dragged her the rest of the way and flung her into the van. Adrienne's shins hit the ledge and she fell to the floor of the stripped van face-first. Anna headed back for Kaia.

Adrienne felt tears rolling down her face as she watched Anna put her knee in Kaia's back and go to work tying her hands. They dragged her to her feet. Kaia was still fighting, kicking and pulling and giving them a hell of a time. Anna squared up and punched her. She hit her three more times before Kaia became subdued enough to yank to the van. All five of the masked people still standing headed for the van, three of them dragged the sixth, the one Kaia had shot. They all jumped inside and slid the door closed with a loud thud.

Kaia landed in front of Adrienne on the floor. She was bleeding from a cut over her eye and her lip was swollen. She spit blood on the van floor. Adrienne's eyes watered again. This was all her fault. Kaia's eyes met hers, and Adrienne felt a contagious calm coming from them. The five WAK members all took off their masks and sat on the milk crates that were serving as seats. Anna was driving, Christina was in the passenger seat. Celeste and two others were in the back, and the body was on the floor by the back door. Adrienne recognized the two with Celeste as Jacob and Sean. They were members Adrienne had dealt to more times than she could count.

"Well, you're pretty confident, aren't you?" Kaia said in response to them removing the masks.

Adrienne couldn't believe Kaia would dare provoke them, but she couldn't help but smile. They looked down at Kaia and smirked.

"Oh yeah, we're confident. You two aren't going anywhere but to a shallow grave."

"We'll see."

"You get a call for help out to your buddies?"

Kaia shrugged. "We'll see."

"Let me show you something, pig." Jacob reached to a blanket covering something. He pulled back the blanket and exposed a chest nearly spilling over with assault rifles, handguns, and ammunition.

Sean laughed. "If your friends try to pull us over they're getting pumped full of lead. And even if they do somehow pin us down, you certainly aren't coming out alive."

Anna was disturbingly quiet in the driver's seat. Adrienne knew she must be the one who orchestrated all this. She must want this with a fire, yet she had barely looked back. She had almost seemed irritated she was needed to tie them up.

Adrienne looked Kaia in the eye again. She wanted to say so much, but she didn't want to talk in front of the Wild AKs. She wanted Kaia to know she hadn't been able to call help. She wanted to hear Kaia tell her she'd done the right thing choosing to go for the gun, but she didn't know if that was true. All she'd been able to think at the time was that if she didn't find a way to fight back and kill these sons of bitches, they would be long gone by the time help got to them. Had she been able to kill them, that would have been true, but in light of her failure to do that she wondered if the radio wasn't the better choice. Now it would be several hours before anyone even wondered where they were. They could be dead by then.

"That one dead?" Kaia nodded to the body at the back of the van.

Adrienne expected a violent reaction, but Celeste just sadly nodded. "Yes."

"Who is it?" Kaia asked.

Celeste leaned over and removed the mask, again surprising Adrienne with her cooperation. It was a member named Cheyenne she'd known and even liked. She had a bullet hole between her wide-open eyes. Something about the way it was placed shook Adrienne up. It brought the reality of guns fresh to her mind, the cold and impersonal way they ate through anything in their path. Adrienne hated that the worst people always seemed to endure while the nicer ones perished. Cheyenne wasn't a saint, but why couldn't that bullet have found Anna instead? Would this even still be happening if it had?

Kaia scanned Cheyenne's face. Adrienne couldn't begin to imagine what she was thinking. She felt a surprising lack of hatred from the WAKs toward Kaia over the death. They hated her as a cop, but she had in some strange way earned their respect by killing members, by surviving Gianna's wrath. Adrienne had no such respect despite sharing meals, parties, secrets, and memories with them. She was nothing to them now. A rat.

Adrienne heard a siren. It sounded a couple hundred feet away and she couldn't tell if it was for them. She couldn't imagine it was. She hadn't gotten the call out. She hated that Kaia might be thinking she had. She was horrified by the idea of Kaia expecting help that wasn't coming. But she couldn't let the WAKs know that they weren't being pursued.

Kaia looked to the front of the van. Adrienne followed her gaze. She was watching Anna's reaction, watching her eyes flash to and from the rearview mirror.

"It's for us," Anna finally said. Kaia smirked and winked at Adrienne. Adrienne's stomach clenched. The cop trying to stop them didn't know who they were dealing with; they couldn't be prepared. Adrienne wanted to feel hope, but all she could muster was fear that another innocent person was going to die.

"You might want to hold on to something," Anna said and hit the gas. The WAKs all reached for something to grab, but Kaia and Adrienne were at the mercy of the momentum, sliding across the floor. Kaia slid into Adrienne until the side panel stopped them both. Adrienne seized the opportunity and whispered into her ear.

"I couldn't get the call off. It's not for us."

"Doesn't matter," she said. Adrienne didn't see an ounce of anything she'd feared, no disappointment, fear, or anger. "They'll be airing it citywide now anyway."

"As what, a stolen car? Will they even care?"

"Oh yeah, they care. Or maybe a kidnapping if anyone saw us. It's going to be nothing but problems for these guys now."

"Shut up down there," Sean yelled, but he was distracted, looking out the window at the cop pursuing them.

Kaia pulled her knees to her chest and started maneuvering her tied hands under her feet until she had them in front of her. Adrienne felt paralyzed. She wanted to tell Kaia to stop, but she knew she couldn't draw attention to them. She watched the three members in back. All were staring out the windows watching the pursuing officer. Kaia was eyeing the gun in Sean's hand. Kaia met Adrienne's eyes and seemed to stop time for one agonizing second, then tore away and lunged for the gun.

Her hands locked on the gun and wrenched it away. Sean tackled her to the ground. Kaia twisted the gun and fired out the window. The glass shattered and the square pieces rained down on Adrienne. Adrienne swung her hands under her feet too, struggling more than she thought she would to do so. With her hands in front, she staggered to her feet. Jacob rushed her, but she quickly put her hands out the window, waving wildly in signal to the officer.

The van careened around a corner and Adrienne fell back to the floor of the van. She heard a gunshot and spun from side to side trying to place if anyone had been hit. Anna hit the brakes hard, then hit the gas again, intentionally tossing them all around the van. The sirens screamed after them. Kaia was still wrestling with Sean for the gun. They both had hands on it, working with all their strength to control the direction of the barrel. Kaia twisted her body and elbowed him in the face. He didn't lose his grip entirely, but she was able to pull it and point it at the front seat. Four more shots sounded through the van. Anna ducked. The windshield spider webbed.

"Are you fucking kidding me?" Anna screamed. "Get her under control!"

Jacob let go of Adrienne and helped Sean wrench the gun away from Kaia. They finally ripped it away and Sean punched Kaia in the face.

The van veered again and Adrienne and Kaia both slid across the floor and hit hard against the opposite panel. Adrienne grunted. Kaia's cheek was bleeding. Her eyes spoke a silent apology. Adrienne surprised her with a quick kiss.

"You're amazing," she whispered.

The van whined and shook, struggling with Anna's demands for speed. "This thing doesn't have it in her," Anna said. "You're going to have to get him to drop off."

Sean, Jacob, and Celeste each reached for the rifles. "Hold on." Jacob sneered at Kaia and Adrienne, then opened the back door. The wind of the highway rushed through the vehicle, and Adrienne tried to find a ledge for her foot to keep herself from sliding. The cop was in an SUV, following closely. Two more cars were behind him, trying to catch up. The cop hit the brakes hard when he saw the doors open, but the front of the SUV was quickly riddled with bullets as all three Wild AKs fired. He veered off and crashed into the concrete barrier. Traffic around him panicked and tried to avoid him, but only managed to sideswipe one another, spin out of control, and block the way for the two police cars behind them.

"Yeah!" Jacob yelled. "What now, pig!" Jacob and Sean reached for the doors and struggled to pull them closed, then finally got them to latch. Adrienne watched for as long as possible, hoping to see the cops catching up again, but the police lights were fading farther into the distance and the van was screaming away. Adrienne searched Kaia's face but found nothing.

The van pulled off the highway and slowed. Everyone fell quiet, collectively holding their breaths. Adrienne strained to hear sirens; the others were no doubt straining to hear silence.

"Not far now," Anna said, glancing over her shoulder at Adrienne and Kaia for the first time. "Not your city anymore, cop, so you can let go of that idea."

"My city isn't the only one looking after that."

"They're just going to get more of what he did if they find us."

"Maybe, but you keep shooting at cops, one of you is going to get some more of what *she* got." Kaia nodded at Cheyenne's dead body.

"Well, luckily for everyone except you, we're almost there," Christina said.

"I'm stopping here," Anna said. "We're remote. I want them tied properly and then we'll keep on. If this bitch shoots at us again I swear it's all your asses."

The van slowed and it felt like they were on a dirt road. She couldn't imagine where they were going, but the chances seemed slim of being found by law enforcement now. Kaia's eyes were flashing wildly around the van. Adrienne couldn't imagine what she was planning, but she'd obviously entered a different frame of mind. Adrienne couldn't read her face anymore. She tried to look around too, to find something useful. She tested her ropes, and while they were much less restricting in front of her, she still found no give whatsoever around her wrists.

The van stopped. Anna jumped out of the driver's seat and walked around. The back doors opened and the other members all jumped out.

"Kaia." Adrienne's voice was weak and squeaky, fear taking it over.

"It's okay," Kaia said.

"They're going to kill us."

Kaia's eyes were soft. Adrienne saw her trying to work up to saying it wouldn't happen, but she couldn't. They had no idea where they were, they were outnumbered five to two, and they were obscenely outgunned.

Anna grabbed Adrienne's feet and dragged her out of the van. She landed on the ground before she even realized she was falling. She heard the scrape of them doing the same to Kaia. The air was shockingly cold against her skin. Her hands were numb and shivers crawled over her. Anna closed the van doors and grabbed each of their shirts, then yanked them so they were upright against the back of the van.

Anna seemed to notice a pain in her arm from the effort. She touched her shoulder gingerly and held bloody fingers in front of her. She shrugged out of her jacket. A bullet had grazed her.

"Look at that, you got me." She turned to Kaia and laughed. "Goddamn, you're a pain in my ass."

"You thought I was going to just let you kill us?"

"Kind of."

"You're a slow learner then."

Anna laughed. "I can appreciate a fighter, but I can't abide one." She kicked Kaia in the stomach, doubling her over. Anna crouched down and forced her to sit again. "All right," she said. "Which one of you killed Gianna?" Anna's eyes went back and forth between them.

Adrienne's heart pounded and her face got hot. She glanced at Kaia for guidance, wondering if they had any shot at denying it.

"I did," Kaia blurted out instantly.

Adrienne was horrified. "No, she didn't. I did."

Anna was still crouched in front of them. "That's cute," she said. "I see what you're doing. But you're going to tell me the truth."

"I killed her," Kaia said again. Anna punched Kaia in the face hard enough that her head smacked into the van behind her. Adrienne cringed.

"It was me, Anna," Adrienne said. "Gianna wanted to kill me, you know she did. She came for me, we fought, I won."

Anna laughed. "You fought and you won, huh? That simple? That's pretty hard to believe."

"I used the lid of the toilet tank. I hit her as hard as I could and she went down. I didn't mean to kill her, but I did. I'm the one you're looking for."

Anna turned back to Kaia. "What's your story?"

"That's true, except it was me, and I *did* mean to kill her. She went after Adrienne. I found them and hit her with the toilet tank lid. That's why the blow was to the side and back of her head."

Anna looked back to Adrienne. Adrienne just shook her head. "It was me. You know it was me. She's just trying to save my life."

"How do I know you're not just trying to save hers?"

"She is," Kaia said. "Adrienne, just stop it."

Anna laughed. "You can both stop. I'm killing you both either way. You were both involved to some extent, and you're both going to die for it. Tell me the truth and I'll make it fast."

Adrienne looked at Kaia, begging her to stop lying. Anna was already prone to believe Kaia. It made more sense to her since she thought of cops as killers, but Adrienne couldn't let her believe it. She knew Anna had something special in store for the one who killed Gianna and she couldn't let Kaia take that for her.

"What's it going to be?" Anna asked. "Can we get on the same page? Who did it?"

"I did." They both said the words again in unison.

Anna was visibly frustrated. She stood up and paced, then came back and crouched again. "I guess I just have to torture you both then. I was only going to torture the one who killed her and put the other down quick, but since I can't be sure, you both get it. How's that?"

She glanced from one to the other, waiting for one of them to change their story, but neither did. Anna directed the guys to hold Kaia while she retied Kaia's hands behind her much tighter than before.

When she was bound again, Anna took a knife from her pocket and flipped it open. She cut Kaia's sleeve and exposed her shoulder. She put the blade to Kaia's skin and dug in. Kaia only winced at first, but it quickly turned to screams as Anna dragged her blade horizontally, peeling her skin.

"It was me!" Adrienne screamed. "It was me, it was me! Anna, you know it was me!"

Anna finished dragging the blade through and held up the patch of skin she'd removed. Adrienne thought she might throw up. She looked at Kaia's shoulder. Blood was pouring down her arm from the two-inch square of missing skin. Kaia was pale and her eyes were closed.

"Well, pig? You ready to change your story? Plenty more where that came from."

Kaia opened her eyes and spit in Anna's face. "It was me."

"No!" Adrienne yelled. "Damn you, Kaia! It's not true."

Anna stood and kicked Kaia in the head. "I know you did not just spit in my face." She knelt over Kaia and started punching. Kaia fell to the dirt, unable to protect herself. Adrienne heard herself screaming, but she couldn't control it. A fist connected with her face.

"Shut up," Anna said. Kaia was unconscious on the ground, spatters of blood flung across the dirt around her.

Anna paced in a rage, yelling at Kaia's unconscious body. "Fucking shot me. Spit on me. Out of your fucking mind. Wake her up!"

"Anna, she had nothing to do with it," Adrienne said. "Please. It was me. I swear it was me. It's all because of me. Just let her go."

"Let her go?" Anna walked over. "Let her go? Are you crazy? Even if I take your word for it that you killed Gianna this one's still not going anywhere." Anna crouched in front of her again. "You know, you were supposed to love Gianna. You were with *Gianna*. You were with her for years and then you two just kill her like she's nothing. You don't even shed a tear. How long before you were fucking the cop?"

"I—"

"Shut up! You're a snitch. You're a disloyal scheming bitch. You killed my best friend, who loved you, and you don't give a shit, but you're fucking falling apart for this chick? Why is she so important, huh? Guess what, I don't care. If she's the only way to tear your tiny cold heart apart, then get ready." Anna stood back up and walked over to Kaia. She rolled her onto her back and slapped her face, trying to wake her.

"Get her up, I said!" Anna yelled and stood upright again, pacing like a maniac. The members scrambled for water and splashed Kaia's face until she stirred. "Get her up."

Sean and Jacob each grabbed one of Kaia's arms and dragged her to a standing position. Kaia was covered in blood from the beating and the knife. Anna squared in front of her and started hitting her, over and over again. Kaia grunted from the impacts but didn't say a word. Adrienne yelled until her throat was raw. Her cheeks were wet and hot with tears. Anna's knuckles were bloody.

Adrienne heard a siren. It was far in the distance and utterly useless to her, but it seemed to remind Anna what she was doing. Kaia was limp in Sean's and Jacob's arms. Her eyes were barely open, her face was bruised and bleeding. Anna pulled her knife out again.

"You ready, Blondie?"

"No, Anna, please!" Adrienne screamed. "I'll do anything."

Anna looked over her shoulder at Adrienne. "All I want from you is the look on your face when you see this." Anna turned and stabbed downward, sinking the blade into Kaia's chest. Adrienne felt herself screaming, but everything sounded quiet. Kaia looked at the knife buried in her and then met Adrienne's eyes. They were still filled with that same relentless calm.

Jacob and Sean let go of her and she fell to the ground. Anna turned back to Adrienne and walked over as if nothing had happened. She swung the van door open, grabbed Adrienne's shirt, and yanked her up. Adrienne's legs were numb and useless. Anna struggled with her weight but managed to drag her back up and into the van.

"We're going for another ride," she said. "Where we can take our time with you."

"What do you want to do with her?" Christina nodded at Kaia.

"Leave her," Anna said. Adrienne felt like she was breathing fire. She couldn't tell if Kaia was already dead, unconscious, or awake and struggling to breathe. Was she feeling death take her? Was she slipping out of life to a backdrop of blood and screams?

"I love you, Kaia," Adrienne yelled. She didn't know if Kaia could hear her. She didn't know if her words would even matter, but she had to try.

"Oh, Jesus, shut up." Anna shoved her farther into the van. Adrienne watched Kaia's body on the ground, searching for signs of movement. She couldn't see any. The door slammed shut.

She felt the engine rev and the van take off. She had no idea where they were. Even if she could find a way to escape or get help somehow, how could she tell someone where to find Kaia? Even if she was alive now she'd bleed out or freeze to death overnight.

"How you doing, girlie?" Anna beamed over her shoulder from the driver's seat.

"Fuck you."

"That's the spirit."

"You're going to die for this," Adrienne said. "I'll find a way."

"Look at that, Gianna did teach you a thing or two, didn't she? You can save it though. I'm not taking chances with you. There's not a thing in this world you can do to stop me."

Adrienne couldn't stop crying. The tears just leaked down her face even as rage became her primary emotion. She kept flashing back to Kaia, wondering if she died yet, guessing she probably had.

"Hey, Adrienne," Anna said. "Who killed Gianna? Your girlfriend is already dead now, it doesn't matter anymore. Was it her?"

Adrienne didn't answer.

"You were convincing and everything, but you were desperate to save her. So how about it? Who was it?"

"It was the cop," Christina said. "This one doesn't have the sack."

"It was the cop, huh?" Anna asked.

"You're never going to know," Adrienne said. "If that's the only thing I can take from you, I'm taking it."

Chapter Thirty

Kaia woke up on the ground. The freezing air bit at her skin. The stars were an explosion of glitter above her. Seeing so many of them scared her. She was too far from civilization. But as that fear started to grab her, she pushed it back. They hadn't driven that long. It couldn't be as bad as it looked.

The tire tracks were fresh, leading back to what she assumed must be a paved road. It would lead her back to help, but beyond a main road, she wouldn't be able to track Adrienne. She carefully sat up. The mixture of numbness and pain tingled through her whole body. She was stiff and sore. Her arm was bare where Anna had cut away her sleeve to peel her skin. The chunk missing from her shoulder was deep, but had stopped bleeding. The skin around it was blue. Her arms ached from being tied so tightly behind her, and she'd long lost circulation in her hands. More pressing, Anna had stabbed her and the handle was sticking out of her chest, near her collarbone.

It was too high to have hit her heart, and judging by her ability to breathe, it had also missed her lungs. Just looking at it made pain radiate through her chest and shoulders, but she took a breath and breathed past it. She hadn't even felt it a moment ago; it was all mental. She knew she couldn't remove the blade or she'd risk bleeding out. Anna should've known to take the knife with her, but she had been too emotional to think clearly.

Kaia staggered after the van tracks. Why would they take Adrienne to a second location? Why not just kill her here? Kaia suspected Anna knew Adrienne had been the one to actually kill Gianna and had a long, grueling session of torture planned. She wanted to scream thinking about Adrienne being tortured, but she knew she needed this to be true or Adrienne would be dead before she even found her way off this land.

Her feet were throbbing, the cold was excruciating. She was quickly short of breath and became paranoid it was related to her injuries, that she was going to flicker out and die somewhere along the road. She couldn't let that happen. She forced herself to keep walking. When the knife caught the corner of her eye, she decisively ignored it. She was going to survive. She was going to find Adrienne. Nothing else was acceptable.

It was at least a half mile to paved road. She saw the trail of dirt from the tires veering left, but it quickly stopped leaving any trace, and her connection to Adrienne was severed. She followed the road searching for cars, street signs, or people. It felt like it took years before she finally saw a set of headlights coming her way. She walked into the middle of the street to stop them. The truck slowed all the way to a stop several yards away, like they were afraid of her. She imagined her silhouette did make her look like a serial killer since she couldn't raise her hands and wave at them.

"Help!"

The driver's door opened and a head popped out as the person stood half in the truck, half out of it.

"What in the hell happened to you?" The voice sounded like it belonged to a teenager, but the headlights were blinding her and she couldn't see him clearly.

"I need you to untie me." Kaia turned so he could see the rope.

He stepped around the open truck door and jogged toward her. As he neared her, she saw she was right. He was just a kid. His hair was wild and his pale skin made his acne stand out like fireworks on his face.

"Holy shit." His eyes were the size of silver dollars. Kaia turned around.

"Untie me."

"Right."

His hands were trembling as he tried to maneuver the knots loose. His fingers felt like fire against her skin, and she couldn't be sure if it was because of the cold or the lack of circulation. In either case, she wasn't sure her hands were going to work anymore once they were free.

"What happened to you?" he asked again. "I should call you an ambulance."

"No," she said. If she let him do that she'd be stuck dealing with the responders. She'd have to fend off demands for reports and be dragged to the hospital and drugged to sleep. She didn't have time for that. "I'm a police officer. I'll call myself."

Just as she felt herself about to lose her patience with him, she felt the rope loosen, and she was free. She glanced at her hands, but they were so blue she couldn't let herself look. She couldn't let anything distract her. She hobbled to his truck and slid into the driver's seat.

"Where do you live?" she asked.

"Just up the road."

"Good, I need your truck."

"What?"

Even the simple motion of putting her hand in her pocket and producing her badge was excruciating. The teen's eyes flashed over her badge, but she knew he was too shaken up to really look.

"You'll get it back." She reached out and grabbed the door handle and pulled it closed. The boy backed away as he nodded his head quickly, his eyes still round and wide.

Kaia put the truck in drive and sped off as fast as she dared. She couldn't shake the image of what would happen if she had to slam the brakes, or even worse, got in an accident with a knife sticking out of her chest. She couldn't let that slow her down. Adrienne might not have much time. Her first urge was to try to find the van, to follow the last road she knew it had been on, but she knew she'd taken too long to wake up, walk to the road, and commandeer a truck. They were long gone. She'd never find them with simple blind driving, and even if she did, she'd be no match for them with no weapons other than the knife in her chest. She had to get to help.

She finally found a street name she recognized and was relieved to find she had been right about the drive time. They weren't too far out of town. She sped until she was parked in front of Reid's house. She stumbled up his front stairs and banged on his door frantically.

"Reid! Let me in!"

She knew walking was still a challenge for him and he could well be on the way, but it was after three in the morning now, and she had to be sure she'd woken him up. She hit the doorbell several more times. Finally, she saw his silhouette through the glass in his door.

"Reid!"

"Kaia?" He opened the door. "Oh, my God." He flung the door open and tried to help her in, but Kaia pushed his hand away, knowing he was barely standing himself. "What the fuck happened? I'll call an ambulance."

"No, let me in."

"There's a fucking knife in your chest!"

"Let me in," Kaia insisted, pushing past him. She went straight for the first chair she saw and slumped into it.

"What happened?"

"They took her. They have her." Kaia's teeth chattered. Reid limped to the couch and grabbed a blanket. He came back and wrapped it around her carefully.

"Adrienne?"

"Yes. Anna has Adrienne. She has her. She's going to kill her. I have to find them."

"Honey, we have to take you to a hospital right now. We'll call—"

"No. I have to find her. She doesn't have long."

"You have a fucking knife in your chest."

"I know, I know. You have to help me."

"We have to call it in," Reid said. "We'll get everyone on finding Adrienne and we'll get you help."

"Reid, please. No one else will be good enough. No one else will handle this like we can. By the time they get a team and a plan together and actually start moving it will be too late."

"Usually I'd agree, but I can barely walk and if you don't get some medical attention you could die. How long has that been there?"

"Forget the knife for a second," Kaia said. "I know it looks bad, but if it was going to kill me it would have."

"I'm not sure that logic holds—"

"I have to get it out, obviously, but I can't go to a hospital. It'll take too long."

"You're not asking me to do it."

"No. But don't you have some kind of contact? Your informant?"

Reid hesitated, dread all over his face. "He patches up criminals that can't go to hospitals."

"That's who I need."

"But, Kaia, he just patches people up a bit. It's not really safe. He doesn't have the materials he needs to really fix you."

"All I have time for is a patch up. I want this thing out of my fucking chest, a Band-Aid, and I'm back on the road."

"You're insane. The guys can work on finding Adrienne."

"No, Reid! They won't find her! You know they won't find her!"

Reid tugged at his hair in distress.

"Please, Reid. I have to save her. I have to. They're going to torture her. To death."

"Shit." He took out his cell phone and dialed. He gave his address and a quick description of Kaia's wounds, then hung up. "This is a bad idea, Kaia."

"I can't let her die, Reid. Please just help me."

"Where were you?"

"They took us from my apartment parking lot. They took us to some land off the highway and did this." She gestured at herself. "They left me, took her, and went west."

"West."

"Yes, on a little back road."

"That's not a lot to go on."

"I know that, that's why I need you."

Reid pulled up his laptop and brought up a map. "Show me."

Kaia pointed to the unnamed road off the highway. He turned the screen back to himself and studied the map. "That's not awful, actually. It's all big parcels of land, farms. If we can find an association between one of those and one of the members, we'll probably have her."

"Hurry, Reid. It's already been too long. I've been too slow."

The doorbell rang. Reid got up and limped over. A scruffy, stocky, tattooed white guy came in and looked her over with a straight face.

"Are you going to be able to handle this here?" Reid asked. "I don't want it done like this if it's too risky."

"Reid," Kaia snapped.

The man sat down and pulled Kaia's shirt away from the edges of the wound. "It's going to be messy," he said. "But I can do it. Your big problem is going to be infection down the road."

"We can handle that later," Kaia said.

He held out his hand in greeting. "I'm Kendrick. I'll be taking the knife out of your chest."

Kaia laughed lightly and shook his hand.

"You're sure?" Reid asked again. "She'll be okay?"

"This is imprecise work, Mr. Castillo, but it's what I do. Lie back." He guided Kaia to the dining room table and had her lie flat. Kaia's heart pounded in anticipation, but she knew this was what needed to happen. She couldn't be locked down in a hospital for days.

"Kaia, please don't do this," Reid said. "Let me take you in."

"Start looking up those addresses," Kaia said. "He'll tell me if I have to go in."

Kendrick nodded his confirmation at Reid. Reid breathed out a long sigh and pulled up his laptop again, but Kaia knew he wasn't looking yet, couldn't focus. Kendrick put his bag on the table and pulled out several clean towels.

"Ready?" Kendrick asked. Kaia nodded. He pressed around the wound with the towel. The pain at his touch was intense, but she could handle it. When he started to remove the blade, she couldn't suppress a yell. Reid jumped to his feet, but the knife was already out. Kaia heard it clang on the table and Kendrick pressed down hard with both hands on her chest. She felt warm blood rolling down her neck, but Kendrick's calm face reassured her.

"Reid, please start looking," she said. "I'm fine."

Reid nodded and turned his attention to the computer screen. Kendrick's weight was steady and strong.

"You doing okay?" he asked.

"I think so."

"Soon as the bleeding slows down we'll get you sewed up. I have something I can give you to help keep the infection away, but as soon as you're done with whatever you're dealing with you have to go in. Don't blow it off, even if you think it's healing."

"Got it."

"That's a nasty one you have on your shoulder too. I'll clean and wrap that for you."

"Thank you."

Kendrick nodded, looking her over again. "They got you good, sweetie."

"I know."

"You getting 'em back?"

"Oh, yes. Even if it kills me."

Kaia couldn't stop watching Reid. She knew his mind was racing and that he was already distracted. She couldn't let herself break his concentration, but it was torture waiting for him to find something. All she could think about was what Adrienne must be going through. She could be getting tortured. They could be peeling her skin, beating her. She could be about to be shot. She could already be dead for that matter. Kaia felt sick.

Reid wasn't just her best friend, he was also a beast at his job. He had found suspects Kaia had thought were gone for sure a number of times with paper-thin evidence to lead him. Kendrick started working on sewing her up.

"All right, I'm going to read these names," Reid said. "Stop me if you hear one you recognize."

"Go."

"Karie Adams, Michael and Robyn Lowell, Robert Henderson, Augustine Vickers—"

"Vickers! Christina Vickers is a member. She was there. She's Anna's right hand."

"Fourteen eight-seventy Dallas Lane."

"That's it." Kaia sat up.

"You want me to call it in?"

"No, I'm going."

"You need backup."

"No, they're up to their necks in guns. If they even smell cops they're going to mow them down and shoot Adrienne. I have to sneak in somehow." Kaia felt Kendrick's speed pick up. He was clearly aware he didn't have long before she rushed out the door.

"I'm your backup then," Reid said.

Kaia cocked her head at him. "I love you, Reid, but you can barely walk."

"I can still shoot a motherfucker, can't I?"

"Yeah, I guess so." Kaia smiled.

Kendrick covered her stab wound with several layers of dressings. He sprayed something into the open wound on her shoulder. Kaia's inhale came in a hiss of air at the shock of pain. He wrapped her in gauze.

"My work is done."

"Really?"

"I mean it's some pretty shitty stitching, but I know someone who's about to bolt on me when I see them."

Kaia hugged him with her good arm. "Thank you for this." Kendrick nodded and hurried out the door, suddenly seeming eager to put space between himself and their problems.

Reid handed Kaia a ballistic vest. It was a spare of Reid's and didn't really fit the way it should, but it was better than nothing. He put his own on and limped down the hall.

"Reid, we have to go."

"I know you're freaking out, but we're not going without guns," he said. She couldn't help but nod and followed him to his gun safe. He emptied it, piling a surprising number of rifles and handguns into her arms.

"Damn, Reid, any other day I'd give you a hard time, but right now I love you. These don't even look legal."

"You never know when you'll need to take out a gang." He reached for the last one, a shotgun, then slung a bag of ammunition over his shoulder.

"You don't have to come. Really. It's dangerous. There aren't going to be any arrests."

"I know that, Sorano. Let's rock."

CHAPTER THIRTY-ONE

The van came to a stop and jostled Adrienne back into awareness. She hadn't been sleeping, just somewhere else. She'd been back on the cold ground with Kaia, holding her. Had she died yet? Did she regain consciousness? Did she struggle? Did the knife hit her heart? Or did she just fade out in the cold?

The back door opened and hands grabbed her ankles. They dragged her to the edge of the van. Her hands scraped the coarse floor, skin sanding away under her own weight. All she could focus on was the constriction in her chest. The grief was crippling, suffocating and numbing.

"Grab her," Anna said. "Let's go."

Hands seized her arms and dragged her to her tingling, numb feet. She couldn't support her own weight. She didn't know if it was the cold or if she just didn't have the will, but Jacob and Sean didn't seem bothered by supporting her.

Adrienne forced herself to look around and be aware of her surroundings. The narrow path they'd driven up was covered in foliage, barely even defined. Trees enclosed her. They were on a footpath now, walking uphill. Her legs screamed at her to stop walking. It was a slow and tedious climb despite the mild look of the incline.

When they got closer to the top, Adrienne saw a roof. Slowly, a large barn revealed itself. The sidings looked like metal painted the classic barn maroon. There were windows on every side of the old building, plenty of places to escape. As they approached, the doors opened. Adrienne's stomach dropped. There were more of them.

The boys shoved her inside and she fell to the ground. She was in a circle of fifteen more Wild AKs. The entire core of the gang had showed up. The five who'd kidnapped her trailed in and shut the doors.

"Where's the cop?" someone asked.

"Already dead," Anna said. "She was raising too much hell. Had to put her down." A sigh circled the room. Adrienne felt sick. These animals had been sitting around fantasizing about torturing a cop. Torturing Kaia. She couldn't bring herself to think what had happened was best, but she also couldn't fight the relief Kaia wasn't here to face these beasts. She would have gone down swinging against anyone, but this many sadistic minds in one room would have come up with something horrific.

She was only faintly aware that those thoughts were aimed at her now, that she would have to face whatever they couldn't do to Kaia. And she was a snitch. Gianna had warned her snitches got their skin peeled, but she'd never known how literally to take it. Seeing Anna take a chunk of Kaia's skin horrified her. How much skin could they take before she died?

She'd calculated her chances of grabbing a gun over and over, but now, surrounded by this many Wild AKs, she wondered if maybe the best use of the gun, should she get one, would be to just shoot herself and end it. Anna entered the circle that had formed around Adrienne.

"Got our snitch," she said. A round of shouts circled around Adrienne.

"This traitor gave our secrets to the police. She betrayed Gianna. She's the reason detectives know where you all live, why you have cops camped outside your homes harassing your families. You're each going to get your chance with her."

Another round of whoops went through the circle. Adrienne felt nauseous.

"I'm going to cut her ropes, and every single one of you can have a go at her, but no one kills her. That's mine." They all nodded in agreement and Anna walked over to Adrienne. She reached in her pocket, searching for her knife.

"You left it in my girlfriend," Adrienne said with venom.

"So I did," Anna sneered. "She shouldn't have spit on me. The shooting I could have gotten over, but she was dead when she did that."

"Fuck off, Anna, you would have killed her either way."

"Yeah, you're right." Anna accepted a knife offered to her by another member and cut Adrienne's ropes. The moment her hands were free Adrienne swung at Anna as hard as she could, surprising even herself when the blow landed full force. Anna lunged at her, but Christina's arm cut her off.

"You're last," she said. "Let them have her."

Anna paced, struggling with the terms she'd just laid out herself. Finally, she relented and waved at the first member to enter the circle. A teenage boy Adrienne knew was brand new came into the circle. He was timid, eyes bouncing from her to the ground.

"You'll want to put your hands up," someone jeered.

"She's a rat."

The words of encouragement continued until he finally rushed her and swung. Adrienne dodged the blow and elbowed him in the side of the face, wanting to protect her hands from the damage of punching as long as she could. She wanted to have something left for Anna. He seemed unaffected and came at her much more aggressively, swinging until he was able to make contact and send her to the ground. Pain radiated through her face, much the way it had when Gianna used to hit her, but now her whole body hurt from being tied up, from the cold, from losing Kaia.

Sean came into the circle. "Get up," he said. She pushed herself to her feet, determined to face this. The only way she could think to honor Kaia at all was to raise as much hell as she would have. She'd do at least some damage to every son of a bitch that stepped into the circle with her, no matter how much it hurt, no matter how much worse it made things. When Sean swung at her she kicked for his balls as hard as she could. His punch followed through and sent her to the ground, but he doubled over too. Adrienne felt her skin split on her cheek and blood roll down. Sean was also reeling, holding himself.

A new person stepped into the circle, too impatient to let Sean recover. A young Hispanic girl had her hands up and was taunting her. "Get up, bitch." Adrienne realized they all wanted a fight. No one wanted to just beat her on the ground. She knew she'd eventually get too tired and hurt to keep this up. Her chances of really hurting someone would go down with every new person, leaving her completely defenseless when Anna was finally ready to kill her.

She took a second to catch a deep breath, then stood. She rushed the girl, letting her punches fly without reservation. She caught the girl in the chin and forced her back on her heels. She stayed after her. If she'd learned anything from watching Gianna and Anna it was to overwhelm with aggression. Her fist connected with the girl's nose and Adrienne felt it snap. A thrill shot through her, and she knew the hatred that compelled these people, the satisfaction of hurting someone you despise with your entire being. Somewhere deep down it disgusted her, but she couldn't think like that right now. Instead, she aimed for the girl's nose again, hitting the mark and sending a splash of blood through the air.

She felt an uneasiness pass through the circle, indecisiveness at whether to intervene. She followed the girl to the ground and struck again and again, determined to cause irreparable damage before she would inevitably be pulled off. The girl's hands rose, blindly trying to push Adrienne away, but Adrienne had leverage that couldn't be overcome. She felt the WAKs' unwillingness to rescue the girl she was destroying. They were losing respect for her. They were disgusted and embarrassed by her. This was their love? This was family? She hated them all. She landed a blow that rendered the girl unconscious, something she'd never done before. An automatic reaction told her to stop, but she overrode it and punched again.

"That's enough!" Anna snapped.

Christina jumped into the circle and grabbed Adrienne, flinging her backward to the dirt floor. Christina's shoe was coming at her face. The impact slung her into the ground hard, like the dirt had rushed up to her, not the other way around. Dizziness and darkness overtook her.

CHAPTER THIRTY-TWO

K aia sped through the back country roads at dangerous speeds, but Reid didn't protest. He watched the GPS unit that was guiding them, dependent on it in the absence of streets with actual names.

"It should be coming up," he said.

Kaia reluctantly slowed. "Think they'll have guards posted?"

"I think we have to assume they will. They had all those guns for something."

"This is going to be a mess," she said.

"You're telling me. We're walking into a lion's den."

"You really don't have to do this, Reid. I can go on foot from here. Take the car home. I can't promise I'll be ethical about this."

"They almost beat me to death," Reid said. "I have no love for them. And no one stabs my partner."

"But your career. You love being a cop. They'll ask you why you didn't call this in."

"And I'll tell them you were right. Showing up here with a team of officers would have just triggered mass chaos and endangered Adrienne's life."

"But—"

"Stop trying to talk me out of it, Sorano. We're family. If we get fired, we get fired. Would you drop me on the side of the road by myself to go take on a bunch of gangsters alone in order to protect your career?"

"Of course not."

"Good, because I'd kick your ass."

Kaia laughed. "All right, fine. So where is this place?"

"According to this it's right here."

They both leaned forward, looking carefully outside.

"I don't see shit," Kaia said, heart sinking to her stomach. They were on a narrow dirt road, surrounded closely by trees.

"Don't panic," he said. "Go slow."

Kaia crept forward, scanning feverishly for signs someone had been through recently. Kaia saw a flash of someone running out of the corner of her eye.

"Don't stop," Reid said, spotting it too.

Kaia resisted the powerful urge to slam the brakes, trusting Reid wholeheartedly. "Why?"

"They don't know it's you. They don't recognize this car and this road goes to other parcels. They won't do anything if you keep going."

"But that's them. We need to go that direction."

"We'll go on foot. The longer they don't know we're here the better. You alert them now they might kill Adrienne and split."

Kaia's chest seized at the thought. She continued straight, forcing herself to keep an even pace as if she hadn't seen anything. It countered every urge in her body to drive away. She spotted a small clearing ahead.

"Here?"

"Not yet."

"We have to walk back. If we go too far you're not going to be able to do it."

"If they spot us it's game over," Reid said. "I will figure out how to do what I need to do."

Kaia consented and continued around the bend. She felt like she was going to explode. All she wanted to do was run straight for Adrienne, destroying anything and everything that tried to stop her. She knew she had to trust Reid's judgment. She was too emotionally invested to think clearly.

"All right, up here," he said. Kaia parked the car and hurried to the trunk. She loaded herself down with as much as she could carry, putting a pistol in her waistband, slinging a rifle over her shoulder, tucking a knife away, shoving extra magazines in every spare pocket, and carrying another pistol. Reid grabbed a pistol, the shotgun, and the sniper rifle.

"You any good with that?"

"Yeah, I'm all right actually."

Kaia nodded. She no longer had any concerns he didn't understand the full implications of her plan. He reached out for a hug. "Let's go get your girl."

They headed into the trees, cutting deep before turning back the way they had come. The air was ruthless, biting the skin, eating at her fingers. Kaia slowed more than once for Reid, but every time she looked back he was right there. She knew he must be in pain, that he was pushing himself too hard, but she couldn't bring herself to tell him to slow down. A few seconds could be the difference between finding Adrienne dead or alive. She could also be long dead already, but Kaia couldn't let herself think about that.

She listened for footsteps, all too aware she might end up running smack into a Wild AK. They were running around out here for some reason. Had they alerted the others a car passed by? Or had Reid's plan successfully made them ignore it?

"God, it's nothing but trees," Kaia whispered. "Where did they take her?"

"Maybe just a clearing."

Kaia hoped not. With the temperature what it was she knew if they were outside the whole process would go faster. She desperately tried to pierce the darkness with her eyes, seeking any signs of a building or maybe a fire. She heard a rush of footsteps and crouched down. She glanced over her shoulder and saw Reid had done the same and was mostly hidden behind a tree trunk. Kaia didn't dare rustle the leaves trying to find better cover. She scanned the horizon for shadows, ears clawing at the air for signs of anyone.

She spotted someone running in the opposite direction. They must be trying to get back to the others.

"Reid," she whispered.

"Got him." He already had his rifle raised. She heard the muted pulse of the suppressor and the person went down. Kaia lost her breath, all of this now made real. The silence between them as they watched to see if the Wild AK would rise was excruciating. He didn't move.

"You okay?" she asked.

"I'm good. That must be the way."

Kaia nodded and crept forward again. She finally spotted a narrow clearing they must have driven through. It swerved up a hill. "I don't like this," she said.

"Me either," Reid said. "Let's go around."

Reid took the lead, again surprising her with the speed he managed. They hustled around and up the hill until they had a straight look at a barn. It was long and rectangular, fairly large. Reid looked through the scope on his rifle.

"How many did you say there were?"

"Five."

"Yeah, not anymore."

"What? How many?"

"I'm seeing at least eight. Four out front and four more through the windows. And I don't even see Anna or Christina, so that puts us at ten or more."

"Shit. Where did they all come from?"

"Don't know, but they're all armed. This is going to be nasty, Kai."

"Can you pick them off?"

"One for sure, but if they run for cover that may be a wrap on that approach and there will still be a ton of them left."

"Follow me." Kaia crouched and led him to a boulder. She lay on her stomach. "Here, they won't know where you are. The one on the left is alone. They won't even see him fall."

Reid looked through the scope and nodded. "I see what you're saying. That's if I can manage a perfect shot. He gets out a yell and—"

"You'll make it."

"Okay, this one on the left, then the one far right. Then whoever is still dumb enough to be around."

"And I got anyone who tries to come this way."

Reid looked through the scope again. It felt like forever waiting for him to line up the shot. The muted shot fired and the body dropped. She held her breath waiting for someone to notice, but no one was the wiser. Reid panned the rifle to the right without a break, aimed, and fired again. Another body dropped.

"You're a beast, Reid." She felt strange congratulating him on taking his third life in a matter of minutes, but she couldn't fight the excitement that they were inching closer to Adrienne.

"This one's going to tip them off," he said. "I'll take the big guy in front so we don't end up having to fight him, but they'll see. They might run inside, but they might charge out here too. You ready?"

She traded the pistol for the rifle. "Ready."

Reid aimed again and fired. It hit center mass. It would probably end up fatal, but it wasn't instant. The guy hollered in shock and touched the pool of blood forming on his shirt.

"Someone's shooting!" he yelled and spun for the barn. Reid fired again and hit him in the back, taking him down.

"The five that took us had vests," Kaia said.

"Got it. Kidnapping crew has body armor, new guys don't."

The last person out front ran inside. Reid sent another round through the window, but she couldn't tell if he'd hit anyone.

"Looks like panic in there," Reid said. "They're going to hunker down."

"Damn. All right, time for me to get down there."

"There's still too many."

"I'll have to be sneaky."

"I'm going with you."

"No, stay here. Do what you're doing."

"Kaia, wait," Reid hissed, but she took off in a low crouch, cutting to the side of the barn.

Chapter Thirty-three

Adrienne woke up in a chair in the middle of a bare room. The walls were thin, silver metal, and the floor was dirt. There was thick rope looped around each arm several times, strapping them to the chair's arms. Her ankles were similarly wrapped so that her movement was almost entirely restricted.

"Well, good morning."

Adrienne had a hard time placing the voice. Her head was pounding. She finally spotted Anna in the corner, straddling a chair like the one Adrienne was tied to. The pain in Adrienne's head and face was excruciating. Trying to breathe sent jabbing pains down her spine and sides. She felt dried blood cracking on her skin as she moved.

"You missed some of the fun," Anna said. "Christina knocked you clean out."

"So they beat me while I was unconscious?"

"It wasn't ideal, but we don't have all damn week."

"I thought you did. Isn't that the point of bringing me to the middle of nowhere?"

"No one's finding you, if that's what you mean. We still have life to live though, deadlines to meet, drugs to sell."

"Big shot like you has deadlines, huh?"

"I take it you heard about Marco."

"Of course I did," Adrienne said. "That was you?"

"None other."

"Why?"

"For Gianna."

"You thought he killed her?" There was a time that would have made her feel guilty, but her hatred for anyone who wore a WAK tattoo ran so deep now she didn't care anymore.

"I did for a spell," Anna said. "Turned out not to be true, but he was still lying, scheming. He wanted Gianna out of the way. He paid." Anna stood up and approached her. Adrienne's heart jumped in anticipation, but she forced her face still.

"Now what?"

Anna took the knife she borrowed from her pocket. "Now it's your turn." She flipped the knife open and put the blade to Adrienne's throat. "You want to beg for your life?"

"What for?"

"You know I never understood what Gianna saw in you. It never made sense. I guess she was blinded by the sex, the cute face."

"You know we weren't just sex. I loved her."

"How can you say that to me when you killed her?"

"She tried to kill me," Adrienne said. "All I wanted was to not be beaten. All I wanted was to be treated like a human, like she loved me a fraction of how I loved her. And when she couldn't do that, all I wanted was out. I was not the betrayer, she was."

Anna hauled off and punched her in the face. "She was the most loyal person on this planet."

"Right, loyal. Do you have any idea how much shit she talked about you?"

A flash of doubt crinkled Anna's face. She shook her head and punched Adrienne again. "Shut up. Don't say another word about her. How dare you."

"You want to talk to me about how great she was and how I destroyed and betrayed that? That's not what happened. You're fucking delusional. Even she didn't think that about herself. She knew what she was."

Anna punched her again. "It really was you, wasn't it? You did kill her."

"It doesn't matter, Anna. She's dead and she did it to herself. If she would have treated me right it wouldn't have happened. If she had let me go like she should have it wouldn't have happened. She brought us to this."

Anna punched her again. Adrienne's head snapped back and the dizziness swirled around her head again. Anna grabbed the collar of her shirt and forced her head upright again.

"You always had it out for me," Adrienne said. "Even Gianna knew she was wrong sometimes. When I had to call the police because she was choking me to death she understood. She let it go. But you, you wanted her to beat me for it. You wanted to label me a snitch. What is your problem with me, Anna? Were you jealous?"

"Of course not. I saw what she couldn't. Yes, I thought you were a snitch way back then and I was right. Look at you now."

"Because I had to! It would have never happened that way if I'd had another choice."

"Bull," Anna snapped. "You would have gone for that cop no matter what, your little high school sweetheart."

"I wouldn't have snitched. I never wanted anyone to get in trouble. I didn't want any of you in jail, and I certainly didn't want you dead."

"Yeah, well, we are. We're all fucking in trouble or dead, Adrienne. Now it's time to pay."

Anna cut away Adrienne's sleeve the same way she'd done to Kaia. "You want a matching scar?"

"Yes, I do." Adrienne wanted to know what Kaia had felt. She wanted to be close to her in any way she could. She felt the cold metal touch her skin, the edge dug in. At first, the blade was sharp enough it didn't hurt, but as it went deep, as it turned horizontal and separated her skin it became unbearable. She couldn't stop herself from screaming. She didn't want to give Anna the satisfaction, but she couldn't bear it. As she gave in, screaming became the best feeling in the world. Anna pulled the skin away and held it in front of Adrienne's face.

"That's just a taste," she said. "I'm taking it all, piece by piece."

The door opened and Christina stuck her head in. "Anna?"

"What?"

Christina gestured for her to come over, but Anna rolled her eyes in frustration. "What? I'm busy."

"We have a problem. There's someone here."

"What do you mean someone here?"

Christina asked Anna again to come over with an insistent nod, but Anna wouldn't budge. Christina finally relented, obviously annoyed. "We have three people down, probably a fourth in the woods."

"What?" Anna whipped around.

"Jimmy, Jamal, and Lynn are dead. Carlos was in the woods keeping watch and hasn't come back."

"This story better end with we have another prisoner to torture."

"Not yet. It's a sniper. We can't find them, and they're all afraid to go outside."

"A sniper?"

Anna looked at Adrienne, seeming to mull over her options. "Who the fuck?"

Christina stepped into the room. "Los Hijos de la Santa Muerte."

"What? No."

Christina lowered her voice. "It was a sniper that took out Kendra. It's a sniper here."

"But why? We had a deal. Why work so hard to make peace if they just wanted to battle? We could have done that from the get-go. They have no reason to do this."

"Maybe they're pissed we handled their cashier."

"So they hit four of my people? No. It's not them."

"Who then?" Christina's eyes were wide. Adrienne could see she was having a hard time staying composed. "Cops?"

"They'd be raiding us."

"Well, whoever it is they killed four of us. We need you out here."

"I'm a little busy."

"Anna, there're four members down."

"Fuck." Anna returned the knife to her pocket. "Have to do everything around here. Get Celeste in here. I want Adrienne watched at all times. If this fucker is here for her I need eyes on her."

Christina nodded and left the room. Seconds later, Celeste came in.

"You have one job and one job only," Anna told her. "Keep watch on Adrienne. If she tries to get away, put one in her kneecap. If someone tries to rescue her, put one in her forehead. Don't wait. She does not leave alive."

Celeste nodded and took the gun from her waistband. She sat on the extra chair in similar fashion to Anna moments before, straddling it with her arms and chin rested on the back. Anna left the room and the door closed with a cold click.

Adrienne's eyes were swollen from the beating, and she could barely see out the narrow slits left to her. Celeste looked uncomfortable.

"Sniper, huh?" Adrienne asked.

Celeste shifted her weight and didn't answer.

"Who'd they get?"

"Newbies."

"You scared?"

"Not as scared as you should be."

Adrienne had no idea who could be doing this, but she had to admit, she was less afraid now. It was comforting someone was fighting back whether they meant to rescue her or kill her too. Her heart was yearning, hoping for Kaia, but her mind wouldn't let her entertain it. The way Kaia had been left, there was no way. But who else could it be? Had the cops found Kaia's body and figured out she must have been taken? But Anna was right. This was not the approach she would expect from the police force.

"Celeste, you don't have to do this," Adrienne said. "This was never you. Do you really want to kill me?"

Celeste met her eyes. "You're right, I never wanted this for you, but you did this to yourself. How could you kill Gianna? How could you snitch? What did you expect? What am I supposed to do now?"

"Just let me go."

Celeste laughed. "Right, then they'll kill me."

"Come with me."

"No, Adrienne. I'm not a traitor like you."

"This isn't you."

"Shut up, Adrienne. Just stop. It's over."

"It's not over. Look around you. All of your friends have warrants or death threats hanging over them. There's someone coming after you right now. Half the people you know will be dead or in jail in a year. You can still get out. You're not in trouble yet. Help me and I will help you."

"You can't just walk away from being Wild. You weren't even a member and this still happened to you. You have any idea what they'll do to me if I help you? If I bail on them? We won't even make it off the land. There are nineteen of them out there."

"Fifteen."

"What?"

"There were nineteen besides you. Now there's fifteen. And there's at least one more person out there on our side."

"You don't know that they're on your side. They might kill you too. It's probably the Hijos."

"Celeste, just think about what you're doing."

"Fuck you, Adrienne." Anger flashed across Celeste's face. "You were down with this life too. You only flipped because you wanted to bang the cop, now you're acting like you're better than all this. You turned your back on your family and now you're getting what's coming to you. I cared about you. I told Gianna to take it easy on you. I recommended you as a member. I tried to help you, and you turned your back on all of it. You don't get to ask for my help now."

A symphony of gunshots rang out in the next room. Adrienne and Celeste both stared at the door, waiting, listening. She heard frantic whispering but couldn't decipher the words. More gunshots sounded, pangs of metal got closer, and Adrienne saw holes punching through the wall. She tipped her chair and let herself fall to the ground, hitting hard, making herself as small as possible. Celeste dove to the ground and pointed her gun, but had nothing to shoot. She crawled on her stomach closer to the window. She slowly raised herself up and peered out.

"Who is it?" Adrienne asked.

"Shut the fuck up," she hissed. Her head swiveled back and forth as she searched desperately for the mark. Suddenly, Celeste's head jerked back; a mist of blood sprayed through the air. Adrienne jumped in shock, and Celeste fell to her back. A drop of blood rolled slowly down Celeste's face and into her open, glassy eye.

Adrienne fought the fear and paralysis. If there was a chance, this was it. She was still sideways on the floor, tied tightly to the chair. She tried to scoot across the floor, gaining only an inch at a time. She had to make it to Celeste, to her gun, maybe a knife. She didn't know if she'd be able to free herself, but she had to try.

She shifted her weight forward. The legs of the chair creaked in protest. The floor grabbed the legs, building a pile of loose dirt and resisting her progress. Soon she was soaked in sweat and had barely moved a foot. She heard a scattering of gunshots in the main room next door. She wondered if they had posted guards in the other rooms to keep someone from sneaking in, but from the sound of the shots, they hadn't. Had other people been shot through windows? If so, how depleted were their numbers? And was Celeste right? Was this the Hijos? Was she just as likely to be killed as the next person? Adrienne switched her approach and thrust her weight into tipping the chair, attempting to roll to Celeste rather than scoot to her. The jolt of the chair turning and crashing back to the ground was painful, but she saw what had to be the handle of a knife peeking out of Celeste's pocket.

She saw a flash of blue run past the window. She froze. WAK members were moving outside in pursuit of this mystery sniper, and she could do nothing to conceal herself, but they didn't notice her. They were gripped by fear, unable to do anything but scan the forest for the gunman.

As soon as they passed, Adrienne couldn't help but crane her neck to see what they were after. They came back into view when they got farther away. They were heading for a particularly thick cluster of trees. Adrienne saw what must have drawn them out. It was a faint outline of something. She wasn't sure what she was seeing, but it was out of place and wasn't natural, possibly the outline of an arm. The two Wild AKs approached now in a sprint. The outline sprang to life, stepping from behind the tree, knife blade flashing in the night.

Adrienne's chest froze. She knew that outline, that dirty blond hair. It was impossible, but it was her. Kaia thrust the knife viciously into the first WAK's throat and slashed through, dropping him instantly. The second WAK tried to raise her gun, but Kaia was already attacking. She grabbed the blue shirtsleeve and yanked down, pulling the member off balance and veering her aim into the ground. Kaia sunk the blade into the back of her neck. It was ruthless, a kind of ruthless she would've never imagined from Kaia. Adrienne knew Kaia must be thinking she was dead. She'd known that rabid need for violence when she'd beaten the girl in the ring half to death.

She felt tears she hadn't noticed falling down her face. Kaia was alive. She was alive and here and moving like she'd never had a knife in her chest in the first place, like Adrienne had just imagined it all. She wouldn't stay alive at this rate, though. She was taking on way too many people by herself. Adrienne had to get free. She had to do something.

Chapter Thirty-four

Kaia slid her knife out of the Wild AK's neck, letting the body fall next to the first. The blood snaked over the frozen ground. Kaia dragged the bodies out of sight. As far as she could tell, they had spotted her and acted alone just as she'd hoped they would.

Kaia made her way around to the back in search of more vulnerable WAKs or a way in. She knew at some point her only option would be to make the plunge inside, but the fewer WAKs alive when that happened the better. She could just sit outside as long as it took, picking them off one by one, but some small part of her had hope Adrienne was still alive in there, and she had to move fast to keep it that way.

She didn't see anyone in the back of the barn, but she found it hard to believe they wouldn't have at least one person watching it by now. She peered through the scope on the AK. It wasn't nearly as powerful as Reid's sniper, but it was vastly better than her eyes. She spotted someone through a window. He seemed alone and was pacing, glancing nervously out the window occasionally but clearly afraid to linger by it. She didn't have a shot at him, but she could get in that room.

Kaia searched for the best line to the door. There wasn't a way to avoid exposure. If she missed someone it would be deadly. Gunshots sounded from the front of the barn. They saw Reid, or they thought they did at least. She didn't have time to worry about him. She seized the distraction and ran for the barn. She braced to hear bullets chasing her heels, but none came. She made it to the barn, then plastered her back to the metal and sidestepped to the door. She took out her knife. The longer she resisted gunfire the longer she could be a secret. She grabbed the doorknob and burst inside.

The Wild AK spun. It was Sean, still in body armor. Shock crossed his face. Kaia charged. He raised his gun but she plunged the knife into his neck. His eyes went wide. Kaia had firm control of the direction of his gun, but he managed to pull the trigger. The shot rang loud and hollow, announcing her. She held her breath and guided his weight slowly to the ground, hopeful the sound was lost in the racket of shots from the front.

The house went silent for a moment, then Kaia heard whispers and footsteps coming her way. The room had a door on each side of her, the one to her back that she'd just come through and would take her back outside, and the one in front of her, which led to the interior of the barn. She closed her eyes and took a breath, then raised her gun at the interior door, waiting for them off to the side in case they came through shooting.

She heard at least four voices. Her heart thundered out of control, the gun rattled in her shaking hands. The door burst open with a kick from the other side. Kaia fired, dropping the first one. The gun kicked into her shoulder as she continued fire. The person behind the first went down too before return fire blasted through the doorway. She heard the pangs of bullets punching through metal. Kaia lunged out of the way, seeking protection behind the door they'd just kicked open. Three more WAKs forced their way inside, stepping over their friends' bodies.

Time became a blur. Her vision was hyper focused and tunneled. She felt like she'd fired a thousand rounds. She kept pulling the trigger and two more WAKs went down. Two bullets pounded into her and knocked her backward. She was afraid they went through the vest, though she didn't feel pain. Vests could only take so much before they failed and this one didn't even fit as it should.

Her rifle clicked, out of ammo. She had plenty more but no time to reload. She dropped the rifle and reached for a dead WAK's weapon, but the wall of muscle that was the last Wild AK alive in the room rushed her and kicked the gun out of reach. He swung his gun at her head, apparently out of ammo too. She ducked, but he shoved her into the corner behind the door and slammed her against the wall, crushing her throat with the gun.

She slashed at him with her knife, but he grabbed her wrist and pinned it to the wall, still using his remaining hand to press the gun across her neck. She struggled to reach the pistol in her waistband with her free hand, but it was pinned tightly between her back and the wall. She needed air. Her vision was fading. The black was closing the corners of her eyes. She clawed at the gun, trying to ease the pressure, but she was getting weak. Everything went dark and she felt her arms drop, unable to bear their own weight. She distantly heard a single gunshot and she fell to the ground.

She felt like she'd fallen into a lucid dream. She knew her eyes were open, but she saw nothing. She knew she'd fallen, but she couldn't move. She knew she'd heard a gunshot, but she couldn't feel the pain. Cold fingers touched her face. They were soft and gentle.

"Kaia." She heard a familiar whisper. It was Adrienne. Kaia swam through the dark, reaching for consciousness but unable to find it. It was like she'd dived into deep water and lost track of which way was up. She fought it, but it only seemed to get worse, and as it got worse a kind of panic threatened to take over.

"Breathe, Kaia."

She wasn't breathing? Was she dead? No. She hurt too much to be dead. She screamed at her body to come back, to breathe, but she couldn't remember the sensation. She was stuck in the dream.

"Baby, breathe!" Adrienne's voice got more urgent. Adrienne shook her. The feeling brought back an awareness of her body and she forced her lungs to take in air. She felt herself gasping, rasping through the pain of her crushed throat. Adrienne's arms tightened around her, holding her.

"You're okay," she said. "Slow, deep breaths."

Kaia's arms automatically wrapped around her, clinging to her. Slowly, her vision came back. Sound came back in full force. Gunshots were still sounding from the main room. It felt too loud, like it was echoing around her head an octave higher than the sounds should be.

Adrienne's face finally came into focus. She had splotches of black, blue, and purple scattered across her face from several different blows. There was a tangle of ropes hanging from her arms that she'd only managed to get halfway out of. Adrienne smiled as she recognized Kaia processing her.

"God damn it, Kaia, you have to stop scaring the shit out of me. That's the third time I've thought you were dead."

Kaia's eyes watered. "What did they do to you?"

Adrienne squeezed her tighter and kissed her quickly on the forehead. "Later. Can you walk?"

"Have to." Kaia struggled to sit up, letting Adrienne steady her.

"There're still more of them. They'll come check on these guys soon when they don't go back."

"Reid is distracting them." Kaia reached for the AK-12 she'd just been choked with. "He's the sniper." Kaia couldn't help but smile as hope filled Adrienne's face.

"Come on, let's get out of here." Kaia nodded at the door she'd come through, the one that went outside. Adrienne took a step out, then blasted into Kaia in urgent retreat.

"They're outside," she whispered and carefully closed the door. "That way," she silently mouthed as she pointed to the back wall.

Kaia heard shuffling in the next room, the clatter of empty magazines being discarded. "They're still inside too."

"Now what?"

Kaia went to the window and carefully leaned forward enough to peak outside. Adrienne gripped her arm. She glanced outside and pulled back. No one was looking her way. Half were facing the house, half watching the woods.

"Big players are in here," Kaia said. "No sign of Christina or Anna out there."

"How many outside?"

"Five."

"Shit."

"Do you know how many we started with?"

"Twenty."

Kaia counted off bodies she knew about, then shrugged. "So five out there, three inside."

"Should we just wait for Reid to take care of them? He shot Celeste in the head through the window."

"I don't think he can reach them. That's probably why they moved to the back."

"What do we do?"

"I'm going through this door to the main room to take out the three in here. You stay here and shoot anyone that comes for this back door or the window."

"No, please don't."

Kaia touched her face. "The only way out of this is through them. They're too well positioned for us to run."

Gunshots shook them both, followed by Christina calling out. "Oh, Adrienne." A loud crash marked her kicking through a door in search.

"Where's Anna?" Adrienne barely even breathed the words.

Kaia shrugged. "Maybe Reid got her."

Adrienne shook her head. Kaia agreed it was unlikely. Anna knew how to protect herself without looking like a coward. More and more, Kaia had to admit Anna was in some ways worse than Gianna, more tactical. She was probably quietly searching for them.

"We know you're still here, Adrienne," Christina yelled. Kaia changed the plan and went to the window. She aimed the AK at the group of Wild AKs guarding the back. She didn't want Adrienne responsible for the five people outside. Even though Christina and Anna were more skilled, they seemed to be separated at the moment. She looked to Adrienne, who raised her gun at the door for Christina's inevitable rush inside. She nodded.

Kaia leaned out the window and fired at the WAKs in back. Two fell to the ground and struggled to back away from further fire. A young girl raised her pistol. Kaia ducked inside for an instant as the shot rang through the air, then leaned back out and fired. The young one ducked and ran. The rest watched, at first in horror, then followed. The injured ones struggled to scramble after them. The door from the main room kicked in behind her. Adrienne's gun sounded from where she waited.

The door to the outside kicked in too and Anna burst inside, gun raised. Kaia threw herself in between Anna and Adrienne, taking another round to the vest. She rushed forward and slammed Anna into the wall. Anna was covered in blood and furious. She head butted Kaia, landing the blow to her nose with excruciating success. Kaia fought the automatic recoil and leaned her weight into Anna, determined to keep her away from Adrienne and trusting Adrienne completely to handle Christina even as their grunts betrayed a life or death struggle.

Anna dropped the gun and shoved her palm into Kaia's chin, twisting her head away, pushing for space. Kaia was forced to drop her gun too and shook her hand off. She reasserted her weight into Anna.

She tried to drag her to the ground, but Anna was relentlessly strong. She looked to have an average build, but years of fighting made her the kind of tough that was infuriating to the point of feeling futile.

A thud and cry from Adrienne drew her attention for the span of a quick glance. Adrienne was taking blows from Christina from her back, but she was dragging her over by her sleeve in an effort to even the leverage. Anna pushed Kaia enough to give herself space to punch. Anna's fists came in a flurry, catching her on the chin. Kaia regained her balance, but Anna turned away and rushed for Adrienne, raising a foot to stomp on her face. Kaia dove after her and grabbed the ankle Anna was standing on, pulling as hard as she could. Anna crashed to the ground and kicked her entrapped leg for freedom, but Kaia held on. Kaia felt the pistol in her waistband come loose and slide to the floor, but she couldn't risk reaching for it without being sure she'd get it. Kaia used her body weight and one arm to keep control of the leg and took her knife from her pocket with the other hand. She stabbed Anna's calf and pulled the blade through the flesh. Anna screamed.

"You bitch!" She tried to claim the blade from her own leg, but Kaia ripped it out and stabbed again. She felt the blade biting into flesh, tearing through the resistance of skin and muscle. Anna screamed again and dove for Kaia's arms, trying to still the blade.

Kaia accepted the elbow to her face, refusing to let go of the knife. Anna's finger plunged into the stab wound in Kaia's chest, pressing hard enough to rip the stitches even through the gauze. Kaia screamed and slashed crazily with the knife in an effort to reach something more vital than her leg, but her elbow was pinned. Kaia thrust her weight into Anna and toppled her over. She wrestled for the top, but Anna was strong, battling just as hard. Kaia sank her weight into her knee and drove it into Anna's injured leg. Anna screamed. Kaia pushed again, using Anna's leg as a platform to push off, and finally succeeded in rolling Anna onto her back. Her knife arm was free. She overpowered her natural reaction to hesitate and stabbed downward as hard as she could, ignoring Anna's arms trying to stop her. She slashed past them by sheer force.

Kaia's knife sank in. The room felt frozen. Kaia looked down. The knife was in Anna's chest. It had hit center and Anna's face was twisted in pain and shock as she looked down at the hilt in Kaia's hand. Anna's hands hovered around Kaia's, around the hilt, afraid to touch it, afraid not to. Kaia tightened her grip and pulled the knife out as she stood up. Anna's chest rose as Kaia ripped the blade free, then she collapsed back to the ground. Blood spurted from her mouth and she choked and gargled on it.

Christina yelled and fell away from Adrienne. She crawled to Anna's side, seeming to forget everything else. Adrienne scrambled away, more than happy to break from the violence and catch her breath.

A gunshot pierced the air. Kaia felt the burning sensation rip through her. The heat of it radiated through her entire arm. She spun to locate the shooter. The young Wild AK who had fled was now standing outside the window with her gun raised, prepared to take another shot. A gun appeared on the outer edge of the window frame and fired. The girl's brain and blood sprayed through the air and her body fell out of view.

Kaia was shaken by the visual though she knew it saved her life. She frantically tried to reach the pistol she'd lost in the fight, but Reid's face in the window drew her attention away. She breathed in relief.

"Reid!"

She heard Christina shuffling beside her. She turned in time to see her reach for a gun and spin it on her. Kaia lunged but she was too far away. Adrienne kicked Christina's hand fast enough to make the shot miss. She kicked again, this time hitting Christina in the head. Christina was dazed but still struggling to aim the gun, still trying to shoot Kaia in spite of Adrienne's attack. Kaia rushed to help, but Adrienne acted in a flash. She grabbed Christina's arm and wrenched the gun around so it pointed at Christina. She squeezed Christina's finger and force pulled the trigger. Christina's head shot back from the impact and her arm fell limp.

Adrienne backed away. She backed right into Kaia. Kaia grabbed her shoulders and forced her to turn away. She guided Adrienne's head to her chest and held her.

"It's okay," she whispered. Adrienne buried her face in Kaia and held her.

Reid came through the back door and put his hand on Kaia's back. Adrienne let go of Kaia and hugged Reid.

"Thank you," she said.

"Hey, you got it," he said with a sad smile.

"You saved her life," Adrienne said. "You saved both our lives."

"I did my best." He smiled. "Not as good as I'd hoped. You're shot, Sorano."

Kaia looked down at her shoulder for the first time. Her entire sleeve was soaked in blood, and it hurt like hell. The stab wound in her chest hurt even more, but she couldn't bring herself to look.

"I think one may have made it through the vest, too," Kaia said. Reid frowned and tried to peek under the vest, but she waved him off. "Just a graze if it did."

Adrienne pulled up Kaia's sleeve to get a look at the accessible bullet wound. Worry filled her face.

"It's just my shoulder," Kaia said.

"Let's get the hell out of here," Adrienne replied. "You need a hospital."

"There are still some out there," Reid said.

"A few ran when I tried to take down the last group out back," Kaia said to Adrienne, who hadn't been able to see.

"We can't stay here," Adrienne said.

Reid took another look at Kaia's shoulder. He seemed troubled by the blood now dripping from her over-soaked sleeve. "All right," he said. "Let's make a break for the car. Hopefully, they're long gone. They're obviously scared of us and probably Anna too now that they ran on her. I don't think they'll be a problem anymore, but we'll be careful."

They loaded themselves down with every weapon in sight and cautiously ventured into the night air. The temperature had dropped even more and they were not properly dressed.

"How far?" Adrienne asked.

"Maybe a mile."

"Shit." Adrienne's concern was plain on her face as she wrapped her arm around Kaia to steady her. Kaia was in pain but overall fairly convinced she was going to be okay, though the looks on Adrienne's and Reid's faces were making her doubt herself. Was she losing too much blood? Pale? Not acting normal? She couldn't tell, but as Adrienne took some of her weight she realized she was lightheaded. She couldn't do much to watch their backs or scan the woods; all she could focus on was walking through the pain, putting one foot ahead of the other and refusing to think about how much farther was left. Reid had his gun raised and was looking almost manically in circles, but he didn't seem to see anything suspicious.

Kaia couldn't say how long it took, but they were approaching the car. Adrienne opened the back door and climbed in with Kaia. Reid got in the driver's seat and pulled onto the dirt road. None of them spoke as they drove down the road, forced to pass by the barn yet again as it was the only way back to civilization. Finally, the drive smoothed out and Kaia realized they were on paved road again.

Kaia felt unbearably heavy. She couldn't hold herself up. Even as she was aware she didn't need to exert anything to simply sit in the car, she felt exhausted by the effort of being. She slumped into Adrienne, who cradled her. She felt Adrienne's fingers in her hair, touching her face, caressing and comforting her. Kaia breathed in her smell and relaxed into the pain. At least the fighting was over. The relief that Adrienne was safe was enough to overshadow every bruise, cut, and puncture. They'd done it. They got her back.

Sleep pulled at her and though she was afraid to fall into it, it took her.

Chapter Thirty-Five

A drienne sat by Kaia's hospital bed. She hadn't worried that Kaia fell asleep in the car, but when they couldn't wake her at the hospital she'd about gone into a panic attack. The hospital staff had pulled her from the car and whisked her into the emergency room in a flurry that was both comforting and disconcerting.

They'd taken her into surgery without consulting anyone, which told her Kaia was in danger of dying, but by the time they filled Adrienne in, Kaia was already stable again. She'd been waiting for her to wake up all night with no signs of change.

Cops had been coming and going, trying to check on her, but they'd mostly stayed in the hallway, receiving their updates from Reid. They had left Kaia's room to her.

The nurses urged her to go home, to get sleep, to eat something. It seemed as much a part of their patient care as actually tending to patients. They were always telling family to take care of themselves though they had to know it was futile.

Reid was right by Adrienne's side most of the time, calming her down when the panic threatened to take hold again. She knew he was afraid too, but he'd been a strong and steady force in the face of her anxiety.

"She's tough as nails," he said. It seemed to be his mantra that got him through the hours of waiting.

Adrienne turned to him and put her hand on his shoulder. "I know."

He smiled. "So are you."

"We all are."

"You should have seen her when she showed up on my doorstep. She had a Goddamn knife sticking out of her chest and all she could think about was you." He laughed. "I thought she was insane. I mean she literally had a knife in her chest." Reid motioned to where the knife had been on his own chest, shaking his head in disbelief.

"I know," Adrienne said. "I saw Anna do it. It was horrifying. I thought she was gone for sure."

"I don't think anything could have stopped her from coming to get you."

Adrienne smiled and looked back to Kaia's serene face, deep in medicated sleep. "I would have done the same for her. I hope she knows that."

"She does," Reid said. "You may not have had a knife in your chest, but she knows you risked your life for her when it counted. You killed for her when it counted."

Adrienne smiled and gently rested her head on Kaia's thigh. Reid squeezed her shoulder and left them alone. Adrienne brushed the stray hairs from Kaia's face and rested with her.

She didn't realize she was drifting into sleep until Kaia's cough stirred her awake. Kaia struggled for breath, seeming panicked by the tubes attached to her.

"You're okay," Adrienne said, rushing to stand up and reassure her. "You're okay," she said again. The pain and fear crossing over her face broke Adrienne's heart. "You had surgery, love. You're probably really sore, but you're okay."

Kaia grabbed Adrienne's hand and slowly calmed down. "I had surgery?"

"Yeah. They had to. We couldn't wake you up when we got here. You lost a lot of blood and you were pretty torn up."

"Wow." Kaia seemed shaken by the information.

"You're okay now."

"What about you?" she asked. "Are you okay?"

"I'm fine. They checked on me."

"Reid?"

"He's better than either of us. Don't think he has a scratch he didn't already have."

"Glad one of us came out unscathed." Kaia smiled. "Has anyone talked about what happened yet?"

"Yeah, Cruz and Davis were both here. Reid handled it."

"What do you mean handled it? There are like fifteen bodies in the woods."

Adrienne shrugged. "He's handling it. They were more worried about you than the bodies, honey. You're a mess. You have a stab wound and two gunshot wounds. My face is more purple than flesh tone. They know we did what we had to to get out safe."

"It's got to be more complicated than that."

"Doesn't look like it. And if it is it will be later. For now they just want you to get better."

Kaia smiled weakly and closed her eyes. She looked like she might doze off again, but she opened her eyes and reached for Adrienne's face. Adrienne moved into her touch and let Kaia pull her into a careful kiss.

"You sure you're okay? All of you?" Kaia patted Adrienne's chest by her heart.

Adrienne had been struggling with the images, Gianna's cracked skull, Anna plunging the knife mercilessly into Kaia's chest, the feeling of forcing Christina's finger to pull the trigger on herself, all the blood. It had been trying to overwhelm her, but just looking at Kaia made her feel safe again.

Adrienne looked Kaia in the eye and smiled. "I will be. I never thought I would see that much blood or death, but I would do it again in a heartbeat to save you."

Kaia kissed her forehead. "Me too."

"I would do anything for you, Kaia. I was so afraid I lost you. Over and over again, I kept thinking you were gone. I thought it was going to kill me. I was more afraid of that than I used to be of Gianna, or Anna, or dying or killing, any of it. None of it felt like it feels to lose you. Or to think I did."

"I know." Kaia touched her face. "I felt it too. I thought I lost you. I thought I was going to be too late. It took so long to get back to Reid and then to find you. It was torture thinking of what they were doing to you, and I couldn't do anything to stop them. I was so afraid I was going to do all that and end up just finding your body. I—" Kaia choked up. "I just thought I was going to be too late. That it was going to be revenge, not a rescue. I thought I was going to fail you."

"You could never fail me." Adrienne kissed her. "I know you're in a dangerous line of work, but if you could please not almost die for at least a few months my psyche would really appreciate it."

Kaia laughed and wrapped her arms around her. She pulled Adrienne close, overriding Adrienne's fear of hurting her. "I don't want to do anything for the next few months except get better and love each other."

Adrienne relaxed into her embrace. "We can do that."

About the Author

Nicole is a lifelong storyteller who is most happy when exploring the hidden corners of life. She lives in Denver, Colorado, where she is a collector of jobs that inspire her writing. She has worked as a 911 operator, police dispatcher, EMS dispatcher, and martial arts instructor. Most recently, she and her wife started a music video production company and love working together as producer and director.

Website: http://www.nicoledisney.com/

Books Available from Bold Strokes Books

Alias by Cari Hunter. A car crash leaves a woman with no memory and no identity. Together with Detective Bronwen Pryce, she fights to uncover a truth that might just kill them both. (978-1-63555-221-8)

Death in Time by Robyn Nyx. Working in the past is hell on your future. (978-1-63555-053-5)

Hers to Protect by Nicole Disney. High school sweethearts Kaia and Adrienne will have to see past their differences and survive the vengeance of a brutal gang if they want to be together. (978-1-63555-229-4)

Of Echoes Born by 'Nathan Burgoine. A collection of queer fantasy short stories set in Canada from Lambda Literary Award finalist 'Nathan Burgoine. (978-1-63555-096-2)

Perfect Little Worlds by Clifford Mae Henderson. Lucy can't hold the secret any longer. Twenty-six years ago, her sister did the unthinkable. (978-1-63555-164-8)

Room Service by Fiona Riley. Interior designer Olivia likes stability, but when work brings footloose Savannah into her world and into a new city every month, Olivia must decide if what makes her comfortable is what makes her happy. (978-1-63555-120-4)

Sparks Like Ours by Melissa Brayden. Professional surfers Gia Malone and Elle Britton can't deny their chemistry on and off the beach. But only one can win… (978-1-63555-016-0)

Take My Hand by Missouri Vaun. River Hemsworth arrives in Georgia intent on escaping quickly, but when she crashes her Mercedes into the Clip 'n Curl, sexy Clay Cahill ends up rescuing more than her car. (978-1-63555-104-4)

The Last Time I Saw Her by Kathleen Knowles. Lane Hudson only has twelve days to win back Alison's heart. That is if she can gather the courage to try. (978-1-63555-067-2)

Wayworn Lovers by Gun Brooke. Will agoraphobic composer Giselle Bonnaire and Tierney Edwards, a wandering soul who can't remain in one place for long, trust in the passionate love destiny hands them? (978-1-62639-995-2)

Breakthrough by Kris Bryant. Falling for a sexy ranger is one thing, but is the possibility of love worth giving up the career Kennedy Wells has always dreamed of? (978-1-63555-179-2)

Certain Requirements by Elinor Zimmerman. Phoenix has always kept her love of kinky submission strictly behind the bedroom door and inside the bounds of romantic relationships, until she meets Kris Andersen. (978-1-63555-195-2)

Dark Euphoria by Ronica Black. When a high-profile case drops in Detective Maria Diaz's lap, she forges ahead only to discover this case, and her main suspect, aren't like any other. (978-1-63555-141-9)

Fore Play by Julie Cannon. Executive Leigh Marshall falls hard for Peyton Broader, her golf pro…and an ex-con. Will she risk sabotaging her career for love? (978-1-63555-102-0)

Love Came Calling by CA Popovich. Can a romantic looking for a long-term, committed relationship and a jaded cynic too busy for love conquer life's struggles and find their way to what matters most? (978-1-63555-205-8)

Outside the Law by Carsen Taite. Former sweethearts Tanner Cohen and Sydney Braswell must work together on a federal task force to see justice served, but will they choose to embrace their second chance at love? (978-1-63555-039-9)

The Princess Deception by Nell Stark. When journalist Missy Duke realizes Prince Sebastian is really his twin sister Viola in disguise, she plays along, but when sparks flare between them, will the double deception doom their fairy-tale romance? (978-1-62639-979-2)

The Smell of Rain by Cameron MacElvee. Reyha Arslan, a wise and elegant woman with a tragic past, shows Chrys that there's still beauty to embrace and reason to hope despite the world's cruelty. (978-1-63555-166-2)

The Talebearer by Sheri Lewis Wohl. Liz's visions show her the faces of the lost and the killers who took their lives. As one by one, the murdered are found, a stranger works to stop Liz before the serial killer is brought to justice. (978-1-635550-126-6)

White Wings Weeping by Lesley Davis. The world is full of discord and hatred, but how much of it is just human nature when an evil with sinister intent is invading people's hearts? (978-1-63555-191-4)

A Call Away by KC Richardson. Can a businesswoman from a big city find the answers she's looking for, and possibly love, on a small-town farm? (978-1-63555-025-2)

Berlin Hungers by Justine Saracen. Can the love between an RAF woman and the wife of a Luftwaffe pilot, former enemies, survive in besieged Berlin during the aftermath of World War II? (978-1-63555-116-7)

Blend by Georgia Beers. Lindsay and Piper are like night and day. Working together won't be easy, but not falling in love might prove the hardest job of all. (978-1-63555-189-1)

Hunger for You by Jenny Frame. Principe of an ancient vampire clan Byron Debrek must save her one true love from falling into the hands of her enemies and into the middle of a vampire war. (978-1-63555-168-6)

Mercy by Michelle Larkin. FBI Special Agent Mercy Parker and psychic ex-profiler Piper Vasey learn to love again as they race to stop a man with supernatural gifts who's bent on annihilating humankind. (978-1-63555-202-7)

Pride and Porters by Charlotte Greene. Will pride and prejudice prevent these modern-day lovers from living happily ever after? (978-1-63555-158-7)

Rocks and Stars by Sam Ledel. Kyle's struggle to own who she is and what she really wants may end up landing her on the bench and without the woman of her dreams. (978-1-63555-156-3)

The Boss of Her: Office Romance Novellas by Julie Cannon, Aurora Rey, and M. Ullrich. Going to work never felt so good. Three office romance novellas from talented writers Julie Cannon, Aurora Rey, and M. Ullrich. (978-1-63555-145-7)

The Deep End by Ellie Hart. When family ties become entangled in murder and deception, it's time to find a way out… (978-1-63555-288-1)

A Country Girl's Heart by Dena Blake. When Kat Jackson gets a second chance at love, following her heart will prove the hardest decision of all. (978-1-63555-134-1)

Dangerous Waters by Radclyffe. Life, death, and war on the home front. Two women join forces against a powerful opponent, nature itself. (978-1-63555-233-1)

Fury's Death by Brey Willows. When all we hold sacred fails, who will be there to save us? (978-1-63555-063-4)

It's Not a Date by Heather Blackmore. Kade's desire to keep things with Jen on a professional level is in Jen's best interest. Yet what's in Kade's best interest…is Jen. (978-1-63555-149-5)

Killer Winter by Kay Bigelow. Just when she thought things could get no worse, homicide Lieutenant Leah Samuels learns the woman she loves has betrayed her in devastating ways. (978-1-63555-177-8)

Score by MJ Williamz. Will an addiction to pain pills destroy Ronda's chance with the woman she loves or will she come out on top and score a happily ever after? (978-1-62639-807-8)

Spring's Wake by Aurora Rey. When wanderer Willa Lange falls for Provincetown B&B owner Nora Calhoun, will past hurts and a fifteen-year age gap keep them from finding love? (978-1-63555-035-1)

The Northwoods by Jane Hoppen. When Evelyn Bauer, disguised as her dead husband, George, travels to a Northwoods logging camp to work, she and the camp cook Sarah Bell forge a friendship fraught with both tenderness and turmoil. (978-1-63555-143-3)

Truth or Dare by C. Spencer. For a group of six lesbian friends, life changes course after one long snow-filled weekend. (978-1-63555-148-8)

A Heart to Call Home by Jeannie Levig. When Jessie Weldon returns to her hometown after thirty years, can she and her childhood crush Dakota Scott heal the tragic past that links them? (978-1-63555-059-7)

Children of the Healer by Barbara Ann Wright. Life becomes desperate for ex-soldier Cordelia Ross when the indigenous aliens of her planet are drawn into a civil war and old enemies linger in the shadows. Book Three of the Godfall Series. (978-1-63555-031-3)

Hearts Like Hers by Melissa Brayden. Coffee shop owner Autumn Primm is ready to cut loose and live a little, but is the baggage that comes with out-of-towner Kate Carpenter too heavy for anything long term? (978-1-63555-014-6)

Love at Cooper's Creek by Missouri Vaun. Shaw Daily flees corporate life to find solace in the rural Blue Ridge Mountains, but escapism eludes her when her attentions are captured by small town beauty Kate Elkins. (978-1-62639-960-0)

Somewhere Over Lorain Road by Bud Gundy. Over forty years after murder allegations shattered the Esker family, can Don Esker find the true killer and clear his dying father's name? (978-1-63555-124-2)

Twice in a Lifetime by PJ Trebelhorn. Detective Callie Burke can't deny the growing attraction to her late friend's widow, Taylor Fletcher, who also happens to own the bar where Callie's sister works. (978-1-63555-033-7)

Undiscovered Affinity by Jane Hardee. Will a no strings attached affair be enough to break Olivia's control and convince Cardic that love does exist? (978-1-63555-061-0)